The Red Mitten

The Red Mitten

by Sarah Birdsall

McRoy & Blackburn, Publishers
Ester, Alaska

The Red Mitten
Copyright © 2006 by Sarah Birdsall

paper (vi + 202 pp., 6 x 9), ISBN 0-9706712-7-x
(13-digit version: 978-0-9706712-7-1)
cloth, ISBN 0-9706712-6-1
(13-digit version: 978-0-9706712-6-4)

Published in Ester, Alaska by
McRoy & Blackburn, Publishers
P.O. Box 276 • Ester, AK 99725 U.S.A.
mbe@mosquitonet.com
www.alaskafiction.com

Printed in the United States of America by
Thomson-Shore, Inc.
7300 West Joy Road
Dexter, MI 48130-9701
www.tshore.com

Book design and production by
Deirdre Helfferich
Ester Designworks
P.O. Box 24 • Ester, AK 99725
editor@esterrepublic.com
www.esterrepublic.com/designwelcome.html

Dedicated to the memory of my wonderful mother, Carol L. Durr, and to the rest of my family—Chris and Jenny especially—with love and thanks.

With thanks also to Sondra Porter, who first gave me the idea that I could be a writer, and to Ron Spatz, who told me that's what I was.

Who says that time heals all wounds? It would be better to say that time heals everything except wounds. With time, the hurt of separation loses its real limits. With time, the desired body will soon disappear, and if the desiring body has already ceased to exist for the other then what remains is a wound... disembodied.

—from the Chris Marker film, *Sans Soleil*

WHEN KATIE FELL ASLEEP ON THE PLANE, SHE DREAMED OF NICKY. In the dream she was in the waters of Ilmenof, down deep below the surface, where everything felt thick and slow and opaque, like liquid glass. There were dead fish like the ones she and Billy and Nicky used to see in the early winter beneath sheets of clear ice—spawned-out salmon, their decomposing state suspended by the frozen water until spring.

And there she found Nicky, finally, after all these years. Found him and reached for him and realized with amazement that he still lived, he was moving in the water, his face turning to look over his shoulder at her—

Hey, Katie. Whatch you doin', eh?

And then she noticed there was blood in the water, red swirls that fanned out from his head like the tendrils of his thick black curling hair, and she said: *You didn't drown.*

Didn't I?

At this point in the dream Katie began to pull herself away, even though she wanted to be there, in the dream with Nicky, wanted to ask him how he was, wanted him to tell her it wasn't her fault, wanted him to be, after all this time, *back.*

But she felt herself reaching for consciousness, scrambling for it the way a drowning person rushes toward the surface.

She opened her eyes and she was on the plane, the noise of it droning in her ears, and for a moment she had to register her thoughts, remember everything: she was on a plane going to Ilmenof because her mother was dead, dead, dead, and there was a tin of ashes in her backpack that was once the flesh and blood that had loved her. Then the dream took over her thoughts like a black cloud swallowing the sky. It was because she was so close, she reasoned; even in the air in the plane she could imagine the smells of the spruce and the tundra and the water pulling at her—as Nicky was, too, pulling at her. Dead Nicky. Dead like her mother, but lost so many more years ago.

She remembered the blood coming from his head in her dream, and knew why she would have dreamt it. How often had she thought it? That her father killed him. Or even Billy, in an insane rush of grief and rage.

Those thoughts were her secret. Because in the end it all came down to her and the thing she did.

Katie turned toward the window and stared at her reflection—a pale and tired-looking ghost in the small filmy oval. Her gray eyes burned back at her, gray like the color of the water of Ilmenof during breakup. Inherited from her father, like the widow's peak that sealed the shape of her face. When she drew herself, she drew a heart perched atop a long, thin neck.

She looked down past the dirty white wing of the plane. They were still flying over the mountains; between breaks in the wispy cloud cover she could see the bright white peaks of whatever range they were flying over—how odd that she didn't know its name. She didn't know its name but she knew the look of it, could remember, clearly, the first time she saw it when she and her mother flew this same route so many years ago. Winging their way into the Alaska dream. Katie's father's dream, in which she and her mother were simply the co-stars in his great production.

Ooooh, her mother, Vivian, had said: *Oh*. Katie still remembered her mother's lips being round with the word, her eyes large as she looked at the cold snowy peaks below.

Vivian who was now dead. She was running to catch the bus to ride to her job at the hospital, where she worked as a nurse. She suffered an aneurysm, fell to the sidewalk. Katie heard the sirens from the apartment they shared. But she didn't know that the ambulance was for her.

The burst of a vein and Vivian was dead, and just as it had been death that took Katie away from Ilmenof, it was death that was now bringing her back. Soon, she knew, the mountains would turn into foothills and the foothills would turn into stretches of green and red and orange and gold tundra, broken here and there by the occasional boggy marsh or the cluster of wind-beaten black spruce. The wind. Katie knew they would feel it soon, knew it would grip the sides of the plane and bounce it around in the sky. She wished she could have managed to stay asleep; that would be like a miracle, to sleep then wake and be there, the flight over. But then she would still have one more flight to go—this next one in a small plane across the width of Ilmenof.

Katie thought again of her mother, of their years-ago arrival. Manny, Katie's father, was waiting for them at the Ilmenof airport; he'd arrived ahead of them to prepare for their coming—which basically amounted to pitching a tent and digging a hole for an outhouse. Manny stood on the dirt runway, smiling up at Katie and her mother from the bottom of the plane's steep metal steps, wearing a white canvas cap and a tan canvas shirt. Katie could remember trying to look serious and grown up as she descended the stairs, but every time she looked at him a smile pushed itself against the corners of her mouth.

He'd brought a boat for them to go back across the water. Vivian looked at the lake and said, again, *Oooh*. The boat didn't seem big enough.

My age, Katie thought, thinking of her parents. *Back then, they were not much more than my age now.* It hardly seemed possible. By the time they took the plunge and moved to Alaska, Katie's parents had already lived what seemed an entire life; Katie, on the other hand, felt as if she was waiting for her life—her real life—to begin. Twenty-nine and she'd been back living with her mother. What did that say about her? There was no marriage, no children, no property purchases, and no career to speak of. She'd kept thinking Boston was temporary—that she and her mother were back for just a little while, and that someday they would return home to Ilmenof to live. But temporary became a dozen years, all of Katie's twenties, and the rest of her mother's life. There was supposed to be a moment, Katie thought, when you became a grown-up, an adult, a decisive force, the person you were supposed to become. In jeans, a hooded sweatshirt, a T-shirt and black canvas basketball shoes, Katie hardly felt like a woman. And at five-one, size three, her thin fine hair pulled back in a ponytail, she could have passed for someone's teenage child. Someone's child. Was she even that, now that her mother was gone?

Her father would be there, at the end of this journey. But she no longer knew who he was; she wondered if she ever did. He'd had his own surprises. Still, she never thought it would be so long. She always thought something would happen, break the spell, and give her back her life—Nicky, her father, Billy, too—and the woods and the wind and the water. But with Vivian dead there was nothing now that she could save.

Of course Nicky was dead, too, had been dead for all the past twelve years. But unlike with Vivian, Katie never saw him as someone dead; Katie never touched his lifeless skin, felt the weight of his flesh with the blood stilled in his veins, had no proof of his nonexistence, like the ashes that traveled here with her now. For all she or anyone knew, Nicky could have risen from the water and walked away.

She saw, now, out the window, glimpses of the expected tundra. The other passengers moved in their seats, crowded themselves over to one side of the two-aisle plane to get a better view. These passengers were men, mostly—fishermen from the states, geared up in new khakis and bright flannel shirts, ready for their Alaska adventure. Katie knew them, knew their hopes and dreams. Her father, once, had been one of them.

She wondered about balance, like in a boat, if the plane could roll over in the sky. She barely finished the thought when the plane began to shake and the passengers scurried back to their seats. She closed her eyes and tried not to think about the little plane in the big sky, tried to think instead of the sound of the wind across water, the sound of the wind in the tops of the trees.

But the thoughts brought a voice, coming across years, a flash of dark eyes, hair:

Windego, eh, Katie?

Nicky.

She opened her eyes, turned quickly to the window, as if somehow she might see him there.

Ray Twigg woke up and heard the wind. It seemed to circle his house, like Indians around wagon trains in movies he had watched as a boy. He heard cans rolling, saw out his window the trees bending as if in prayer. He thought: *I'm late.* At the same time he wondered if he had left anything important wandering loose outside. After all his years here, he should know better.

He stretched in his narrow cot and made a weak attempt to free himself from the wool army surplus blanket tangled around his legs. He had woken up earlier—but then it was too early. There was no reason to get up before he had to. Still, he hadn't meant to cut it this close; now he would have to get up and get out of there if he were to meet the plane. The wind was a devil out there. The Visqueen stapled over the outside of his windows—the Alaska storm window of choice—was rattling away. Middle of June already and he hadn't taken it off yet. There was no sense in doing it now, he thought; it would soon be time to put it back on. Even two weeks ago it had been too late.

Story of my life, he thought, then wondered why. When he was younger he'd been right in it, right on top of everything. Plunge right in, tomorrow couldn't be waited on. So he'd had that, once. And if things had turned out different, then, he would be different now. He was sure of that. It was nothing that could be helped.

But he had that new plane, finally, he reminded himself. The new plane and the plywood office right in town. The sign out front: *Flights,* it read; *sightseeing, fishing, hunting. Experienced bush pilot.* Necessary things now—an office and a new plane. It seemed every summer new pilots were coming to Ilmenof. Trust fund kids from places like Colorado with hot-shot planes and vans and rustic-chic (did he have that word right, he wondered?) little offices. Playing bush pilot on a wide-open playground. As some of them had learned too late, no place to play. Gotta know the winds; gotta know the winds.

Windego, he thought, then checked himself. Was he joking, saying that? He didn't know anymore. There was a day earlier in the summer when he thought he saw something. He still wasn't sure. He was flying in the new plane, over the lake. It was calm; he was thinking about its being calm and clear at the same time—unusual. It was a day when you could see down into the depths of the lake, something he didn't like to do. There were bodies in the lake. Drowned people who had never been found, whom the water refused to give back. He knew he should look, fly a little lower; there were families who still wondered, who still longed for that final confirmation. But he felt that after a certain time the lake became the grave, the resting place. And there was something else. He couldn't explain it. Out in the middle of the lake the bottom had never been found; the depth there, immeasurable. There was something private there, mysterious. Like a soul. It made him feel hollow inside even to think of it.

That day in the new plane, the wind came out of nowhere. It was as if it had been hiding behind an invisible curtain and suddenly he was like dice in a cup, shaking and lurching, out of control. Then something glommed onto the nose of his plane: a horrific face stretching toward the thin windshield in front of him, white swirling arms reaching for the wings—

But it was fear; what he'd seen was his own face, reflecting back at him. His own fear of disappearing into the waters of Ilmenof.

"Damn wind," he said now, forcing himself to get up. When he first came to Ilmenof—how many years ago was that, now?—he'd found a comfort in the insistent blowing. It was like a steady *shhh* in his brain. He'd needed that, then. But now the wind reminded him of things he hadn't done, and he worried, too, about the new plane, tied down in a cove, bobbing on the waves. Though he'd never lost a plane to the winds. Yet.

He sighed, stood and stretched, his bony knuckles skimming across the rough ceiling near the peak. Why he didn't make the height of his house more suitable to his own is another thing he wondered about; fear of the cold, it must have been. When he'd first arrived, he'd heard *build small, stay close to the ground.* And that's what he did.

One room, low ceiling, a cot, a bookcase, a wood stove. Plywood counters still unfinished. Small propane cookstove, one propane lamp screwed to the wall in the kitchen area, a cluster of kerosene lamps with sooty globes on his small square table. Everything had been the same for so long. Maybe that's why he spent so much time in the little office in town, sitting at his desk and staring out the big, eye-like front window. Because this place was so small, he reasoned, though he knew the office was even smaller.

He caught a glimpse of his face in the mirror on the wall and took a step across the room toward it. The mirror had cracked years ago, before he'd gotten it safely hung; he'd mended it with a ribbon of epoxy. When he looked at himself the crack divided his long angular face lengthwise, like a clear but jagged scar, one light blue eye on either side of the line.

He saw it was time to rebraid his hair. He tried to do this every three days, when it began to look too much like an old, frayed rope hanging down his back. That, and a shower at the gas station when he did his weekly laundry. It reminded him that he was once from someplace else. The reminding was necessary, though there were days he attempted to avoid it. But he was not here to forget. It wouldn't be right, to forget.

He decided to wait another day to mess with his hair. It didn't look too bad, and sometimes it took him awhile to get a new braid right.

When he was a young man in Georgia, his hair was cut loose around his face, and it curled and flipped in the humid heat. He saw himself suddenly as he had been—distantly, as if looking at something across a field. His legs like stilts. His hair a crown of gold.

He'd grown the hair, in part, to make up for the absence of a beard. A little more something between himself and the cold.

He had often thought, though, about cutting off the braid. It would be easy; he had a pair of sharp scissors. He imagined feeling lighter. Maybe he'd look younger without it.

No. He caught himself. He wasn't going to start doing things like that.

He pulled open his door, stepped outside into the wind. His feet were white and ghost-like against the dark earth. He took a few steps down the trail that led to his outhouse, turned his back to the wind and pissed into a cluster of short, scrubby, wind-beaten bushes.

Back inside, he poured water into a basin and splashed it onto his face. He found himself sighing again. He needed to get over to the airport. Katie was coming home today, and he was to take her across the lake with him when he did the mail run. It wasn't that he didn't want to see Katie; for years she and Billy and Nicky were a favorite part of his life—they would always be there, when he brought in the mail, the three of them always together. He would play uncle and bring them things from town—candy and gum, comic books if he could find any. It seemed a happy time, in retrospect, though he was still suffering severely at that point. The lesson he learned was never to think that things could not be worse, or that any individual person had an exclusive grip on sorrow. But as with many things, he felt there must have been something he should have been able to *see*, and therefore something he should have been able to do, that could have changed the course of events that led to Nicky's death. Maybe, maybe not. Maybe. But he knew his feelings of responsibility were nothing compared to what the others felt, and he understood the shutting off, the years of silence. He'd been there; he was there.

You don't know what happened, Katie had said, on one of the last times he had seen her.

Well, no, sweetheart; no one does—

How do you know? How do you know no one knows? Katie'd said then, and he'd chalked it up to shock and sorrow. Over the years he'd thought about what she'd meant; he'd chalked this up to her own feelings of guilt and self-blame, the wanting to believe that there was some reason other than a course of events and an accident that changed the world forever.

These feelings he knew as well—he had been there; he was there still.

———————————

Twigg was there to meet her when Katie got off the plane. He recognized her instantly as she came through the open doorway and began to descend the metal steps. *Such a small thing*, he thought, and he realized at once how little she had changed: thin, pale, angry looking, the way she had been the last time he'd seen her. It was like a time warp, and he realized that wasn't right. People do change; people should change, especially between the age of seventeen and what? Thirty?

Twenty-eight or twenty-nine? The thought seemed unreal to him. How was it that time just kept going by? As he watched, he saw her pause midway down the steps and grab the railing. Her head seemed to tilt back and it looked to him that her eyes were closed. People jerked to a stop behind her. Twigg began to walk toward the stairs. Then she began to move again, and when she reached the bottom and saw him she rushed over, threw herself against him as if she still were only a child. Twigg felt his heart hurting for her. He laid a big palm on her tiny head and patted her back with the other. "Hey now," he said, gently. "Hey now, Katie. Let's get you home." She nodded, pulled away, and he was surprised to see she managed to hold back her tears, though her eyes blinked fast and her lips were stretched tight in something that wasn't quite a smile. And there, down the length of her cheek, was the scar he'd heard about, from something she had done to herself, locked in a bathroom not long after she and her mother had left Ilmenof. Cut off her hair and cut the side of her face. All that, now this. *Oh, Katie*, he wanted to say. *Don't lose the world.* Had she even, in all the years between Nicky and now, ever gotten it back?

He decided the best thing was just to get her in the plane and get her across the lake, though what was waiting for her there was anybody's guess. Manny never quite had the parent thing figured out, Twigg thought. But surely, under these circumstances, he would put in some effort. At least he didn't have a girlfriend or anything, didn't seem to want to change that. Hardly noticed the new public health nurse in town, Margaret. Lots of luck there anyway, for any of them, Twigg thought; he knew who had caught the woman's eye, and it wasn't Manny and it wasn't him. A thought came to him then, as he and Katie silently grabbed her gear from the pile of baggage and walked toward Twigg's truck, and he felt guilty for the lift in his heart. Katie's coming back was certainly a bend in the road. Just when he thought things were heading a certain way.

But that, too, could go bad. He realized he'd recognized the angry scowl on Katie's face: Billy wore it, too.

They hopped into the cab of his truck and began the drive down to the water. Though it was cloudy, Katie put on a pair of dark sunglasses, and Twigg felt as if he were chauffeuring a mysterious celebrity.

At one time, after the accident, Katie probably held that kind of status, but the story now had been laid to rest among the myths and legends of Ilmenof, buried under things that had happened since, Nicky's missing body just one more on a list of those the lake has taken.

Twigg noticed the splattering of earrings along the outsides of Katie's ears and tried not to stare. He wasn't so secluded that he hadn't noticed the trend of multiple piercings, but there was something determined about the row of holes along her ears, the tiny silver baubles clinging there. Twigg had a sudden flash of Katie as a child, a memory of something he used to say about her: *As stubborn as the snow in the shadows in the spring.* That was it, he thought; there was something stubborn about all those holes.

The road into town was still unpaved. The old truck lurched and bounced. The terrain was flat, barren; a few stretches of scrub spruce held tight against the wind. As they neared town, houses began to appear—shack-like structures made mostly of plywood, some with back yards riddled with dog houses, others with broken snowmachines waiting to be fixed. Anybody with money lived closer to the lake, where the various hunting and fishing lodges looked glossy and out of place. There used to be just one lodge that had been built, owned and run by the same people for years. Now that lodge was lost among and dwarfed by the newer buildings, and the family, seeing a change in the tide, sold out and flew south. Twigg wondered if the day would soon come when he would be run out of business by a newer, slicker operation. He had one thing on his side: experience. That was something all the trust funds in the world couldn't buy.

When they came into town—which consisted mostly of one street with a graying and fading post office, a trading post with a warped front porch, and a telephone booth—Twigg waited until what he thought was just the right moment to point out his new office.

"See that?" he said, pointing up ahead.

Katie looked, said: "That's different."

"That's my office."

For the first time she smiled. "You're stepping up the world, aren't you?"

"Just tryin' to survive." But he did feel big inside, showing that to her. The office was a good move for him. It *said* something—something more than survival. Success. He was successful in this new life he had created for himself; he had stood the test of time, and he could hold his own. And of all the pilots at Ilmenof, he was the one the locals chose to fly with. That said something, too—something that meant much more to him than his bright little office.

"This town hasn't changed," Katie said

"Well, you ain't seen the lake front yet."

With that they passed his office, and the road continued on toward the cove where Twigg and various other pilots tied down their float planes. They could see the water now, gray with whitecaps on the waves.

"Is Billy around?" Katie asked suddenly.

"Yeah—yeah, he is."

"How is he?"

Twigg thought for a moment. "You know it's always hard to tell, with Billy."

"He's not fishing."

It didn't sound like a question. "No—no, he isn't." In the past Billy would be in Bristol Bay, commercial fishing with his father, Jake. But he quit going for the whole season some time ago, goes now only for the ten-day/two-week peak.

"Marla finally leave Jake?" Katie asked. Marla was Jake's third wife.

"Yeah—lasted longer than anybody thought, though." Twigg looked sideways at Katie and tried to think of a way to say something about Billy without being obvious. "Just a bunch of men over there, these days," he said. It sounded natural enough. But he could see that Katie's thoughts were already someplace else; they were nearing the crescent of cove, and the rest of the shoreline was unfolding.

"Jesus," Katie said, looking at the row of lodges that gleamed even in the gray.

"Welcome to Disneyland, Alaska style."

A short time later they were in the air, flying over the gray waters of Ilmenof. Forty miles wide and seventy miles long, the lake was a formidable presence: magnificent. Dangerous. Like so much of Alaska. Twigg felt he had come to an understanding with his adopted state: never expect anything to be halfway. Never expect anything to be

complacent and tame—*comfortable*. Always expect an edge. In this way
he had learned to get along.

Katie's family had settled on the opposite side of the lake from
the town in a large corner of the lake called Tangle Bay, a name inspired
by the many islands that riddled the area. From the air the islands
looked like puzzle pieces of varying shapes and sizes.

Twigg flew first over open water. Whipped by wind, the gray
mass moved and seemed to breathe beneath them, like a large animal
stirring in sleep. Katie was silent and Twigg made a few fumbled efforts
at small talk. But when the islands began to appear she sat up straighter
in her seat, and despite the dark glasses covering her eyes he could see
on her face all they had in common: love, loss, the being gone from
someplace held dear; the being gone a long damned time.

Billy Johnson stuck his knife into the belly of a salmon, pushed
the blade toward the gills. The insides spilled onto the stained plywood
table: intestines, the tiny purple liver, two sacks of bright orange eggs.
He reached inside and pulled out the heart, thought the salmon moved.
He waited, heart in his hand. Nothing. He wondered if it was still alive
when he'd sliced into it; he didn't like it when they were still alive. But
sometimes he couldn't tell.

He dropped the heart onto the table—which stood between the
low-roofed cabin of his childhood and a wide, swift stream—and heard
the sound of a low plane. He'd been waiting all morning to hear it,
dreading it, knew it was coming and there was nothing he could do.

When he picked up the knife again, his hand was shaking. He
tried to steady it as he sliced up the back of the fish, then up around
the gills, splitting the salmon into halves connected by the tail fin. He
pulled out the skeleton, still attached to the head. He had a place for all
the parts of the fish. The head, the skeleton, organs, and guts went into
an old 55-gallon drum, to be cooked later for dog slop; the sides went

into a barrel of salt brine before being hung in the smokehouse. He had a gallon-sized mason jar for the eggs, already half full.

He distributed that fish, then started another. He liked to clean as he went.

Fuck, Bill, just pile 'em up, eh?

He could see Nicky across the table from him, for an instant. Hair in his eyes, hands covered with blood and slime. Tipping his head to the side as he talked. Knife moving so fast.

Billy's own knife slipped as he started the next fish; the tip of the blade stabbed into the palm of his hand, just under the thumb. He pulled it out and looked, pain shooting up his arm. A pool of blood formed and began to trickle over the sides of his hand. It looked as if he was holding something red and shiny. A red spider, maybe, or something once solid now dissolving there, in his hand.

He closed his eyes and fought an urge to tip the table over, to kick at it and at everything. Katie wasn't supposed to be staying long, he reasoned; it could be that he wouldn't even see her. Or it could be that he would see her, and it would be okay. So much time had gone by. Sometimes it seemed he had lived a whole separate life, once, a long time ago. Other times it seemed as if he was right there again, on the beach, in the wind and the rain with the ripping feeling in his heart, kicking and kicking at Nicky's baidarka until finally he felt something breaking there, in the boat's skeleton.

I didn't kill him. He has told himself this more times than anybody could count.

He heard the sound of the plane again; this time it was coming his way. He rinsed his hand in the clear, fast-moving waters of the stream and watched the blood fan out from the wound and wash away. He took a clean bandanna out of the pocket of his jeans and wrapped it tight around the clean wound, then walked down the trail that followed the stream to the lake.

The Johnsons had no dock. Years ago Billy's father had tried and tried to make one that would hold up against the strain of the wind and the water, but he could never get it right and eventually gave up. They always pulled their boats onto the shore or anchored them and waded in. When he was younger, Billy made dock designs in his head for when he had his own place, his real place, not the place he'd built upstream from his father's, where he still lived now.

He'd had some idea, then, that his real life was yet to happen. He knew now that it was only what it was.

Twigg landed on the wide stretch of water in front of the Johnson's place and began taxiing the plane toward the shore. Billy hurried in that direction, pulled his hip boots up his thighs and waded out to meet the plane, which he grabbed by the brace beneath the wing. Twigg popped open the door.

"Hey, Billy," Twigg said. "How's it?"

"Oh, not too bad," he said. "Lots of fish today."

"Hear anything from your old man?"

"It's been good," Billy said, referring to the commercial fishing in Bristol Bay. "Some big runs, eh?" Fishing with his father was something he had lived for when he was a boy, but there had been only a few seasons when he'd got to do it before Nicky died and Katie left. He still remembered the feeling of having *everything*.

"Here's your mail," Twigg said, handing him a small bundle secured with rubber bands. Billy took it with one hand, kept his hold on the wing with the other, which was the cut hand, and he could feel how the bandanna was wet. A moment of awkward silence passed between them, and Billy thought how Twigg didn't have to say anything—there was nothing that needed saying.

"Well, I just dropped her off," Twigg said.

"Manny home?"

"Well, no, not exactly—on his way, though; he did manage to catch me on the radio to say he was just finishing up with a client and would be heading home soon."

Billy nodded, but didn't know what to say. He could feel the pressure of unasked questions in his throat. There had been no words between him and Katie since the day Nicky died and no real words between them that day, either. He had dreams of asking her what happened. Not to Nicky, but to *them*.

"So I should push you out now, eh, just a little maybe, you got good wind," Billy said.

Twigg sighed; Billy's ears caught the sound and he saw without looking how Twigg shook his head. "Yeah," Twigg said. "I got good wind today, I'd say, no shortage of good wind 'round here." He smiled at Billy and pulled the door closed.

When Billy returned to the splitting table, he dropped the bundle of mail onto the ground. He saw there was a letter for him from Margaret; he left it with the rest. He tightened the bandanna around his bleeding hand, holding one end with his teeth. He threw some fish onto the table, worked without cleaning, filling the table with piles of parts.

After a time he quit, hands aching. He stared at the messy table and imagined Nicky.

We did good this morning. Billy'd said this once; he remembered the feel of the words. Early that terrible summer, before the salmon, before Billy'd left for the bay, when they set the net for other fish.

You, Billy, you did good. Nicky had just returned from a night in town; it took Billy a moment to see the bits of dried blood on his face, the swollen, bruised lips.

So what's this now, eh, Nicky? You been fighting again—I see it there, your lips, you should look at yourself. For chrissakes, Nicky, you been back a month and that's three fights now, three fights. Back a month from his winter in Anchorage. Billy had had to go get him, bring him home. Drugs and fights; Billy didn't want to know.

It's nothing. It's not shit. No big deal, eh? It was nothing.

Keep this up, and Dad'll be sending me back from the bay, check on you.

Words said without thought. Nicky looked at him then stabbed his knife into the table.

Hey—hey, Billy'd said. He shook his head, fast. *Don't do that. Don't get started. All right. That wasn't so good a thing to say. I shouldn't—*

If he's so fucking worried then why the fuck doesn't he just have me go down there where he can keep a fucking eye on me himself, eh?

I don't know.

You know. Everyone knows.

No, Billy'd said, then: *It'll be right, eh? It'll work out. Don't leave again. Wait for winter, eh? We'll do some stuff. Build a winter camp, do some trapping, run some dogs. It'll be right.*

Nicky'd tipped his head, spit, pulled the knife out from the table. Suddenly he smiled, fresh blood oozing from a split in his lip. *So, Katie, eh?*

Yeah.

That must be fucking weird… Glad she finally grew her teeth.
Among other things.

Billy would have said something then, but he was glad to have the subject change, glad Nicky was smiling.

Goin' over there?

Yeah, when we're done.

I'll do this.

You sure, eh?

Nicky had nodded. As Billy's knife had touched the trout he held, it began to twist and flop with sudden violence, the insides seeping out of the cut he'd started.

You always think they're dead. Nicky came around to his side of the table, pinned the fish down, whacked it on the head with the butt of his knife. The tail twitched, the mouth moved, the eyes flickered, and then nothing. Nicky said: *You don't hit them hard enough, Bill, you got to crush them skulls right in.* Then he kicked the side of the tub that held the fish. A few tails flinched, a few mouths moved.

Billy did this now, kicked the tub. A ripple of movement shuddered through the heap of scaly bodies. Billy chose one, put it on the table, and with the butt of his knife he crushed in the skull. But there was no twitch, no flicker—it seemed it was already dead.

⸻

The house was dim, cold from lack of a fire. Katie slid her pack down her shoulders, dropped it to the floor. Her father was not home.

He had made radio contact, though, with Twigg on the flight across the lake. The sound of his voice was startling to her. When he had called after her mother's death, Katie couldn't really feel the effect of his voice at that time; she'd felt as if she had been bludgeoned into a state of numbness. In Twigg's plane the voice scratched at her soul and filled her with dread. Yet at the same time it almost brought her to tears. She was filled with the longing of a seven-year-old child who'd spent one too many nights away from home. Now that she was here, she didn't know what she felt.

She had only seen Manny once in the twelve years of her absence. He'd come to Boston for the burial of his own mother—Katie's grandmother. Katie had been gone from the lake, from him, for three years. She hadn't been ready to see him.

So what have you been doing with yourself, Katie?

Nothing.

Nothing?

Nothing.

She remembered a window in a restaurant where they were having lunch. The snow falling on the sidewalk outside. Manny's reflection, uncomfortable and struggling. The scar on her face, like a neon sign.

Now, the house felt as if it would crush her. Everywhere she saw her mother, saw Nicky, saw Billy. She gritted her teeth. She knew it would be hard, knew there would be pain. She remembered what she told herself: *take it.* Think about pain. Think about the feel of a needle, pushing its way through skin…

She stood there in the silence. After a small time she felt she could breathe again, started to see the house for what it was: walls long void of the life that once lived inside them.

Coming in on the plane, she had thought how the knoll that the house sat on looked like a cupcake, turned upside down and decorated on the sides with tiny trees, random clusters of pretend brush scattered across the top by the house. The trail that wound up from the cove where the dock stretched into the water was like a dirty piece of string; the house itself looked old, tired and gray, and much smaller than Katie remembered. Again, she'd wanted to cry.

After Twigg reluctantly left her alone on the gray and sagging wooden dock, and the plane taxied out of the small cove which provided shelter from the winds that whipped off the main water, Katie had shouldered her pack and proceeded to face the storm of memories that spilled over her as she began the climb up the knoll. The smells were especially powerful. Spruce needles. Birch leaves. Various scents that rose up from the dry and dusty trail. Katie had remembered all the dust in town, too, despite the grayness that indicated recent rains. All of Ilmenof was like that. Dry. Despite all the water, in the lake and in the sky, anywhere the ground was uncovered the earth would turn to dust.

When Katie had climbed the hill and reached the house, she didn't allow herself the chance to pause and examine the structure, to remember the doorway and the comings and goings, to visualize her mother there, or Nicky, or Billy before she betrayed him, or the ghost of who she used to be. Instead she pushed against the rough wooden door without altering her pace and tumbled inside, snagging her pack and almost tripping. But there she stopped.

There was a sour smell in the house; dirty dishes were piled across the homemade counters in the little corner kitchen. Across the room from her the table sat in front of two large, single-paned windows; a group of kerosene lamps with dirty chimneys were clustered in the center.

She remembered walking into the Boston apartment, a week or more after her mother's death, after the service and the arrangements and her aunt's return to her own home. She'd been out doing errands, a normal thing. Groceries. It was late afternoon. She came through the door. Silence. Silence and gray light. That was all. Where her mother once was there was now nothing.

Nothing. Her mother said this. Once. *I don't want anything.*

There must be something, Katie had said. It was after they'd left, when the pain began to settle and it became clear that they would not be going back. They had left so much at Ilmenof. Katie wanted it back. She didn't want her father to have it all.

Her mother had said, *No.*

Katie moved across the floor, and wondered now what she'd wanted. The floor creaked and she saw how it warped toward one of the walls. The house had never been quite square. Before Alaska, Manny had been an architect; there was an office Katie could remember, up high in a tall building, an image of her father in a white shirt with a tie. After their arrival here he commercial fished for awhile, with Billy and Nicky's father, but he was now and had been for some time a guide for the lodge on this side of the lake, spending his days with men such as Katie had seen earlier, on the flight to Ilmenof.

She went to her room and pulled open the curtain hanging across the doorway. Her room was a small extension on one side of the house; her parents had slept in a loft over the main room. Dust from the curtain rained into the air as she entered. She felt a weight in her heart. The room was apaparently used now for storage; cardboard boxes were stacked on what once was her home-made cot, and other things—tools, an old chainsaw, winter boots—littered the small floor area. Katie wondered what she'd expected. She leaned her pack against the boxes on the bed. She'd have to wait until her father came home to clear out the other stuff. She told herself it was okay. *There is my window. There is my bed. There is the braided rug my mother made me, underneath a box.*

There have been bigger rooms in the different apartments in Boston; her mother would always let her have the nicest room, would always say, *Oh, isn't this nice,* and then would add: *It's only temporary, Katie, until we see what happens.* They talked of better apartments; they talked of homes in the country, good neighborhoods. They didn't talk of Ilmenof.

In those rooms in those apartments Katie would lie awake at night and listen to the sirens screaming down the city streets. In her mind she followed the swirling lights, imagined the trouble, the catastrophe. The sirens were something she could never get used to, the sirens and the phones—they went together somehow, in her mind. Maybe it was the noise, the alarm; maybe it was because of the way her mother would look, picking up the phone, hesitant in her hello, as if expecting only something bad. As if that's what phones were for, bad news and emergencies.

When she got the call about her mother, from the hospital, she was just on her way out the door to walk to a bookstore and do some other errands before having to get ready for her own job at the Chinese restaurant where she waitressed. It was one of her mother's co-workers, a friend; Katie didn't get it at first, what the woman was saying. "She should be there," Katie said. "She left the same time she always does." But as the voice on the other end explained again, and it began to register, Katie felt herself slipping down against the wall toward the floor, her mouth open and unable to move.

Katie's mother's ashes were in a tight urn in a zippered bag buried deeply in her backpack. She'd had this horrible feeling that she was doing something illegal, bringing them silently stashed in amongst her things. But here she was. Here they were. She still wasn't sure why she thought her mother would want this.

On a shelf in the room that ran just below the ceiling Katie saw some of her old stuffed animals and wondered why she had left them—wondered, too, why her father hadn't thrown them out. They stared down at her with dusty, cloudy eyes: a kitten, a bear, and a giraffe—the giraffe had been her favorite. There was a stump in the room and she stood on it to pull them down off the shelf. Dust flew everywhere and the toys smelled thickly of wood smoke. She wiped their worn, familiar faces with the threadbare sleeve of her sweatshirt.

They reminded her of Norma, Billy and Nicky's cousin from the village. Her friend. Once. Then her father's lover. Norma would fuss over the stuffed animals, things she didn't have.

Why did Norma leave, too, after Nicky died? She knew this because her mother kept track, through her friend Shirley who ran the original lodge on the other side of the lake. They both thought, but never said aloud, that Norma would end up replacing them both. But it didn't happen, it hadn't happened, and that was another unclear shadow in the backdrop of Katie's thoughts that have to do with Nicky's death, another area where she wanted, but didn't want, to go.

Katie put the animals back into the dust on the shelf and returned to the main room. She leaned against a wall, squeezed her eyes closed, forced her mind to clear. She was aware of pain in the center of her stomach; she'd pierced her belly button several weeks after her mother died, and it wasn't healing right and kept getting infected. She was considering the fact that she might have to let it grow over. But for now the pain seemed fitting—she felt pain all over.

She opened her eyes, as if starting again, looked and saw: there were things here she could do. Build a fire in the stove, heat some water and wash up the dishes. There is little one can do, besides such things as these.

Katie had learned how to pierce herself from a girl who lived down the hall in the first apartment she and Vivian had lived in after they left Ilmenof. The girl's name was Marsha Fay and she, too, lived with her mother. She was several years younger than Katie but knew about all the things Katie didn't know about, from growing up at Ilmenof: eyeliner, stockings, the best kind of tampons, and how to give yourself a permanent. While Katie's face was healing, before she went out looking for work, she would wait for Marsha Fay to come home from school in the afternoons. Katie would first help her with her homework—home-schooling had been good to Katie, she had excelled—then there would be a small space of free time before their working mothers returned home. It didn't matter which apartment they hung out in. Each was similar, and similarly empty.

One of Marsha Fay's favorite things was to "improve" Katie. It was Marsha Fay who fixed the tattered self-inflicted haircut into something passable; multiple attempts were made to put make-up on Katie, but always Katie would look in the mirror, not like what she saw, and immediately wash it off. They both pretended the wound on Katie's face, with the stitches freshly removed, wasn't there.

Marsha Fay would often use her own round and semi-plump face to demonstrate techniques and improvements in the hopes of winning Katie over to the other side—that world of girls who fussed and fretted, who enhanced their lashes and dyed and curled their hair and sculpted cheekbones with the right shades of blush. It seemed to Katie that Marsha Fay was looking for a face that wasn't her own; Katie was resigned to hers, her pale skin and the small nose that seemed off-center on her face, her protruding upper lip. Now with the scar it seemed especially futile to try to "improve" herself, or "make the most of what you've got" as Marsha Fay would say, and make-up was something she opted not to indulge in. But one thing about Marsha Fay's adornment of herself that Katie did like were the multiple piercings on the edges of Marsha Fay's ears. Katie decided to start off with one, and Marsha Fay had her hold an ice cube on the lobe until it felt numb. But it wasn't numb, not all the way through; when Marsha Fay began to push the needle in Katie felt it, and she took a sharp breath.

"Hurt?" Marsha Fay had asked.

"It's okay."

"Do you want me to stop?"

"No." Katie focused on the pain. It seemed pure and clear. Later, when the hole became infected, that too became a pain she could focus on. Her other ear piercings Katie did herself, watching her face in the mirror as she pushed the needle through her skin. She did several piercings soon after the first; after that she did them more sparingly, saving the space on her ears for when she needed something to consume her thoughts. Gradually, her hair grew back, and little by little the scar from her cheekbone to her chin lost its redness, though it never completely faded.

Round about the time Marsha Fay and all her girl gadgets moved away, Katie had six holes in one ear and seven in the other, and she'd also learned how, with needles and ink, she could create her own do-it-yourself blue tattoos. By the time she met Khoi, at the Chinese restaurant that was owned by Khoi's uncle, she had a three-inch width of blue tattoo bracelets on her left wrist, all composed of patterns and shapes in variations of the letter "N." Her mother was not approving (*You're going to get blood poisoning, Katie!*) yet at the same time she let it go. Katie was well into her twenties at that point, had had her own apartments when she could afford them, so there was nothing to be done but express motherly concern and hope the phase would pass.

Khoi, on the other hand, understood and embraced what she'd done. But he also turned it around, buying her small silver earrings with auspicious symbols and protective creatures, gently putting them into her ears himself. "You can wear your altar," he said, kissing her forehead. "Let it bring you good things." The scar on her face and its origins he took as proof that not all Americans were hollow. Despite the difference in their cultures and backgrounds they had a common ground: they were both on the outside of East Coast American life—strangers, intruders, people who didn't quite fit.

Now, back at Ilmenof, Boston took on a faded, dream-like quality in her thoughts as Katie stood outside her former home, examining the woodpile. The woodpile was stacked under the eaves on the west side of the building. It used to be one of Katie's jobs to stand there with

Manny while he split the bongo-shaped chunks of spruce and birch; Katie had to grab the pieces after they came flying off the chopping block and put each piece in its proper place under the eaves. Spruce was kept separate from birch, and the freshest cut, greenest wood had to be as far to the end and as close to the bottom of the pile as possible; as it seasoned it had to be rotated up and forward. Seasoned wood had less creosote in it when it burned; there was a danger of chimney fires if too much creosote built up in the stovepipes. Manny would lecture Katie about creosote as she stacked and organized the woodpile. If their house were ever to burn down from a chimney fire, she had been sure it would be her fault.

But now Katie found the woodpile completely disordered. Spruce and birch were all mixed together, and wood that was obviously well seasoned remained buried on the bottom. It was unsplit except for a neat little pile, near where the ax leaned against the wall. As Katie's eyes took in the graduated thicknesses—from sharp thin kindling pieces to nicely quartered chunks—she saw also a weathered piece of paper secured with wood on top of the pile. She felt her heart drop and her knees wanting to buckle as she recognized the handwriting: Billy's. She gently removed it from the pile.

Hey, Manny—
This should last you awhile now it's warmer, but when it
gets low let me know, eh? It's no problem—
Bill

Katie stared at the note, ran her hand over the writing. She tried to stay focused on the question the note raised: Why was Billy chopping wood for Manny? But the sight of it, and the sound of it, the feel of the words and she was filled with Billy again, of the missing him, of the wanting to explain it somehow to him, of the dream and the desire and the weeping longing for forgiveness.

It was evening and several more flights before Twigg tied down the plane in the cove, back where he'd started from, and saw a smear of blood on the brace beneath the wing.

Billy. He'd noticed the bandanna, but forgot to ask. Was too distracted to ask. He'd kept seeing the other Billy, the Billy whose face was like a clear morning, clean and bright and full of hope. The Billy who'd said, twelve years ago, when he'd come back unexpectedly from fishing in the bay and Twigg saw him in town:

Seen Katie, eh?

Well yeah—off and on—

How's she?

Fine—as far as I can tell—you come back just to see her?

And then he'd smiled, and laughed, and shook his head in a helpless sort of way.

You got it bad, Twigg had said, and he remembered how he felt amazed, that two people could know each other as long as Billy and Katie had, and then one day it all becomes different. And then with another day, it's different again.

Twigg then thought, too, of this: winter, years ago, another mail run. The December sun weak and low, already sinking away. Landing the plane on the snow-covered lake. Seeing the kids coming on the dog sled. Billy and Nicky on the runners; Katie a princess in the basket. The dogs' breath white clouds. The feeling: *This* is Alaska! Boxes for Katie's family, unloaded onto the ice. Oranges, ordered from the trading post in town; soda pop. Billy and Nicky in thin coats and worn boots, watching. Katie in her fur coat and mukluks, ripping open the boxes, giving gifts to the boys—oranges and soda pop, held in their arms like treasure. Billy smiling, Nicky frowning, but four dark eyes always on Katie.

As he climbed into his old blue pickup, Twigg thought about stories, how someone once told him that every person's life was like a story, with characters and cause-and-effect sequences all woven together, winding toward climaxes and final unravelings.

Some people's stories end long before their lives, one last paragraph enough to sum up the end of one's existence. Twigg could see how this was possible. It had been Cindy, he realized; *Cin* who told him this. He sighed, shifted his truck into gear, bounced and bumped his way into town. Tired, hungry, thinking about dinner, what he might fix, when suddenly there was a small boy running into the road directly in front of him—

No! He slammed on the brakes, lurched forward and bashed his chin on the steering wheel. Shaking and fumbling, he put the gears into park and stepped out of the truck. The boy was all right. Twigg leaned against the cool metal of the door. The boy stood in the road and stared. Dark eyes and black hair: Native, at least in part. Twigg didn't recognize him as one of the local gangsters who would leave piles of mud by the door of his office. Sometimes piles of dog shit. Now and then he would pull a trick of his own back at them; they have fun. But this boy wasn't one he knew. The boy turned and ran away. His small flannel shirt, tied around his waist, came loose and sailed down into the dusty road.

"Hey!" Twigg said. The boy kept running. "You dropped your shirt!" He heard his own voice, weak and trembling, unfamiliar. He pushed himself away from the truck, stepped into the road and picked up the shirt. It was old and worn, but recent dust excepted, clean, and there were small, careful patches on the elbows where holes once had been. Twigg shook it out, looked around, but the boy had disappeared.

He drove the remaining short distance to his office, slow, foot wanting the brake. His hands still shook as he unlocked the door. He brought the shirt with him, laid it on his desk. Then he leaned back in his chair, put up his feet, closed his eyes.

He kept seeing the boy there, running into the road, over and over.

He opened his eyes and stared at the shirt. After awhile he grabbed it, buttoned up the tiny buttons, folded it neatly and put it in the top drawer of his desk. He sat back again, then sat abruptly forward, took the shirt from the top drawer and moved it into the bottom drawer, set it beneath a little-used phone book and slid the drawer shut. Then he sat and stared out the window, at nothing in particular.

It was after eight before her father got home; Katie was at the table looking out the windows, watching the lake. She had seen terns and gulls fly by, swooping up over the crest of the knoll, then diving back down to the water beyond the edge. It would not get dark, but there was duskiness outside, like a gray wash layered over the lighter gray of day, and it was dimmer yet in the house. Katie knew lighting the lamps would do no good. Cloudy summer evenings were an elongated version of what passes so quickly in winter: the transition time between light and dark, day and night, when it is neither one nor the other but somehow both at once. Katie felt as if she were dissolving into it.

The door opened, and a dark moving mass stepped in. Katie had neither seen nor heard the arrival of the skiff; nothing unusual, given the sound of the wind rattling the washtubs hanging on the outside walls, the limited view from where the house sat on the knoll.

Katie looked toward the door and said, "Hi." She was aware of the nervous beating of her heart.

"Hello, daughter."

He came across the room to her; she stood briefly and he kissed the top of her head. He smelled of fish and sweat and home-rolled cigarettes. He was unshaven; the stubble on his chin pricked her scalp. He sighed, patted her shoulder, took a seat at the opposite end of the table.

"Well," he said, "well." Katie was grateful for the dim lighting; she was fighting an urge to cry. "So how are you doing, Katie?" he asked, the words slurring out the side of his mouth. He pulled a tobacco pouch from the breast pocket of his tan canvas shirt.

"I'm all right."

"Good; that's good. I've been worried, you know." His eyes landed on the scar on her face.

She slumped a little in her seat, crossed her arms in front of her.

He sighed again, the air whistling through his bottom teeth. "I always thought she'd outlive me, by a good ten years or so." He sprinkled tobacco into the valley of a cigarette paper, rolled and licked, pulled a lighter from the pocket of his jeans. In the brief flash of fire Katie saw the weight on his face, the dull edge of gray in the combed-back hair, the way the widow's peak had grown more pronounced by the thinning on either side.

He took a long drag from the cigarette, tipped his head back, and blew smoke out into the air. "Even so I thought there'd be some kind of a warning—something. Aren't there warning signs for something like that?"

They'd already had this conversation, on the phone. "Sometimes, sometimes not," Katie said.

"Christ almighty—surviving a Boston winter and dying in the spring. There's something contradictory about that."

"I know."

They let some moments pass. There was a clock somewhere; Katie heard it ticking.

Manny said, "So what do you have in mind, anyway?"

Katie shrugged. "I don't know. A little grave or something, maybe. Maybe a little cache so she could see the lake."

"I thought you were supposed to—scatter ashes or something. Isn't that what people usually do?"

"We can do anything we want, I think. I don't think she wanted to be just scattered around."

"Why do you say that?"

Katie looked at him. Again she noticed the aging, the dullness in his once-glossy hair. But his brows still arched and his eyes still glinted; even in the dim light she could see their sharp-edged gray color as they examined her. "I don't know," she said. "I just think she would have liked to—keep herself together."

"Well, I knew your mother. I don't think she'd care much."

Katie bit at her upper lip, looked at her father. He was looking out the window now. "But there's no problem, is there, with a little grave or something?"

He smiled slightly from the side of his mouth, nodded his head and took another drag off his cigarette. Katie saw how the rolling paper was burning unevenly; a line of red ripped up one side. He put some spit on his finger, tried to slow the burn. "Yeah," he said. "There's a bit of a problem there all right."

"What do you mean?"

"I've had an offer."

Katie looked out the window, looked back at him, narrowed her eyes. "You're always getting offers," she said. Because of the Alaska

Native Land Claims Settlement Act, there was little land available for sale on this side of the lake.

"Oh, yeah, but—" He paused a moment. "I'm getting tired."

"What do you mean?" She felt a rush of panic, like a hand on the back of her head.

"I mean I'm tired. Tired of making conversation with people I don't know, tired of unsnagging their lures and gutting their fish. You know they keep getting younger, these guys. Used to be I'd feel pretty good about the whole bit, taking some nice old gent out for the adventure of his life, give him something to tell the grandchildren back home. But these guys are faster and younger, got all this fancy gear and I tell ya, they want their fish *now*. There's no sitting back and relaxing about it. And well, you know, Phil's gone—heart attack—and I can't see myself working for that kid of his much longer."

Katie thought about Dean, wondered what he was like now. "So is it Dean who made you the offer?" Katie asked. She couldn't picture Dean as a grown man, imagined him as he'd looked at twelve.

"No—are you kidding? He can't handle one lodge. That place has been going downhill ever since Phil died—I'm lucky as hell there're any clients at all."

"Who, then?"

"Some Japanese investors. They were clients, actually, a few summers ago."

"Would you sell to them?"

"No one's offering me the kind of money they are." His head was tipped back a little, and the smoke swirled around his face. "I've got no retirement, you know."

Then Katie noticed his hand, the one holding the cigarette. The knuckles looked swollen, giving the hand a gnarled appearance. "What's wrong with your hand?"

"Arthritis. Hurts like hell."

"Where did that come from?"

"Didn't come from anywhere. Just have it, that's all. Another reason why I need to start looking at other things. It's hard to fix a line sometimes."

Katie thought about the woodpile. She wondered how long Billy had been helping him. "But what about Mom, then?"

Manny took a deep breath, then puffed again on the cigarette, smoke spilling out as he talked. "Katie, your mother knew about things like this." He got up and walked to the kitchen area where he filled a wineglass from a bottle of white wine. Katie had noticed the pile of empty bottles—all from white wine, as had been his habit and evidently still was—in the kitchen when she cleaned. "She knew that wherever she is now she's way beyond caring what happens to a pile of ash that was once her flesh and bone," he said. "You cleaned out here," he added, looking around. He tipped his head back and drank before refilling his glass and returning to the table, the wineglass looking odd and out of place with his person. "She knew about death. She knew what it meant to be a part of things."

Katie felt a tightness in her throat, swallowed hard against it. "She would not have wanted to die."

"That's only natural."

"But—"

"She knew what it was really all about. She's all right with it, Katie; I knew your mother. She's all right with it."

Katie rubbed her forehead, pressed it hard into her hand. Her eyes slid to the side, looked out the window, stared past her own reflection at the gray and moving world beyond the glass.

Later, Katie lay in her bed and heard how the wind had calmed. She heard, too, a loon somewhere down on the water, its howl-like cry rising into the night. Up in the loft that was his bedroom, her father was snoring.

She left her bed, maneuvered through the boxes that cluttered the floor. She grabbed a flannel shirt off the top of her pack and threw it on over her T-shirt and boxers, then walked barefoot out the door. The resting of the wind had allowed the mist to form and gather along the shore; it stretched out onto the water, like the reaching of ghostly hands. Katie walked to the cove and sat on the dock, remembered being little and watching the mist, remembered the things she imagined to be in it: spirits mostly, the ghosts of people who drowned in Ilmenof.

There was a couple they had met one summer, from Idaho, who came to Alaska for water and adventure. They had a kayak. Katie's father had warned them, told them they'd better stay close to shore.

The woman's name was Colleen Smith. They found her fiancé, and the kayak, but she was never found. She had braided Katie's hair, when she and her fiancé stayed with them. After she died, Colleen's father came to Ilmenof every summer for five years, trying to bring her home.

Katie used to imagine her in the mist, Colleen and the rest of the dead. They'd made a mythology of the drowned—she and Billy and Nicky. Stories of people they never knew, or people they'd known most of their lives. Of what became of their bodies, down under the water. They often looked for them, in Billy and Nicky's old wooden skiff. A white rock glimpsed on the mucky bottom was a skull; a washed and worn stick, touched by an oar, was a bone from an arm or a leg. They found a certain fun with it all, though Katie had cried about Colleen.

How could they have known that Nicky, too, would one day join the unfound dead in the waters of the lake? And how could they ever have imagined the chain of events that would take him there?

If that's even where he is. Katie had thought this, too, though everything pointed to the lake. But with no body, you can never be sure. With no body, there is always that space, that living space, where imagination runs rampant.

And over the years she had imagined plenty.

The loon cried out again, and Katie searched the mist now for it, but didn't see anything in the cove. She began to walk on the cold rocky shore, toward the main body of water. Her feet were tender and she picked her way carefully. She was almost there when the loon rose, near the cove's mouth, a black and white buoy bobbing on the waves. Katie waded a little into the water. It was cold; her feet and legs were white inside what looked like another world.

The loon cried out. An answering call came from down the shore, beyond the cove. Katie turned toward it, staring into the mist.

He should be here. She let herself think this. An image of Nicky, drifting in his skiff, in the quiet of night. *It shouldn't be the way it is.*

Then she heard a splash, like a paddle in the water. Then another. She stayed still. A shape formed in the mist—the bow of a baidarka, and she thought: *I am over the edge, this time.*

A pale kayak of wood and bone and skin; the dark-haired, broad-shouldered shape of the paddler. A thrust forward, then a swift and silent retreat swallowed back into drifting white.

Katie's eyes tried to follow; she had seen no ghost. She knew those shoulders. Broader than Nicky's. She knew those shoulders.

When Katie woke in the morning, she heard something in the room with her; there was a scurrying sound, then a scraping, like something on the other side of the wall, trying to get in. She lay still. Then the sound changed, and she lifted her head to see a weasel, brown in its summer coat, moving across the floor. It stopped and turned, looked at her, then slipped beneath the curtained door. Katie rose and followed, quietly peering into the other room.

Her father was up already and sat alone at the table, eating. He was in the chair Katie still thought of as hers; there was the smell of bacon and coffee. She saw the weasel, climbing up the chair opposite, coming onto the table.

Manny didn't flinch. "Well, Buster, what are you up to today?" he said. He took a piece of bacon, put it on the table. The weasel grabbed it and darted away. Manny returned to his breakfast.

His face was in profile to Katie, silhouetted against the window. She watched his jaw move as he worked his food, noticed again the heaviness there, the downward feel of his face.

Before she died, Katie's mother had begun to look much the same; Katie visualized her at the cheap dinette, a drink in one hand, a cigarette in the other, still in her nurse's uniform, sweaty and dusty from her ride home on the trolley.

Hello, sweetheart. She could still hear her mother's voice. She wondered: would she always?

As she watched her father she imagined the world outside the window changing, from the blue-bright of this morning to the white-gray of winter, beyond his profile the swirling, falling snow.

He looked up at her. Smiled. Katie could see the effort there.

"New roommate," he said, nodding in the direction the weasel had gone.

Katie sat down at the table and Manny offered to cook her something to eat. She accepted a piece of bacon and a cup of coffee; the bacon was already cooked, and he walked over to the kitchen stove and poured her some coffee from a tin pot, despite her attempts to say she could get it herself. "Still like a little coffee with your milk?" he said.

"Yes—" she said. She watched as he dumped a good portion of a can of evaporated milk into her cup, then brought it sloshing and spilling over to her.

"Here ya go," he said.

"Thank you."

He smiled again, and Katie sipped the coffee, which was surprisingly good. She glanced in his direction; he caught her eyes and, again, smiled. "Coffee okay?" he asked.

"Yeah—"

"Sleep okay?"

"Yeah."

"Got plans for today?"

"No."

"I've got clients, but you could tag along if you liked."

Katie froze. Here it was. Did he want her to stay, or did he want her to go? *Make up your mind, will ya?* he used to say to her, and invariably it seemed she always made the wrong choice, though he would never really say.

"I think I'll hang here today," she said quietly.

His face gave no visible reaction. "Okay—that's fine. I'm not sure exactly when I'll be home, though. You could always radio the lodge if you needed to. Remember the call letters?"

"KBC72?"

"Yep. Well, I need to get a move on."

"Okay."

"You'll be okay then?"

"Yeah—fine."

"All right—I'll see you later." He moved to the door, put a cap on over his thinning hair, grabbed a raincoat and left. Katie's lungs pulled for air as the door closed, as if she'd forgotten to breathe.

She sat for a while in the quiet of the house. The wind was much easier than the day before; the ticking clock—still unseen—was the dominant sound. She listened for the weasel, but it seemed not to be around.

It was difficult for Katie to just sit. She'd always been bent this way, but it became worse after her mother died. It was as if there was something spinning at loose ends inside her, unable to stop, yet unable to wind back onto the spool. So she stood and walked across the room, made for the door. As she opened it she stopped, noticed a picture on the wall nearby. A Polaroid of the three of them, January, their first winter at Ilmenof, the outside of the house new-oiled and gleaming. The bright glare of the sun on the snow.

There they were, Katie thought—"bucking the tide" and "going against the grain." Her parents had talked like that, then. This was something important they were doing. They thought.

She slipped the rest of the way outside and stepped into a world of sound. Leaves rustled, chickadees and camprobbers whistled and squawked, and every lull in the breeze brought mosquitoes buzzing near her ears. She walked down to the cove, where water lapped against the dock. She went down the length of the dock's rough boards, stretched out on her stomach, painfully aware of the infected hole in her navel, and peered over the edge. At first she saw only green. The reflection of trees; the furry green muck on the bottom beneath. Then her focus shifted and there were pieces, fragments of something between the movement of small waves. Herself—her face—unrecognizable at first. She stuck her hand into the water. The image rippled and faded.

She'd lost a necklace, once, in the thick muck on the bottom of the cove. It was a birthstone necklace—her first piece of real jewelry, a gift from her parents on her eleventh birthday. Something she liked despite her tomboy ways; there was something important about it, because it was "real." And the sapphire stone was as deep a blue as she could ever imagine blue to be; it winked and glittered in a dark magical way that reminded her of clear winter skies at night. The stone was surrounded by tiny silver petals, and these reminded her of roadside flowers from her early East Coast childhood: Black-eyed Susans along country roads, smiling and nodding at her on hot summer days. The silver chain was delicate and shimmery like a tiny bright stream. The day she lost it she'd been lying on her stomach as she was now, staring at the water, but at some point she'd also been pretending to sword fight on the dock.

Both Dean and Norma were here with her that day. The three of them looked and looked, but it was as if the necklace had fallen into a black hole.

Her father had made a remark, about how he knew she was too young for "real jewelry." But her mother helped her look again after Dean and Norma had left, although the effort was futile.

Sometimes, if they had nothing else to do, Billy and Nicky, too, would help her look for it, wading out with their jeans on, bare chests and shoulders catching the sun. Billy thinking, Nicky diving and splashing.

You're stirring it up, eh?

Nicky laughing, shaking the wet from his hair.

Now, Katie took a breath and lowered her face down into the water, opened her eyes. Shadowy shapes of sticklebacks flitted past; she saw the outlines of rocks, of drowned wood. The thick dark muck rose in fingery wisps, waving in the breath-like current.

Maybe you come with me, eh?

She pulled her face from the water, scrambled to her feet. Had she heard the words, or just remembered them? Behind her the trees moved in the wind; she looked over her shoulder.

Are you there? Bushes swayed and rustled, the millions of green leaves in the birches shook and whispered. But beneath the sound Katie knew there was that silence, that same silence that filled her mother's apartment, that same silence that lurked beneath the surface of the water with all the drowned things that lingered there—

She steadied her breathing. She reminded herself that she knew it would be like this, that around every corner she would hear Nicky and see Nicky. Being here was like being awake inside her own dreams or like walking in the pages of her sketchbooks, where Nicky appeared like a ghost beneath the surface of everything she tried to draw.

She pulled up the bottom of her T-shirt and began to wipe the lake water off her face. She wiped, then wiped again.

Twelve years previous

Clouds in the water, feathered by wind—Katie watches their travel across the sky, refracted and reversed. Face wet from looking for the lost necklace. The wind is cool but the sun is warm; she rolls over on the dock, to see the sky as it really is, feels something, pushes herself up with her arms.

Nicky crouches at the edge of the woods, watching her. Black hair blowing; face pale, eyes dark and bright.

She says, "Oh."

He smirks, rises and approaches. She pulls herself to her feet, crosses her arms over her chest, feels her cold nipples push against the thin fabric of her tank top. Her flannel shirt hangs from the branch of a bush, alive in the moving air.

"Still looking for that necklace, eh?"

"Not really."

"That's long gone, that one." He stands close; she feels his eyes on her bare shoulder, feels her own hair whispering across her skin. "You heard from Bill, eh?"

"Not yet."

"So should I call you 'Sister'?"

She frowns. "No! We're just talking, that's all."

He smirks again, tips his face toward the sky. She sees the veins pulsing in his neck, the fine curve of his Adam's apple. "Maybe you come with me, eh?"

"What?" The words rush over her, like a wave of warm water.

"I'm going to the village. Maybe you'll come, eh?"

She swallows hard against a dry throat. She's been wanting to go to the village; she needs desperately to see Norma. "Yeah, sure. I'll go. Just let me get my boots on and tell my mom." She moves past him, her arm brushing his, the air she breathes full of the scent of him—water, wind, something like the tea that grows on the tundra. She feels him watching her. She puts the shirt on, grabs her socks and boots.

"Whatch you wanna do, eh? Slit her throat?"

The words startle Katie. Of course Norma would have talked to him. Norma told Nicky everything. She used to tell everything to Katie.

Katie's cheeks burn. Without looking at him she says, "Do you know what's going on?"

"Norma's not saying." Nicky had been with Katie when they stumbled upon Norma and Katie's father in an embrace in the shed by Katie's house, where the fishing gear was stored. "I haven't seen her," he adds. "It might not be what you think, eh?"

The moment in the shed. How they'd turned and looked as she and Nicky innocently lifted the canvas tarp that served as a door. Katie wished she could remember it as it was, without the filter of her own reaction, her own interpretation.

"I hope you feel better," Manny had said, putting quick distance between him and Norma.

Katie had said, to Norma, "What's wrong?"

Norma just said, "My life is stupid." Then she hurried out of the shed. Katie'd looked at her father, but he acted as if nothing happened. When she'd looked at Nicky, she could see his mind working, saw the way his eyes flitted about.

"I need to tell my mom," she says now, referring to the trip to the village. Though the other thing is heavy on her mind. She has not mentioned it to her mother, and she had begun avoiding her father. "Where's your skiff?"

"Just there." Nicky tips his head. Katie is surprised to see the skiff so close; but then again it was Nicky's tendency to shut the outboard off and paddle or just drift with the wind.

"Be right back," she says, and runs up the hill.

Vivian is outside, hanging clothes that they'd washed earlier in the cove onto a line to dry. Shirts and underwear flap in the wind. In the winter, the laundry would freeze, sometimes almost instantly, and they would bring things in a little at a time to thaw and dry by the wood stove. Katie often thought about how her jeans became some-thing else in their frozen state; she could break the legs right off if she wanted. Then they would thaw and be unmendable, and what was done when they were in the altered state would be permanent.

Vivian is hanging a pair of dripping jeans when Katie approaches. "Mom?" she asks.

"Hmm?" Vivian says. She looks over at Katie. Katie thinks her mother looks pale, tired, despite the blue bandanna tied neatly over her soft hair, despite her lipsticked attempt to look bright and cheery.

"Nicky's running over to the village. Can I go with him?"

Vivian turns and looks past the knoll to the water beyond. She is judging the wind, judging the water, something she has had to learn how to do. The village is ten watery miles away. "All right," she says. "Don't be late, though."

"Okay," Katie says.

"Be careful."

"We will."

And Katie is gone back down the knoll, to where Nicky is wait-ing for her beside the skiff.

On the way to the village there is a place that always frightens Katie: a point of land, reaching like a long arm, surrounded by rocks lurking below the surface, making it necessary for boats to turn toward the open waters of Ilmenof.

Katie knows how it is there, in the open. The lake is worse than an ocean in a bad wind, the absence of salt taking predictability from the waves, giving instead lightness and speed. She sits in the bow of the skiff and hangs onto the sides as Nicky begins that turn. She is wishing now for Billy, wanting to look over her shoulder and see him there.

Nicky stands while Billy would sit. They move farther from the shore. Nicky is saying something.

She looks back. "What?"

"There's some waves, eh? Sit on the floor and use my raincoat, if you don't want to get wet."

She does as he says because she doesn't want to see. She sits facing him, her back to it, knees against her chest. She drapes the raincoat over her shoulders.

She watches him then, as he stands and steers the skiff, which lurches amid the wind-whipped waves. There is something beautiful; she recognizes it as such but doesn't understand. Something in the way he moves with the skiff which moves with the water, the way his face is, alert and focused, yet calm as if he is at home there, on this water, in this wind. She is no longer afraid.

When they get to the village, children come down to the dock to see who it is. They tease Nicky, stare at Katie. As Nicky ties the skiff some young men Nicky's age walk over, stand watching with hands shoved deep into the pockets of their jeans.

"What's this, Nick-eee?" one of them says, looking at Katie. "She don't look like whale bones and seal skin to me!" A wave of laughter. Katie looks at Nicky.

Nicky spits off the side of the dock, pulls tight the knot in the rope. "Go drink some whiskey and beat up some women, eh? You keep out of my shit."

"Sounds better than sitting with some old man, playing Indian."

Nicky straightens, stands close to the speaker. Katie waits, eyes wide, heart pounding. A moment passes. Then Nicky tips his head, says, quiet and low, "Aleut. Not Indian. Aleut."

In all her life Katie has only been to the village a handful of times; she walks through it now, trying to remember the way. Before they parted Nicky had said: *Know where you're going, eh?* Katie had said yes, she did, was annoyed at the sneer in his voice. He went off—to where, she doesn't know.

The village has gone quiet; dust drifts down the empty street. She feels eyes on her, from behind the glass of dirty windows, of layers of cloudy Visqueen, left over from winter. It is like a dream, where the place you are is known and familiar, yet all mixed up somehow, like a puzzle with the pieces out of place.

Then she sees the low rise in the land off the side of the road, the thin trail wavering uncertainly to the door of a gray shack that sits crooked on the ground, as if it is sinking into or being swallowed up by a toothless mouth of earth. She stops. The feeling of Norma blows through Katie, like wind through a thin cloth, and she imagines: Norma with hands on full hips, black hair whipping loose around her heavy face, knit shirt stretched tight across large breasts.

Whatch you want, eh, Katie? You want to spit in my face?

A row of calico kuspuks wave from a drooping line; Katie remembers Norma's grandmother, old and thin, even years ago. Rusty washtubs lean against an old gray wall—there is something hollow in the sound the wind makes as it slips around them, there is something sad Katie feels in the scattered tufts of stubborn grass, fighting for space among the tundra mosses. Norma wants grass. She wants grass, she wants clothes, she gazes hungrily at pictures in magazines: women in high heels, cleaning spotless toilets in spotless bathrooms, smiling. Norma wants men.

You don't know shit about men, Katie, I know what they like—

Katie sees herself with Norma inside the shack, in the curtained corner that was her room, Norma changing, pulling her shirt up over her head, unhooking the back of her bra.

She'd smiled at Katie, holding her breasts like a prize won at a fair, then bent her head and flicked her tongue across her own nipple. Katie had looked away.

They like these. But maybe Billy's different, eh? You'd better hope so. You don't have shit, girl.

Katie threw something, in play, but the room became stuffy, strange; Katie wished she were home instead of there, wished for the open tundra, for Billy and Nicky, and to be eight years old again, all of them.

Today, Norma doesn't seem to be home; there is silence and stillness around the small shack; even the grandmother, who raised Norma, is apparently not there. Katie is flooded with relief. What would she say, anyway? But that really wasn't it, to actually saying something. What

Katie wants is to look at Norma's face, listen to her voice, look for something—anything—that might be indicative of something—anything.

She turns, starts back through the village. She walks fast, tries to be quiet, but her steps seem to grate against the earth, and dogs chained near houses bark and growl, strain to break free. She hears someone yelling and stops, turns around to make sure the yelling is not for her. The shouts come from within one of the houses—shacks— small plywood buildings with low metal roofs, weathered and crouched low to the earth. Improved conditions, the benefits of the white man. Real homes for the savages. Katie feels like a glare on the street, can't imagine why she would not be hated. She sees movement behind the window in the house where the yelling comes from, hears a woman's sob, the sound of breaking glass. She turns away, is startled to see at the next house up an old man, sitting on a stump, whittling. She looks over her shoulder. There is a face now, in the window, framed by the darkness within the walls, the glint of eyes, looking at her. She turns again and rushes away, sees with relief the blue of the water.

She sits on the empty dock and waits for Nicky. Up the shoreline children play, an old woman walks; laughter drifts down with the wind, then sobs, then laughter again. Katie begins to settle inside, turns her face to the sun and closes her eyes.

After awhile a young couple appears, hand in hand, the woman with jet-black hair and dark narrow eyes. She is small and slight while her companion is tall and broad—Katie guesses that she is Aleut while he is Athabascan, Ilmenof being a melting pot of sorts for Aleuts and Athabascans and Yup'iks—why she is not sure. The couple walks down the dock and Katie stands, smiling, feeling glad when they both smile back.

"You waiting for Nicky, eh?" the woman says. She wears long beaded earrings, swinging against her neck.

Katie nods.

"He's down at the river, eh, fighting with some boys." She tips her head; the two laugh a little and walk past Katie to the end of the dock where they take off their shoes and sit together, feet dangling.

Katie knows where the river spills into the lake, knows it would be quicker to walk through the village but she goes up the shoreline instead, the smell of fish in her nose as she gets close. Once at the mouth she sees Nicky, up-river where the village drying racks shine like clean skeletons, red slabs of salmon decorating the bones. Just as the woman said, there is fighting; Nicky and another young man, the one who had been at the dock earlier, roll across the sand while a group of others laugh and watch. Katie rushes over, stops and doesn't know what to do. Nicky has the other man pinned now, pulls back his arm, hand in a fist.

Then someone says, "Hey, Nick, your girl's here."

He looks up and sees her. There is an instant when their eyes meet. Then his fist comes down onto the pinned man's face and there is a dull muffled sound, not like the sharp thwacks! heard in movies, and Katie looks away. When she looks back Nicky is standing, the other one lies on the sand, there is a sound like crying which Katie realizes is laughter—the man Nicky hit is laughing, lying there on the silty river sand, laughing as the blood trickles down the side of his face.

Nicky says, "You keep out of my shit." He snatches up his flannel shirt, left in a heap by the rushing water. "Bill's girl," he says. "This is Bill's girl." He looks at her, tips his head, says "Come on," and begins to walk. Katie, arms crossed in front, passes the staring group of young men and follows.

The trail winds along the river, through tall grasses that sway and bend in the wind. Katie smells their greenness; smells, too, the sun-warmed earth, sees small swirls of dust rise from where Nicky's feet had been just moments before. She has trouble keeping up, is behind him always, glimpsing his black hair from time to time, catching his scent on a stilled breeze. Now and then a mosquito swoops past, or a bee, here and then gone; beneath everything is the low, drowsy drone of the river, visible only at those times when the trail cuts close to the bank. When they were still near the village they'd passed houses, heard dogs barking and whining, the rattling-chain sound of dogyards, but for some time now there has been nothing, though Katie knows there is a destination.

Nicky's Uncle Pete's. She'd been there once, long ago, riding on a dog team up the frozen river.

Ahead of her Nicky's voice: "Uncle!" Soon Katie can see grayed log walls, a sod roof covered with grass and fireweed and wild roses, dainty little birches framing all, white amid the green. A cache sits perched atop long, leg-like poles, and an old aluminum skiff drags against the current, held back by a rope wrapped securely around a tree. A low fire smokes near the water. Beside that is what looks to Katie like some sort of beaver house; she feels for a moment the sensation of dreaming, the effect heightened when Nicky's uncle emerges from it, wet and steaming, as if just being born.

He is naked; Katie looks away. A moment later he stands beside them, wearing shorts now, looking hard at Nicky's face.

"Ech, Nicholas, ech—" he says, as if the punches have fallen on him. Then he looks at Katie; she smiles shyly, remembering being afraid of him, but not remembering why. "The wolf girl," he says, and offers his hand, which is warm and wet, strangely soft. She isn't sure at first what he means, then it comes to her: One winter when she was little, there was a white wolf. Only Katie had seen it, finding it somehow against the snow. Twice; she had seen it twice. Both times were the same—she was checking rabbit snares, set along a snowshoe trail that ribboned through the woods, and stopped for some reason between sites, feeling the silence like a cloak on her shoulders, the presence of the trees, alive in the stillness. And something else. A quiet turn of her head. The figure of the wolf finding shape against the white of the snow, the eyes, nose and mouth sharp and dark, like lines of black ink.

Katie had stared, frightened but curious. The wolf looked at her a moment, then disappeared.

Her father had said: *It's more likely your imagination, you know, than an all-white wolf.* Though wolves were not uncommon at Ilmenof. Timber wolves, gray and white and rust.

Billy had said: *I think maybe I've seen the tracks, eh.* And once when Katie was at his house, and Pete had come over from the village,

Billy told him about the wolf and he looked at her and said: *I saw a wolf like that once.*

She wonders how she had forgotten this, what Pete had said. It had been important, to be believed. But she hadn't forgotten the wolf; in dreams sometimes she sees it, even now, like a ghost of something, a white shadow of something—someone—left behind.

Later she lies in the sun by the river, listens to the low voices of Nicky and his uncle, murmuring like the water, whispering like wings of small birds. She is warm and it is so quiet. Everything is far away, everything that is not here. The inside of her eyelids tell of light-dappled leaves, the waving shadows of tall grass. There is a bee, near then not; another sound—other wings, she thinks. *Dragonfly*, and an image flits across her thoughts—a blue one, then green, then one blue-green, the two together. Somewhere Nicky is laughing, and Katie feels a smile.

She drifts, dozes, wakes after what seems to have been moments but was—she quickly sees—more; the coolness of the evening rises from the ground, and she is surrounded now by the buzzing of mosquitoes. The light is soft and diffused, like pale watercolors brushed loosely on grainy paper; there is still the sound of the river, the quiet voices of Nicky and his uncle.

She hadn't asked what they were doing, before; she'd felt shy, out of place, intrusive. Now she sits and watches, unnoticed, suddenly fascinated by what looks like a giant rib cage, over which they both work. She feels witness to a creation of sorts—sees the scene as an illustration in a book: *And then the gods bent the trees to the shape of their own ribs, drew the flesh of animals tight across, creating*—what? She has no idea.

As she watches Nicky she feels something like pain. He looks like the boy she knew, absorbed in his project, dark curls forever falling into his eyes, the slimness of his shoulders, the hole there, in the faded black T-shirt.

He looks up, sees her, allows a quick smile. Shifts his eyes away, says: "We should go, eh?" and grabs his flannel shirt from the ground. Katie rises, tries to hear—but can't—the quiet words exchanged with his uncle, then Nicky heads for the trail, walking swiftly. Katie looks at Pete, surprises herself by asking, "What is it?"

The old man smiles. "Ikayak," he says.

Before Katie can ask, Nicky, already past her, stops and says: "Baidarka. Like a kayak."

"Oh—"

"Don't tell Bill." Nicky walks away. Katie looks quick at the uncle but feels Nicky disappearing down the trail, so she lifts her hand to say goodbye and hurries to catch up, still foggy-feeling from sleep.

Near the village she almost runs into him; he stands still, head-tipped, listening. Katie stops, hears it too: Music, strange and haunting, almost off-key but not, fiddles and guitars.

"Athabascans," Nicky says.

"What?"

"From the Interior. They play this music up there."

Katie nods but doesn't understand, follows Nicky's movements as he hunches down behind the grasses, walks silently forward.

Soon they can see: A big fire by the river, near the drying racks; musicians and dancers, the whole village, it seems, children running everywhere, laughing.

Nicky looks at her, eyes narrow and the slant of a smile. "Let's dance, eh?"

"No," Katie says. "I don't."

But he grabs her hand and pulls her from the grass and into the moving group, the way he pulled her once, when they were little, into the stream where it was shallow and they could catch salmon with their bare hands. The fish were strong; they twisted from her grip. Nicky laughed as he threw his to the shore.

They slip in among the dancers hardly noticed; he puts a hand on the small of her back, the other one into her own and begins to drag her along with him. "Don't think about it," he says. "Listen. Shh." She puts her free arm up around his neck, feels her feet begin to move with his. She feels, too, the warmth of his closeness, the leanness and the lightness of him, the gentle way his hand holds hers. She tilts her head up and watches him watch the dancing, old people and young people, all together, and she sees how this makes him happy, and she feels how his being happy makes her happy and how she wants him, always, to be happy.

Their feet make prints over those of others, get lost and buried in the changing shuffle in the river sand, theirs close now and in unison, the temporary trace of a story.

Morning, and twigg sat in his office and stared out the window. There was a smudge on the glass where he'd killed a bug. He wiped at it with the loose cuff of his flannel shirt. He liked to keep the office clean. Clean and empty, the varnished plywood honey-colored new.

Looking down the dusty main street of town, he saw a figure at the far end and recognized the lavender mountain parka, the full denim skirt waving in the wind: Margaret, the public health nurse, somewhat new to Ilmenof. He watched her, hoping, then it seemed she really was heading his way, and he thought about trying to re-braid his hair real quick, about taking his feet off the desk, sweeping off the dirt from his muddy boots. But he did nothing—only waited, watched. Her head was down into the wind; she was breathless when she came rushing in and pressed the door closed behind her, leaning back against it.

He thought maybe he knew why she was here. "Mornin', Margaret," he said.

She smiled. "Doesn't it ever quit?" she asked, referring to the wind.

He tapped a pencil on his desk, attempted to return the smile. For five months now she had been asking him this. "Western Alaska," he said. This was the expected reply.

"Maybe I should try the Interior."

"Be up to your armpits in snow."

"Southeast."

"Rains like hell."

"All right—Southcentral. Homer sounds nice."

"You'd do just fine in Homer." He pointed the pencil at his extra chair. "Have a seat. Like some coffee?" He saw how she looked at his old electric percolator before shaking her head. Margaret made coffee in a glass pot, a "carafe" she called it, grinding her beans in a little white electric thing.

She sat across the desk from him. The wind had mussed her cap of light brown curls, brought spots of color into her soft round cheeks, the tip of her small nose. When she smiled there were wrinkles around her eyes; she was nearly forty. Older than Billy, younger than Twigg. Girl-like still; tall and willowy and carefree, something Twigg liked and didn't like at once. He never wanted to be so carefree. He wanted the weight of responsibility, the solidness of it. So many people these days didn't want it; they wanted freedom and free time—"space." He's had plenty of all that. But he never would have chosen it.

He wondered what she had in mind, with Billy. He tried to gauge what she might already know, about Billy and Katie. Billy and Katie and Nicky. Probably everything, he thought; there were no secrets in Ilmenof.

Which he didn't think she'd realized yet. It made him feel guilty and that he should warn her. But what would he say? *Margaret, I know about you and Billy. Everybody knows about you and Billy.*

No; there was nothing he could do.

She said: "Well, I just thought I'd stop in and see what's new."

She knows already. Gossip spread fast around Ilmenof.

"I just needed to take a break," she added quickly. "So many teens with so many problems. And they all come to me—the girls, I mean. And they're not looking to hear about safe sex and birth control—they want advice about their delinquent boyfriends. Sometimes I think this town needs a mental health counselor more than a public health nurse."

"It's not easy, being Native. Being young and Native," Twigg said, before she could go much further. "It wasn't that long ago it was a different world for them—for all indigenous people."

"Indigenous? Ray—you surprise me. Have you studied anthropology?"

He hesitated, then shook his head. "I just read a lot. When I was in college, I studied justice." He had told her this, he thought, sometime or another.

"Oh, I could just see you. Some country lawyer or something."

"I like being a pilot just fine." He tried to keep smiling.

"Well, anyway," she said, "not all the young Natives have problems."

He had the distinct feeling she wanted to say, *Just look at Billy Johnson*, even though he, like Katie, was hovering somewhere on either side of thirty. And he wanted to say, to that unspoken thought: *He's got problems, Margaret, a world of 'em.* But she wouldn't see it like that, Twigg thought; she would throw out some psychological terms, say there was nothing going on with Billy that a little counseling—some "opening up"—couldn't cure. She would see herself as the one for the job, the healing angel, cleaning out those old wounds. Twigg wondered if she had ever known sorrow, and thought not. Maybe that's why he was so taken with her. She'd managed to dodge what he couldn't avoid; her track record was clean, spotless. Maybe that's what Billy saw in her, too, though Twigg knew that the attraction there was mostly one-sided. He knew Billy. He was kind to Margaret, gentle with her aggressive pursuit of him, but he was not smitten.

"So—you had the mail route yesterday."

"Yep." She was getting to it now; he wondered how direct she'd be.

"So is that Manny's daughter that came in?"

Direct enough. "How'd you hear about that?"

"Oh—one of the girls, you know."

He could drag it out, he knew, torture her a little for making him feel like an ignorant country bumpkin—which is what he believed she sometimes saw him as—but he reminded himself that he wasn't that kind of a person, and that any relationship that involved the necessity of games was one he didn't want. "Yeah—it's her. Why'd you ask?" He wanted her to think—for her sake—that he had no idea.

"Oh—just curious, I guess. I've heard a lot about her. Well—about her and Billy's brother. A lot of the local girls think that's some story."

"Yeah, some story all right." For Twigg the story was like a weight, a confirmation, like a body, of something that sent him farther and farther away from the person he saw himself as once having been. The long-legged young man with the gold hair, playing softball in the sun.

Margaret's cheeks flushed; his tone had stung her somehow, though he had not meant anything to seem directed at her. He fidgeted for a moment, scratched his forehead, plucked at his bottom lip. But he felt tired, suddenly, and couldn't seem to come up with any niceties to smooth over whatever it was he'd done. He pulled his feet off the desk, wiped the dirt onto the floor, grabbed his baseball hat and his old canvas vest. "I guess I'd better be hittin' it," he said, trying to sound like the person she expected him to be. Folksy, quaint. "Got a flight to the village."

"Okay," Margaret said and stood. She smiled sweetly, lingered, pulled open the door for him. "How come you don't like to talk about it?" she asked.

He was taken aback a bit, but she seemed so innocent in her question. "Well," he said, stumbling. "I loved Nicky. I loved all them kids. The whole thing was—just a shame, really; a shame." He did sound old, he realized; maybe that's what he was.

———————

Twigg gassed up his plane, pumped the water out of its floats, then found himself back in his office, waiting for his client to show. He realized he should have made better arrangements, more specific. The woman's voice was on the other end of a bad connection; a cell phone or a radiophone, he couldn't tell. But he'd been tight with the conversation. He'd just wanted to get on with it.

Now he felt as if he had been tight with Margaret as well. It was true he wanted to be ready for whenever the client showed, but he'd played it loose before and no harm came out of it. Now with every minute that passed with no word from his client, he thought about wasted time.

He picked at a splinter in his finger. He could hear other planes taking off. His office had no window looking out at the lake; he wondered, sometimes, if this was a mistake. Clients noticed this—they would keep glancing at the wall, searching for the lake, the reason they were here. But that solidness felt good to him, like having his back turned to the wind. And though the lake is a great meter of the weather he had learned to read the wind without it—all he needed was the bend of the trees, the dust on the street out front, his own ears.

He had driven slowly when he was out. Kids on three-wheelers roared past, flipped him off. He didn't remember being like that when he was young. Arrogant and naïve at the same time. Naïve—he guessed he was probably naïve. Both he and Cindy. Thinking how important it was, that thing between them. But it was nothing God—if there was a god—would notice. Or maybe He did.

No, Twigg thought; if there was a god he was not a god of punishment—he would never believe that. Yet it was like a punishment, what happened. And it happened because and only because he and Cindy had fallen in love with each other.

Naïve. He wondered if it were possible that he was still that way. He remembered the day Margaret arrived, and how by chance he was at the airport, turned and saw her walk in the door, fresh and clean and brisk, like a new wind that hadn't yet rolled across the ground. She looked right at him and smiled. And he felt like an old dead battery suddenly jump-started to some kind of life, and he began to think crazy—naïve—thoughts, like that she had been sent here for him, as in a fairy tale with the expected sex roles reversed.

Christ. Twigg shook his head, felt the corners of his mouth pulling down hard. The splinter wouldn't come out without a needle and tweezers, he realized. He looked away from the finger, turned to the window.

There was a woman walking toward his office. Native, heavy, black hair blowing in strands like long snakes. She was familiar and strange at the same time. Beside her was a little boy. Twigg sat up. It was the boy he had almost hit. He pulled open the bottom drawer, yanked out the shirt, unbuttoned the buttons, and laid it casually across his desk.

The woman knocked. Twigg hesitated, then stood and walked over. Opened the door and saw at once who it was.

Norma Nicholi. He said it: "Norma Nicholi."

"Hey, Twigg. Long time, eh?"

"Yeah—" He thought about it: Katie one day, Norma the next. Like something from a movie, all plotted out. "How are you, Norma?" Her face was puffy-looking, pasty; where there was once a voluptuous sheen to Norma there was now only heaviness, the once shiny black hair greasy-looking and dull.

She didn't answer. Looking around she said instead: "An office. Pretty official, eh?"

"Just tryin' to keep up." The boy hung close to her, didn't look at him. Twigg saw the boy's dark eyes find the shirt on his desk. "So where'd you come in from?" he asked Norma.

"Dillingham. Yesterday, yeah. We missed the mail plane."

"I didn't know you were comin' in, Norma." That would have been something, he thought; Katie and Norma on the same flight across the lake.

"I guess I could have called sooner. You got a phone now, pretty good."

"Yep," he said. "Got a phone." He felt something of an old awkwardness, long associated with Norma: even when she was young she seemed to see the world as being made of two things—that which was male, and that which was female. He remembered the eager way she would look at him sometimes, her face young and pretty then, her body soft and full. Just a kid. He was terrified of being alone with her, afraid that his years of loneliness and the dark of the winter had bred something inside him. "I thought you were in Anchorage all this time," he said, to fill the quiet air, to cover the sound of breathing.

Norma said, "I was there. But I been in Dillingham, long time now. I got relatives in Dillingham." She looked at the floor. Twigg watched her face, saw anger pass over it, like the shadows of clouds across tundra. Then she lifted her eyes and said: "We need a ride, eh? I called. I got money; we can pay."

Twigg looked at her clothes, figured she didn't have much—her wool shirt was too big, her jeans worn and stained. Salvation Army stuff. He thought of the eighty dollars-plus sandals Margaret wore, her clean new socks.

"Well, I'm not exactly overflowin' with business today," he said. "Why don't you just give me a little gas money and we'll call it good. It's a nice day for flyin' out to the village."

He saw how she thought about this; Norma was proud, he remembered, hard to give things to. "It's no sweat," he added. "I'm happy to do it."

Norma nodded, but looked again at the floor. Twigg felt a twisting in his heart.

"We got some stuff, over at my auntie's." She wouldn't look at him, now.

"We can swing by there in the truck. That's no problem."

"All right."

The boy clung to her thigh. Twigg said: "Who's this little guy?"

"Alex," she said. "He's mine."

"You missin' a shirt, Alex?"

The boy said nothing. Twigg handed Norma the shirt, said: "Found it in the road." He had figured on saying more. Felt he should say more. But the words were too hard, even to think.

Norma took the shirt, said nothing.

"I guess we should hit it, then," Twigg said, but failed to move. He stared at the top of the little boy's head, the dark hair, clean but messy. He suddenly remembered, realized: He knew the feel of a child's head. The warmth from the scalp, the soft hair.

Cindy'd had two children, once.

Once.

He looked quick out the window, found the sky. He thought about flying. About how little he felt up there in it, about how endless everything seemed, above and below. It was the flying that saved him.

———————————

Billy lay on his cot, slept and sweated. He dreamed about Nicky. It was a dream he'd had before, fragments of images that repeated themselves, over and over: The falling snow, he can't see; Nicky! They are both little, where is their father? He can't see, he can't find him, the snow is thick and heavy, the white of the lake, the white of the sky, Nicky is there, a shape ahead of him on the ice, like a shadow, then he is gone, where?

Suddenly he knows. The hole in the ice, a circle of gray. Sticks his head into the freezing water, knows what he will see because this happened, really happened, and everything was all right: The red mitten, the one that didn't fall off Nicky's hand, down in the dark gray water; he will grab it, he will pull him out, everything is all right—

But in the dreams the mitten disappears. Sometimes just after he sees it; sometimes as his own hand wraps around it. Always he is so surprised.

It happened! I saved him! I saw the mitten and I pulled him out! It was all right!

When he wakes up from these dreams he thinks: *I did save him. I pulled him out. I remember—*

And then he remembers. It seems so incredibly impossible.

In this dream his own hand turns red, after the mitten disappears, as if it had been painted, and he sees how it is because blood is pouring out of him, the cut beneath his thumb, then he looks closer and sees too the insides of a fish, there beneath his skin—

He woke, breathed. Why was he so hot? His T-shirt was plastered to his skin. Then he wondered: *Why am I sleeping in the middle of the day, anyway?*

He moved his arm and pain shot up from his hand. He pulled back the gauze over the cut, took a peek. It was swollen and red, angry looking. He stood slowly, moved across the room to the kitchen, put some water on the propane stove to boil. He turned toward the window and looked outside. The clear skies of the morning had vanished, and he saw how it was about to rain.

Katie—chased inside by the rain—fell asleep on her cot and then she, too, dreamt of Nicky, and her dream was like this: They were children, and he was chasing her, trying to pull her braids. She rushed over the tundra; it was bouncy and springy and uneven; the low branches grabbed at her ankles. Then she fell and he was there, suddenly, on top of her, grown now, the faint whisper of a mustache topping his upper lip—the long dark curls of his hair. She felt the ground beneath her and his weight on top of her; she was warm—he kissed her and he was warm.

Then she saw him walking across the ice, disappearing into the snow; he looked back for an instant, snow in his hair, and then it was as if she was rushing forward across space and time to be suddenly there, deep in his eyes.

Back on the tundra again, and something was wrong; they both looked up and there was Billy, looking down at them, a faceless shape in front of the sun.

Then she began to dream of Billy. There was a crowded street in Boston; she saw him up ahead, thought at first he was Khoi. Then she realized it was Billy, he was soaking wet, he stopped and looked at her, the people moved around him like rushing water. She wanted to kiss him, but couldn't get to where he was.

She woke still holding that feeling, the wanting to kiss him. She felt confused, then remembered: They had loved each other once, and it was good. There was a tent in the woods, and they'd listen to the rain on the canvas. He always touched her as if she might break. And when she'd do something—anything—she would feel him watching her, as if he didn't believe she was real.

Then she thought about Nicky, let herself, pictured him leaning against a tree, hair falling in his eyes. Watching her stab at the earth, digging up forget-me-nots to transplant into her garden.

Those are some pretty scrawny flowers there, Katie.

His face always like two faces, made separately and joined not quite right; Katie had made a clay face once, in an art class she took in Boston, one side at a time, and when she put them together she saw Nicky. And then she had seen photos where two left sides or two right sides of a person's face were spliced together to show how different each side was—if someone would have done this with Nicky, she'd always thought, you would have two different men. One would have delicate features and be almost feminine, like a medieval prince from a book illustration; the other would look like a roughly carved theater mask— eyes squinted, lips curled either up or down.

That day he'd said: *You know where there are some good ones.*

No, she'd said. *I don't.*

You do. But you forgot. A long time ago we found some. Me, you and Bill. Up there. His head tipped toward the mountain behind the woods. *I'll show you, eh?*

She was thinking about it.

Come on, girl. I don't bite.

As she thought this Katie looked at the rain weeping down her window, saw herself in the glass. She divided her face with her hand.

There are two people, she thought; *there are two of you. Where?*

Her teeth clenched; her hand pressed against skin and bone, the cartilage of her nose. She closed her eyes and tried to see. Then she gave it up, laid her face against the cool glass, thought about Billy, only a mile away, years away, forever gone into the world of what was once, but was no longer, the possible.

Katie walked the beach, barefoot, in a sweater and a raincoat with the hood down. Terns and gulls swooped and squawked; she spooked several flocks of ducks camped in weedy areas near the shore. The scene repeated itself among the islands; birds flying, swooping, ducks scooting across the water. The rain was a drizzle now, dense and steady, the drops like falling needles that slipped into the lake.

She went slow, careful of her feet on the rocks and pebbles. There were twigs and sticks to watch for, too, and the skeletons of salmon from other years. This was a stretch of shore well known to her, familiar despite the years of absence, but now different, somehow, from her memories and imaginings, as if seen there through thick glass. Now it seemed clear, focused, the real way it was supposed to be.

It wasn't long before she saw the tip of Johnson's Point. It disappeared for a moment, as the shore dipped inward, then she rounded a bend and she could see it in its entirety: the spiky silhouettes of spruce; the rushing, rippled surface of the stream; the old Johnson cabin, low roofed and gray, the tin smokehouse, washed with rain; the odd angled squares of cleared earth, where potatoes were planted.

The point was empty and quiet; she looked for the baidarka, wondered where Billy kept it, wishing for just a glimpse of it. She sat down among a cluster of large rocks, felt the rain run down her face. *What do*

I want? she thought, then heard the word, nothing, heard again the echo of her mother's voice, there like a bird caught in the wind.

She let her thoughts wander, plucking images as if from a pile of photographs; she saw for a moment Billy and Nicky in the sun by the stream, Billy's white T-shirt gleaming, Nicky barefoot and bare chested, for some reason gloomy that day, but Billy happy and smiling: *Hey, Katie, how's it going, eh?*

When was that? She couldn't remember exactly. But she could remember it was sometime after she'd first seen Nicky since his return from Anchorage.

I have scraggly hair.

No. Now she was remembering Nicky, another day; they were on a high hill, the place where the forget-me-nots grew. They could see hills dipping into valleys, patch-like forests of green spruce rising into the tundra. The lake, sapphire blue, the islands like pieces of a puzzle, the water stretching forever.

No, he'd said again, then: *Billy can't see this hair.*

Can't what?

Have you ever seen how many colors you have, in this hair?

Colors?

Silk.

Then he was kissing her, on the lips, the cheeks, the forehead, the bridge of her nose. His hands glided over the curve of her waist, the dip of her back, the soft bumps of her small breasts. He lifted her off the ground, then placed her down into it, himself into her, washing her with his smell, his skin, his hair.

Don't tell Bill.

Something he always said, something all the different Nickys she ever knew said—Nicky at sixteen, wiping snow off her face after he smacked her square with a hard snowball; Nicky then, in the forget-me-nots, a grown man. Nicky at nine, when he chased after her to pull her braids, and he pushed her to stop her and she got hurt.

Something moved; Katie turned and looked. There was Billy now, in the baidarka, coming out from the mouth of the stream, gliding onto the waters of the lake. Katie swallowed, watched, dared not move. He headed out toward a cluster of islands; soon his back was toward her, and she breathed more easily. He disappeared. She stood and walked toward the point, unsure of why she wanted to go there.

When she reached the stream she stopped, trying to remember where to cross, where the water was not too deep, the current not too swift. She tried several different places, but found she was quickly up to her thighs. Finally, she gave in to the depth of it, raising her arms above her head, letting the cold, glacier-born water rise up to her waist, the bottom of her rib cage. The rocks were slippery; she moved carefully. She felt a bump against her leg, looked and saw the glint of a salmon—large—thrusting past. She watched it, her breath ragged from the cold. For a moment it seemed to hover in the water. Then suddenly it shot away. Katie looked for it, trying to see past the moving surface, knowing it was still there, not far, but vanished from her view.

The cold was spreading through her. She moved forward, felt the depth decreasing, then emerged, dripping, onto the other shore.

The dogs heard her, began to bark. They were back behind the cabin somewhere, chained; she looked but couldn't see them, then walked past the splitting table, shiny with rain, found the trail through the grasses that led upstream and began to follow it, her feet pale on the dark earth.

The trail followed the stream for the most part, but at times cut through patches of forest thick with trees and berry bushes and green leaves. There was a clean, sweet smell; Katie pulled this deep into her lungs.

At the edge of the woods and fronting the stream, Billy's cabin stood small, square and sturdy. Corners notched tight, cracks chinked against the winter cold.

There were birds everywhere. Chickadees, camp robbers, magpies, swallows. Bird feeders hung from the branches of trees, from long nails next to windows. He had always liked birds, she remembered; she was glad there was something he still seemed to have, felt for a moment a flutter of hope.

But she saw, too, how the place had lost its old crispness, the logs long overdue for an oiling. Firewood lay heaped in unstacked piles; clothes hung haphazardly from a sagging line, the sleeves of shirts dangling down into the grasses.

The glass on the windows was dirty. She remembered how clean everything had been, when he'd finished it that year, that awful year, just before he left with his father to go fishing. She remembered especially the windows. She had stood in the center of the room, looked at the tight-fitting boards on the floor, the small white propane stove, the cast iron wood stove made in Sweden, the small table and the two chairs. At first it seemed the panes of glass were not even there—so clearly she could see the blue stream rushing by, the white bark and green leaves of a young birch. Then Billy had said something, and she'd turned from the window, and when she looked back she saw herself there, suddenly, her face framed in the molding, Billy standing beside her.

What had he said? That it wasn't his real place, it was temporary, some place to be for just a little while.

My real place, that's gonna be something.

He'd wanted a lodge, land, a piece of the lake that was his. And because his mother, long dead, was Aleut, he could get that land through the area Native corporation; all he had to do was decide on a spot, the one that would be right.

Katie touched the wooden latch on the door, shut tight against the bears. She slid it open, noticed the way the hinges creaked as the door swung inward. She stepped in, only a little. The cot was made but not neatly. There was some dirt on the floor, a plate and a cup on the table.

Then she saw the necklace, her necklace, the one long lost. Her eyes went to it as if they knew it was there, hanging from a nail on the edge of a shelf. The delicate chain, tarnished now. The deep dark sapphire covered in dust. She thought of moving toward it, touching it, when she felt something else beside her, on the wall by the door.

A black raincoat. She felt a shock of recognition, quickly dismissed. Then, feeling almost silly, she lifted the sleeve to where she could see—

Oh—

She dropped the sleeve, then lifted it again. She had the sensation of being in a dream.

Nicky's raincoat. Nicky's black raincoat. She would know it, know it was his; he had taken her mother's scissors once, her pinking shears, cut the edge on the cuff of one sleeve to see how it would look and she held that sleeve now, saw the zigzags, felt how she was beginning to shake.

Where was it found? When was it found? How long had it been hanging here, in Billy's house? It was still in decent shape—obviously old, but it had not spent a dozen years out in the weather—maybe not even one. As she stared she remembered suddenly her dream, the red spirals of blood spinning out from the back of his head, and she realized that in all her dreams of Nicky in the water he was not wearing his raincoat.

She dropped the sleeve and pulled her hand away from the coat. She felt suddenly that she couldn't breathe. She fumbled with the door and stumbled forward as she plunged back into the outside world. She hurried back down the trail, running and slipping, her eyes on the ground. Then she looked up and Billy was in front of her.

They stared, each startled by the sight of the other, like two animals on a windy day, surprising each other in the brush.

His lips were parted, almond eyes edged round with surprise. He was pale in spite of his olive skin, his black hair wind-tossed and longer than Katie remembered.

She said: "You weren't home!"

He said, voice cracked and whispery: "No."

She bolted forward; he stepped sideways to let her pass. He, too, was barefoot despite the rain, and as she scrambled past him she felt him there, smelled him—a scent different than Nicky's but just as familiar, just as known to her.

At the end of the trail she walked straight into the stream, crossed, and kept going.

When Katie reached the house, she rushed inside, stood and looked around. She felt like she wanted to explode; she wished desperately that her father were home so she could ask him about the raincoat, but the house was empty and still. She noticed a piece of paper tacked near the doorway to her room. It read: *Had to go to the village. Be back late.* Manny must have come by when she was over at Johnson's Point; she couldn't imagine he had a client at the village, but the point seemed trivial. She had no one to talk to. She paced. Then she went upstairs to her father's loft.

It was messy; an unmade bed and a desk piled high with odds and ends of papers. There were papers on the floor, as if he'd recently been going through them; there was also an open drawer, gaping like an unhinged jaw. She couldn't help herself. She stepped closer and took a look, as if she were spying down into some secret hole.

There was an unorganized pile of file folders and loose papers, all stacked on top of each other; near the top was a card, gold edged and bent a little at one corner. Apprehensively, Katie lifted it from the shuffle of papers. *For My Daughter, on Her Birthday* was scripted across the front. Katie opened it. There was a small poem on the inside, but the card was unsigned. Unsigned, unsent. She wondered which of her birthdays it had been intended for, wondered how long it had sat in the drawer. What it was, exactly, that made him decide not to send it.

She returned it to the pile. An upside-down envelope peeked out from the mess; Katie saw that it contained photographs, which were slipping out of its open end. Katie pulled lightly on the corners, and when she pulled out the first photo she almost dropped it; it was of Norma—Norma and a little boy. Taken with a cheap camera, fuzzy with colors bordering on the garish. But still. They had their faces close together, and they were smiling. The other picture was of the same two—though this time they were joined by a third—an older boy who looked to be just heading into his teens. Both boys looked like Norma, but different at the same time; the older boy she felt she recognized from somewhere. Katie looked further inside the envelope. There was a letter. She knew she shouldn't, knew she was being a bad person, but she pulled it out and unfolded it, recognized, even after all these years, Norma's forced stylized penmanship. Katie read.

Hey Manny—

> *Alex and I are coming to Okhonek. My grammy is not up for the traveling, so we'll come see her instead.*

Okhonek was the village. Katie's hands trembled.

> *I won't bring Nico with me. He's got a basketball camp. I wouldn't bring him there.*
> *You can come see us. It'll be okay. I'll never forget how you helped me and how you never told anyone. That makes up for it—I've got no problem, okay? So I mean it when I say come see us.*
> *Nico's camp is the last two weeks of June. We'll come then.*
> *Norma*

Katie held the letter by its edge. Immediately she knew it was something she should not have read. She felt the proverbial can of worms opening inside of her, the worms spilling out and crawling beneath her skin.

The last two weeks of June. That was now.

She wanted so badly to talk to someone, to tell someone about the raincoat, to ask someone about her father and Norma and the boys in the pictures. She was struck by a feeling of incredible aloneness. *How did this happen*, she wondered, *how did I end up alone?*

Mom, oh Mom. Why didn't she talk to her mother when she had the chance? Why didn't she ask her, *Do you think someone killed Nicky?* Why didn't she ask her, *Do you know whatever happened to Norma?* Had her mother known?

"Mom, Billy has Nicky's coat." Katie said it aloud, just to hear it. "The raincoat. The one he would have been wearing. And Manny's got pictures of Norma and some boys."

But her words seemed without substance, like ghosts of thought, not really there without someone else to hear them.

She leaned her forehead against a rough wall. She thought about the raincoat and then about seeing Billy on the trail. How close he was at that moment. The recognition of him, down in the pit of her stomach, though he looked a different man. He wore a darkness foreign to the Billy she once knew.

Something I did, she thought, because when all was said and done, she was the one who killed Nicky.

Twelve years previous

Katie cannot sleep, and it is not because of the wind. She walks the beach and counts the days since Billy has gone to Bristol Bay.

She counts the days since Nicky took her to where the forget-me-nots grew.

It is past midnight. She walks toward Johnson's Point.

Why won't you eat? her mother had asked. *Katie, why do you look so pale?*

And she couldn't say anything. She cannot tell anyone. She and Billy are talking about leaving together in the fall to go to college; everyone is happy about that.

She thinks she should write to Billy and tell him what happened. *It was an accident,* she could say. But was it?

It has been three days since it happened. Three days of living in this new world.

It is raining out and she is cold and wet and shivering but she is glad for that, glad for that. It's what she deserves.

As she nears Johnson's Point she hears the dogs howling. She thinks maybe there is a bear; she hopes for a bear, for a bear to hit her and slap her and bite her and not kill her but almost. So everyone would worry for her, and so she could tell Billy and he would forgive her because he would be so happy, so happy that she was not dead.

Then she hears another sound, the familiar thwack! of an ax splitting wood, and as Johnson's Point unfolds to her view she sees Nicky, shirtless in the rain, splitting piece after piece of round wood, a pile of divided and splintered fragments growing around him. She keeps walking. She crosses the stream. Nicky stops his work and watches her.

"Fuck, Katie," he says. He breathes hard from his work. Drops of rain drip from his dark curls. Katie can't remember what it is she wants to say, finds her eyes unable to leave the blue tattooed line running from above and below his navel, the other lines fanning out from the main. Tattoos he's done himself, with needles and ink. She is overcome by a

64

desire to kiss him there, where fine dark hairs climb upward from the belt of his jeans and she makes herself look away, to look up at the sky and feel the cold rain slap itself across her face.

Nicky approaches her cautiously. "You right, eh?"

She starts to cry.

"Fuck, Katie," he says again. "Come on, come on, Katie, you need to get dry, eh?"

He leaves the ax by the chopping block, starts walking. Katie follows.

The tent is a short way from Johnson's Point; they walk down the length of the point, then follow the shore to where it forms a little cove. The tent is set back within the trees. As soon as they leave the shore mosquitoes find them; still, she stops as she sees, in a small flat area near his fire pit, his carved little people, and even from her perspective she can see that they are sad figures, like those one would find on a poor street in a bad city—people struggling. She wants to reach for them but Nicky unzips the tent and pulls her inside.

The light in the tent is gray-green; it is dark and dim. She smells his skin and remembers him, wants just once more to have him pressed up against her.

"Touch me," she says.

"I can't," he says. "You need to get dry, eh?" He unbuttons her flannel shirt.

"Just hold me, that's all. Just hold me."

"I can't just hold you, skinny Katie." The flannel shirt falls to the floor. He lifts her T-shirt above her head; his eyes fall on her bare chest and she sobs loudly as he places his warm hand on the space between her breasts and her own hands cover his and hold it there.

"We can't be doing this, Katie," he says.

"I know."

"We're in deep shit with Billy already."

"I know." But as she says it her eyes find the place on his nearly hairless chest where a triangle of delicate dark hair grows; she leans forward and presses her mouth to it, feels his free hand on the back of her head, warm and caressing. She slides her tongue across his chest, across his small dark nipples, across the warm pulse on the side of his neck. They sink to their knees, as if to pray.

T WIGG STOOD IN THE CENTER OF THE STREET IN THE CENTER OF TOWN, RAIN ON HIS FORE-HEAD. He looked at the sky. He looked and looked and looked. Blue behind the gray; there was blue behind the gray. Above it, beyond it. Endless blue that went on forever. This was important to him. That vastness, versus his own insignificance. His *temporary* insignificance. Why do we fuss, why do we fuss, he  wondered, and he thought of kingdoms and wars—lovers—the messy tangles of love.

Why do we fuss?

Yet here he was, showered, with clean clothes, and it wasn't Thursday. An expensive bottle of wine, bought during a trip to Anchorage, held tightly in his arm. He could have said no. But he didn't.

As she knew; as she knew. He sighed and started walking.

Outside Margaret's tiny house he took off his green raincoat, shook off the rain, hung the coat on a nail by the door. He knocked.

"Come in, Ray."

Ray. Margaret called him Ray, a thing contradictory to how he thought she saw him.

Cindy called him Ray, too. *Hey, Raaaaaay…*

Cin.

Margaret's "Ray" was much brisker, sharper—clean and crisp. Like a slap across his cheek, to wake him up. As if she could see how long he'd been sleeping.

He slipped off his rain boots, grabbed the wine, and went inside.

She swished around in a bright, gauzy skirt, with what looked like colored long johns—but he knew mustn't be—underneath. Painted toenails, which peeked out past the wide straps of the expensive sandals. Her feet were long and not delicate. He felt badly for noticing this. It made him want to hold her.

"Well, rumor is Rosie Anelon's pregnant," she said, carrying a bowl of something to the small round table by the window.

"Oh?" Rosie was a local girl; Twigg figured she couldn't have been more than sixteen.

"Of course I couldn't say anything if she'd come to me as a patient, but for once I'm the last one to know. About five people asked me about it today."

"I haven't heard anything." Twigg handed her the bottle, dressed nicely in a burlap sack.

She pulled it out a little, looked at the label. "Nice," she said. "You shouldn't have." She set it on the counter, took a corkscrew from a nail on the wall, handed it to him. "Do you mind? Anyway, I've been thinking, that if the rumor is true and she is pregnant, well—I think she probably did it on purpose."

"Good God, Margaret, why would a girl like her do something like that on purpose?"

She reached for two wineglasses, paused, and turned toward him. For the first time he saw something—what?—there on her face, something like bitterness—

"It's the oldest trick in the book, Ray."

"What?" He began to turn the corkscrew into the cork.

"Oh, don't be naïve."

He pulled the cork and she handed him the glasses.

"Just set them on the table—please. Thank you. What I mean is, Rosie's been scared to death that boy she sees—I can't remember exactly which one he is—is going to just take off."

"I can't see how her getting pregnant is going to help."

"It's not like it hasn't worked before."

"Doesn't always work around here, Margaret. Plenty of single mothers around—here or else they moved on to some place like Dillingham." He thought about Norma. Whose boy was Alex, he wondered. There was no ring on Norma's finger. He wondered what happened to the older boy. Everybody knew Norma'd had a baby, how long after she'd left Ilmenof was unclear. But there was plenty of speculation there.

And there were also—if the rumors about Norma were true—plenty of possibilities as to the father. "I can't see how someone would do something like that on purpose to get someone," he added. "There's no love in that." He thought—without wanting to—about all the things he and Cindy had had to overcome, just to be together. Her divorce. Her broken-hearted children. No money; neither of them had any money. Cindy wouldn't take a cent from her husband, she felt so bad. But their love was like a religion to them—they believed in it, they believed in it more than anything else in the world.

"Love," Margaret said, standing near the little corner counter, bread knife in hand, "is timing, circumstance. Chemistry, sure—attraction. But without timing and circumstance—forget it. All Rosie's trying to do is create a circumstance that will promote togetherness. You can go ahead and pour that now, if you like."

"Doesn't love have anything to do with it?"

"Well, but what is love, Ray?"

He watched the wine spill out into the glasses, red pools held by clear, fingerless hands. He didn't know what to say. "It's something… something important. That's like a gift, a truth. Something that lives inside you, is part of you but not—if it's there, it's there, whether you want it or not."

"You mean like a disease, Ray?" She came to the table now, with another bowl—pasta salad—and sat across from him and took the wine he offered.

"I didn't say it was like a disease."

"Well, it certainly sounds like it to me. Something growing inside of you out of your control."

"Haven't you ever known someone who tried not to love someone, but the love kept living, despite endless efforts to kill it off?"

"*Kill* it off? Now you're making it sound like it's this alien thing, taking over your body." She laughed, sipped from her glass. "But anyway—of course I've known people who tried not to love someone or another. Every jilted lover is someone trying to fall out of love."

"I just mean that if it's real, you can't help that it exists. It doesn't mean it's gonna last forever. Only that it won't be up to you. It will either be, or it won't."

"You make it sound like magic, Ray—it's not magic. It's biology. And timing, and circumstance. And—how you play the game."

He shook his head.

The bottle of wine was gone and she'd opened another one, and they still sat at the table. Twigg didn't drink often. But the wine was good, the food was good, and he'd been feeling edgy lately—he wasn't sure why—maybe it was Katie coming back and resurfacing all of that business. Ironically, he knew if he stayed long enough Margaret would bring it up—it was only natural to be curious.

She said, finally, "So what was it then, that happened with Billy and Nicky and Katie? Love as disease or teenage hormones run rampant?" A bit of late-night sun had peeked through the clouds, falling on her face. She looked flushed and pretty. He forgave her for what he saw as a callous way to bring up something that hurt so many.

"I don't know," he said. He thought, then added: "They were always close—the three of them. It was probably a wonder they held out as long as they did."

"Did anyone see it coming?"

"Billy and Katie? Absolutely. Katie and Nicky? No—that took us all by surprise."

"I um…I searched out the story—you know, in old issues of the Anchorage paper. You know—I'd already heard bits here and there. I was just curious."

"That's only natural." Hadn't he just been thinking that? His glass was empty. He couldn't remember how long it had been empty.

"You know, the whole Manny-hitting-Nicky thing—well, that seemed believable. Fathers do that sort of thing. But that whole bit about Manny…hitting—what was her name? The girl from the village—Norma—that was just—odd. It didn't make sense to me."

"Well—everybody saw Norma's face."

"Manny doesn't seem like the kind of guy who would hit a woman—let alone one barely not a girl."

"Well, Norma said—"

"I know—I read it. That she was hysterical, distraught, blah blah blah, and she attacked him so he had to hit her."

That whole Manny-Norma thing. Twigg never understood it, and it seemed so irrelevant to everything else. An image flashed before him, a memory of the time the whole thing was being sorted out. Norma—younger, prettier, standing outside in the rain in a wet blue plaid wool shirt, crying, one side of her face still swollen and bruised. It was like having a movie start playing in the corner of a room where the main feature was up on the big screen—you could see the same actors, but it was a different story, and your only concern as to the content was whether it mattered to the main story you were watching. Everyone decided that it didn't—it was a tragedy for Katie and her mother, because it had to be puzzled out and exposed because of the coincidence of it and Manny's position of having hit Nicky shortly before he disappeared—but in the end it was just a coincidence.

Margaret poured them both more wine.

Later, walking to his own house, he wondered if Margaret was right; he wondered if maybe what happened between him and Cindy was a fluke, and that love is really a game to be played, a calculation of moves, a balancing of timing and circumstance.

He was not playing well. After he'd told her, Margaret had said: *Shit. Shit, Ray,* and reached across the table to touch his hand. But her eyes had wavered, when they met with his. It was a little thing, but he'd seen it.

The truth will out, his mama would always say. Still, he could have kept it to himself a little longer, let her know him more, first. Held that back, like a weak card in a poker hand.

It was because of the boy, Norma's boy, and how he'd almost hit him that caused everything to start stirring up inside him. He'd kept it down for so long. Now he felt like he was going to drown in it, all over again.

I killed her kids. What he'd said to Margaret. Suddenly she got so quiet.

I mean there was an accident, and they died.

And he'd looked out the window and could feel it again, sweet Georgia summer, air pungent and heavy, roads slick from a passing rain, the seat of the bakery truck, sticking to his back. Coming home for lunch; he was coming home for lunch. To the ramshackle little house in the cruddy neighborhood, because it was summer and the kids were home, and Jon needed help with batting practice and Cindy—she was always hungry to talk to a big person during the day, home with the kids.

The kids were in the habit of meeting him at the corner, double on the bicycle, waiting to race him back to the house.

They loved that big old bakery truck. Jon and Jenny.

He remembered. Trees dripping with green leaves, a piece of paper tumbling down the street. The white paint on houses peeling in the sun; big red sea-spray roses dropping to the ground.

The sidewalk was still slippery. The bicycle flashed in the sun as it began to skid. His foot on the brake, his hands turning the wheel, a car coming up fast from behind—

He always used to let them win.

The walk home sobered him a little. Enough to make him feel the weight of regret in the pit of his stomach. He walked inside and sat down on the cot with his rain gear still on, drops of water sliding down onto his bedding.

How could it be as Margaret thinks?

He'd wanted to explain to her, about him and Cindy. It wasn't that he didn't know other girls, nice girls, girls it seemed he should have been able to love. And Cindy's husband—a real prince of a guy. What was it, then, that kept driving them toward each other?

Cindy never blamed him. How he'd wanted her to; how he'd wanted her to.

He stayed on the cot, let the gray settle and thicken in the house. After a time he noticed the wind moving around outside, realized how quiet it had been. The wind picked up and began to gust. He thought for a moment of the Windego, but let it go.

It's just the wind, stupid wind, he thought. *Just ordinary old wind.*

After leaving her father's loft, Katie sat for a long time in the quiet of the house, watching the rain blow around outside the front window. She had also found, amongst her father's things, a letter Billy had written to her. Katie remembered the letter, could even remember the day Twigg handed it to her off the plane.

> *Dear Katie,*

His handwriting, nicer than hers, the letters always the same.

> *We're in Dillingham now, docked for the night. It's raining like you wouldn't believe…*

She'd left the letter where she'd found it, remembered it now in pieces, like a puzzle.

> *You seen Nick? Boy was he in some bad shit, Katie, in Anchorage. It was pretty bad. I worry about him now, all the time—*
> *—The docks are pretty at night, especially in the rain like this, everything's all clean and shiny in the lights. So many different boats, it's always amazing. I like to walk the docks and look at them, check out the names. Someday I'll name a boat for you, eh? You and my mom. The* Katie Marlene…
> *If you see Nicky, you let me know what he's up to, okay?*
> *The fishing's pretty good near Naknek, we'll be heading out tomorrow, if the weather's not too bad…*

There was more; she couldn't remember exactly. The PS: *I'm sending you something, a surprise.*

He came home when they didn't expect. A surprise. He'd flown into Ilmenof, caught a ride with Dean to the lodge, rendezvoused with Manny, and the two of them came here together in Manny's skiff, where Katie was to have been home alone, her mother helping at a clinic on the other side of the lake for several days.

What she remembers most is the look on Billy's face, and the sudden gush of blood when Manny hit Nicky.

But Manny's blows weren't life-threatening. Katie knew that. Yet she suspected him, back in the corners of her thoughts. She had seen his anger toward Nicky.

Billy was supposed to have been the last one to have seen Nicky. They, too, fought after leaving Katie's house, but Billy claimed the biggest thing that happened was that he—Billy—kicked his foot through Nicky's baidarka, thereby causing Nicky to take the skiff—something that led Billy to say, "It's my fault." If Nicky had been in the baidarka, he would not have attempted to cross the lake. Though a boy in the village said he saw Nicky there. People thought he must have been mistaken.

The general theory was that Nicky, angry and upset, set off for town to wreak havoc of one sort or another, got caught in the bad weather out on the open water outside of the islands, and that was that. It was not an uncommon story in Ilmenof. And it was also one that happened to people who should know better.

What did Katie think? Her memories of the days immediately following Nicky's disappearance are warped and muddled, as if captured in a glass ball. There was a searing sort of pain and the terrible knowledge that she had caused it all. And the thing with Norma and her father was like an explosion in the middle of ground zero; before Katie knew anything, the search for Nicky was called off, and she and her mother were on a plane back to Boston. It was like drifting down a stream and suddenly getting caught up in a whirlpool. Katie could see, as she spun helplessly, the way she should have gone, the safe way, the way around disaster. It was obvious, but it was too late.

She took turns blaming just about everybody. But always in the end she realized she could only blame herself.

She remembered the dream she'd had on the plane, with the spirals of blood swirling around Nicky's head. She had never been willing to accept that it was carelessness that caused Nicky's demise. He felt bad but he wanted to live. Katie was sure of that. He was reckless, but he knew the wind and the water. Katie was sure of that, too.

What if, in the gray of that night, in the time after Nicky left Johnson's Point, something happened? Billy didn't start radioing around looking for him until the following morning. There were possible events in there, lost in the gray mysterious hours.

And now there was the raincoat, with its jagged identity on its sleeve. She could swear she remembered that Nicky was supposed to have been wearing his raincoat. It was a question that was asked: *What was he wearing?*

It was getting late. The gray was thickening, and she was beginning to feel the emptiness in her stomach. She also realized she was cold—chilled—and very tired. She heard the faint sound of an outboard. Manny must be home.

It seemed like a long time later that he came trudging in the door. He didn't see her at first and went about shedding his raingear. Katie watched, and imagined all the days he must go through this routine, home to an empty house. Both her parents had ended up alone. There is so much aloneness in the world, she thought. So many people, and so many of them alone.

"Oh—hello!" Manny said, somewhat startled. He started to say something else, then stopped. "I didn't see you there."

"How did your day go?" Katie asked.

"'Bout as well as could be expected. Crappy weather."

"I know. It's cold in here."

"Want a fire? We can do a fire."

Katie nodded, said: "I can get it."

"If you want. You always did like building fires. You eat yet?"

"No."

"All right—I'll rustle us up some grub. I almost forgot you were here." He said this last as much to himself as to her. He shook his head and smiled as he walked into the kitchen area.

Katie said, suddenly before she lost courage: "Did anyone ever find any trace of Nicky?"

Manny stopped and looked toward her. A moment of silence passed. "No. Not that I know of, anyway." His voice was soft, subdued. "Katie, you know that's been just an ongoing sad thing for everybody."

"I know."

"I never wished him any harm."

"I know. I'll go get some wood." She headed for the door.

"I've been thinking about your mother," Manny said.

Katie stopped. She could hear pain in his voice. Her imagined ambitions of bravely asking all her questions were rapidly dwindling.

"I mean, of course I've been thinking of her. All the damned time—even before all this." He looked away from Katie, shook his head. "Isn't it something," he said, and it seemed to Katie he wasn't speaking to her. But then he looked at her again, and for a moment Katie thought he looked confused. "I mean, I've been thinking about what we're gonna do—with her. I've been thinking, if I'm leaving, then maybe I should just take her with me."

"But where do you think you'll be going?"

"I don't know. North, I think. Up into the Interior. Get out of the damned wind."

Katie remembered something: They used to talk about the Interior, when she was little. *Something like that picture on the syrup can,* Manny would say.

Ooo, wouldn't that be cozy. Her mother's reply.

Katie wondered what they expected, moving to Ilmenof. If they'd found the Alaska they'd wanted. Or if they really were looking for the picture on the syrup can, someplace softer, quieter, not quite so extreme.

But the Interior had its own extremes; she knew this—deep, silent cold in the winter, bugs so thick in the summer you breathe them right in. "I think she would have wanted to come home," Katie said.

Manny shrugged, picked some bits of tobacco off his tongue. "But aren't your people more your home than someplace you once lived? Ilmenof was only a portion of your mother's life, you know."

"I guess," Katie said. She was suddenly swept over with this urge to tell him how Ilmenof would have, could have, *should* have been her mother's home for longer than it was—if it hadn't been for him. She swallowed against a familiar feeling of tightness in her throat, turned and slipped out the door.

She walked out into the rain, looked up at the gray sky. *Right here,* she thought, and felt her feet on the ground. Peel back the years like layers of onion, and they would all be here: her mother, her father, Billy, Nicky, Norma, herself. Happiness, she reminded herself, was not to be expected; whatever you get of it is a gift. Who said that? Khoi, she thought; it was probably him. She remembered her father's voice: *Don't just expect things, Katie—for Christ's sakes nothing's going to be handed to you just because you're a good person. Doesn't work that way.*

Yet her parents believed in the journey of their life, the dream of the great adventure. They expected from their lives, wanted. Maybe not "happiness," but something. Something like weight, substance. Richness. But it all comes down to nothing in the end, she thought, for everyone.

She went to the side of the house, by the chopping block, and decided to split some new wood so as not to use up all that Billy had split. She lifted the ax but then remembered the splitting maul, how that was easier for her to use. She walked back past the door toward the shed. The canvas tarp over the doorway flapped in the wind; there was a sound, too, a hollow sound of air moving through the old rusty traps which hung on an outside wall. A sound that reminded her of dark winter nights, the idea of wolves in the woods beyond the knoll. How she used to feel those things, when she was little; the excitement and wonder of everything, even dark.

As she stepped in the shed she was hit with the memory of seeing her father with Norma. The musty smell, the dim light and their fumbled pulling apart. But as her eyes adjusted she was able to put the memory in its place—the shed was just a shed, with leaning walls and sagging shelves. The maul stood by the doorway. She had a feeling of Billy being there, putting things away.

She returned to the side of the house, set a round of spruce on the battered block. She lifted and swung, brought down the splitting maul. The wood halved and fell to the ground. She kept splitting until she had a variety of thicknesses on the ground around her. The movement felt good; she felt the quiet satisfaction of the accomplishment of a simple thing. She picked up the wood and went back inside.

She built a fire while her father worked the frying pans in the kitchen, and the house, which just a short time ago was cold and quiet, was filling with sounds and smells and growing warmth. Soon Katie and Manny were sitting at the table together, quietly eating and not saying much, but getting full and getting warm, a little bit at a time.

Rain gathered on the window, the drops holding then sliding, rolling into others in the fall down the glass. Billy watched. He counted how long a drop was still after it hit, how many other drops merged with it on its way down. He followed with his finger, tracing the movement down the cool, clear pane, wishing for—what? Nothing possible.

This is how it is, he thought; this is what it has all come down to. A good day was a busy day, when the nets were full and there seemed not enough time. A bad day was when there was nothing that had to be done.

He could have gone to Bristol Bay for the full season, tried it again, but his heart wasn't in it, his heart hadn't been in it, not since Nicky. It seemed like a betrayal, because fishing with their father was something Nicky had wanted so bad, and had never had.

He imagined the feel of the deck under his feet, the slow roll of the waves. The CB radio, alive with static and voices—where are the fish? *The nets are jumping down in Nushugak Bay.* His broad-shouldered father with the salty wind in his hair, pipe clenched between his teeth, grinning in the face of a coming storm—*Adventure!*—he would say as the boat began to toss.

But another year, and Billy couldn't do it. Even the two to three upcoming weeks, he didn't know how to get through.

He was thinking that maybe this summer he would find him. Nicky. Katie coming back was like an omen to him, a message: They were all here now. Even Norma. Billy would find him, and then he would know. And he would bring the bones home, bury them on their land. Bring over the Russian Orthodox priest from town—he thought his mother would have wanted that, from something his father once said, that she had loved the priests and their beautiful robes.

Then maybe he would quit seeing him in the shadowy shapes of the trees in winter; maybe he would quit hearing his voice in the cries of the loons, in the sound of the kettle boiling on the stove. And in his dreams he would reach into the water, grab the red mitten, and pull out his bony remains.

And maybe he would also quit thinking he was with Katie, somewhere, living a life with her, kissing her goodnight and waking to her face, the soft brush of her breath, the fine silk of her hair.

He went to Boston once, because he had to see her. It was after four years. Katie was working in a Chinese restaurant. He watched her go to work. It didn't seem it was really her—hair pinned up, a green silk dress with a pattern of dragons and temples of gold.

Once he saw her with someone. Built like Nicky, black hair. Billy went into the restaurant after Katie had gone. The person she'd been with worked there also; it wasn't Nicky. Similar though—he could see that. Billy had sat at a quiet table where he could look into the kitchen, watched Katie's friend slice fish. Quick like Nicky. It filled him with pain. Was it always Nicky, then, for her? Was she ever with him, or was she always someplace else? He looked for, but could not find, something of himself there, in the person of Katie's friend. Then he'd returned home.

He pressed his forehead against the glass, tried to ignore the throbbing beneath his thumb. He thought of Katie, only a mile away. How would it be, he wondered, to walk in Manny's door and see her there? See her, smell her, the sound of her voice again in his ears. There, in that house.

He almost let himself think it, almost let the scene unfold in his mind. Twelve years ago, he and Manny walking in that door. And there she was. And Nicky, too.

No. He turned his thoughts. A face came to him, the feeling: *Uncle.* He saw his uncle standing in front of the cabin by the river, pipe in hand. Everything nice, neat, Pete healthy and clear-eyed. Nicky was always wanting to go there. Billy would hang back. There were other things to do. He wasn't interested in stories, thought there would be time, later, for all that.

He suddenly wanted to see him, imagined again the old Pete, gone now, gone since Nicky. Billy waited always for word from the village, of Pete's death, that he had fallen out his front door and into the river, that his body finally said: Enough.

Would the same thing have happened if Billy had been the one to drown?

He didn't think so. Pete would have hung in there, for Nicky. After the accident Billy went to him, but it was already too late.

Billy daydreamed, in the winter, of Pete coming across the ice on the dog team, sober again, wanting to see him.

Billy and his father never talked about Pete. Nicky sometimes, his body, the wheres and what ifs, all the nooks and crannies along the different shores. If they could just find him. Then maybe they could fall out of the place they'd been tossed into, where they hung suspended, all of them that were left: Billy, his father, Pete.

Billy looked at the raincoat hanging by the door. Like a million other raincoats in Ilmenof, in Alaska. But this one was Nicky's and only Nicky's; Billy was there when he nipped the sleeve with Katie's mother's scissors. The coat was a black, ominous specter at his door. It was trying to tell him something. Something Billy might not ever want to hear.

Blow. Billy stared hard out the window, looked for movement in the trees. Blow. He wished for wind. He wished for wind and waves, for the lake to turn itself inside out.

Twigg thought about the dead people in the water, bones now, most of them, maybe some of them not even that. He was thinking about the bodies while he sat at his desk, feet up, eating from a box of fudge.

The fudge came every year, from Colleen Smith's family. No note, just the fudge, a thank-you of some kind, as if he'd actually found her.

Or maybe it's a reminder, he thought, that she is still out there, that they still want her home. A reminder, maybe a plea: *Please keep your eyes open. Please think of us, think of her—*

He doesn't want to think of her. Colleen had reminded him of Cindy, or maybe she was what Jen would have been like, if she had lived. Maybe Colleen's father is what *he* could have been—if he hadn't come home for lunch that day—a parent, someone with limitless love.

He went over it again: where the kayak was found, where Brian—Colleen's fiancé—was found, and, two years later, the boot that was found, that was hers. A trace, where with so many there is nothing, none; he imagines far down below the surface of the water a black hole like those found in space. Spitting out the boot.

Sometimes Twigg imagined a passageway through which these people passed that came out in another world—like in a fairy tale he'd once read, to the kids—where there was dancing and laughing. Maybe Nicky and Colleen dance there together. She'd been older than Nicky, when she died, but when Nicky died he was nearly her same age. Twigg wondered—if you existed as yourself after you die—do you get stuck with the age you are at the time of your death? Or can you be young again, or if you never had a chance to grow up, can you try it out, see what it's like? Or are you stuck, always, where you had stopped?

He looked out the window and saw Margaret coming down the street, her medical bag clutched in her hand. There was a well-child clinic today, at the lodge on the other side. He thought about putting away the fudge, but left it there, started in on another piece as she swung open the door.

"Well," she said, "are you ready?" Her eyes found the fudge. "What's that you're eating?"

"Breakfast," he said.

She shook her head, sighed short and sharp. "You're hopeless, Ray; hopeless."

"I know that. Like some?"

"No, but thanks."

"Did you ever like ice cream?"

"Well yes, of course."

"What flavor?"

She thought for a moment. "Vanilla, with chocolate swirls. Fudge I guess—fudge ripple."

Twigg nodded. "Yeah, that's good."

"Why do you ask?"

"I just wondered."

She smiled. "Well, I don't eat much of it anymore."

"I figured."

"There are healthier alternatives."

"There're always healthier alternatives." Twigg stood. "I'm an expert at that. I mean, at not taking the healthier alternative."

She looked at him, then looked at the floor. "I suppose sometimes people can't help themselves" she said.

"Well, Margaret, when what you're really wantin' is a bowl of ice cream, then pasta and that tabouli stuff just won't do, despite the price you know you'll pay." He grabbed a wool shirt, the canvas vest. "I guess I'm just sayin' that sometimes people don't do what's good for them, and they do it full knowing."

She nodded, but said: "Well, sometimes a person just doesn't know what's good for them and what isn't. Simple as that."

"Maybe," he said. He opened the door, caught the scent of her clean hair as she brushed past. He'd gone over this many times. If he'd known how it would all turn out, he never would have smiled at Cindy, at least not the kind of smiles that linger a little, that hold on to those brief moments of eye contact. Even not knowing how it would turn out, he knew full well how it was: She was married—nice husband, nice house, happy pretty children. He wasn't without girlfriends. But for some reason he only wanted her.

"Human nature's a funny thing," he added, and she didn't disagree.

Later, after the clinic, Margaret would try to get him to come with her, have dinner—she would lay her hand on his arm in a way that would touch him and hurt him at once. He would know she was secretly upset, that something passed between her and Katie, at the clinic, that told her something she did not want to know. And Twigg would find that what he thought he wanted was not what he wanted after all: To win by default. Why this hadn't been clearer sooner, he did not know.

She did not love him, would not love him, Billy or no Billy.

"No, thank you, Margaret," he would say. "I'm not up for it. Must've been too much fudge."

***

"Why don't you come to the lodge today?" Manny asked. It was morning and they were having breakfast together.

"What would I do there?"

"Well, Sal's still there, you know, and Dean—Dean told me it would be nice to see you."

Katie heard the negativity in the last part. "You really don't like Dean, do you?"

"No—I don't like Dean."

"Well, if you sold to those investors, then I guess you'd not only not have to deal with him, you'd be hurting his business as well."

"I don't want to hurt him. I just want out from under him. And you know, Katie, I'd give you a share—I would have given something to your mother. Maybe you could go to school or something."

She had always intended on going to school. But then it was as if she felt she didn't deserve it, even if she could have afforded it. As she was trying to think of a response she saw the weasel come scurrying out of a corner and look hesitatingly at the table. "Since when do you let animals live in the house?" she asked.

"Since I've been living alone."

She glanced at him, bit her tongue, then sighed. "All right. I'll ride over there with you," she said. "But we have to decide about Mom." She suddenly had this feeling that she should leave sometime soon, though her ticket was set for the end of two weeks. She had woken up anxious, thinking of dominoes, cause and effect. Billy on the trail; she could see how the sight of her upset him. And if she stayed she felt she might unearth something she wouldn't want to know—something about Nicky, or something about Norma and her father, and then she would be ripped open again.

The feel of Billy, close when she passed him on the trail, had stayed with her, was pulling at her, like a distant whisper in her ear.

"We're not deciding anything today, daughter. And your mother wouldn't want you moping around."

"I know. I'll go." It would fill the day. She realized she would have to start thinking about leaving—really thinking about it.

A little later they were out on the water, cutting diagonally across the bay, weaving around the islands. Katie sat in the bow, remembered the feel of being there, remembered too the puffy orange life vest she used to wear that smelled of the lake. She also remembered the feel and the scent of her mother's lipstick, on her cheek where she'd kissed her goodbye.

Katie looked over her shoulder, at Johnson's Point, distant now on the shore. She wondered what Billy was doing today; she wondered if he thought of her.

When the lodge came into view, it seemed much smaller than she thought it ought to be, the log walls much duller than the gleaming image in her mind. As they drew closer she could see how the logs were badly in need of an oiling. The building also seemed to tilt a bit, as though its foundation was sinking on one side. The two docks, which once seemed like wooden sidewalks stretching out into the water, looked stubby and crippled, like crooked fingers. She wondered why this was more than Dean could handle.

She remembered how the lodge used to seem like a shining castle on the shores of the lake. She had a memory of being small and standing on one or the other of the docks with her father while he talked with other men, could remember the deep drone of the men's voices above her, the smell of gas from the outboard motors around the docks and the sight of the swirling, multicolored patterns on the water where gas had leaked into the lake.

Dean wasn't there when they arrived, but Sal came out to greet them, happy to see Katie. Sal was the cook/waitress/winter caretaker— had been as long as Katie could remember—and she gave Katie a long hug and said: "I was so sorry to hear about your mama, sweetie. I think the lake rose an inch with my tears when I heard."

Katie said: "Lake was still frozen, Sal."

"Technicality, Katie; technicality." Katie was glad to see the stern flat face ("old hatchet face" Manny used to call her) amazingly unchanged despite the lapse of years; Katie wondered how old Sal was now, how old she'd been when Katie first knew her, and why it was she seemed so old to her then, when she couldn't have been.

Manny had some clients to take out; he left Katie there with Sal, to help her get the dining room ready for the well-child clinic. "Remember those?" Sal asked Katie. "Pokes and prods and shots." Katie laughed a little and followed Sal into the lodge.

In the entry area she stopped. There was a wall of black raincoats, like Nicky's—had they always been there, and had she not noticed? They were like dark soldiers, lined against the wall.

"What?" Sal said.

"That's a lot of raincoats," Katie said.

"Well, you know—nobody ever has the right gear. Can't beat those old raincoats."

They walked into the dining room where Sal began to wipe down a table, her lean sinewy arm a blur of brisk motion. "So's Manny sellin' or what?" she asked suddenly.

"I don't know."

"Do you care either way?"

"I don't know."

"It's been tough since Phil died. Manny and Dean—I don't know. There must be somethin' there I don't know about."

"I wouldn't know, Sal. Have all those raincoats always been there?" Katie was still looking toward the entryway.

"Yeah—I think so. There's only nine or ten there. Some have gotten lost, some have gotten replaced, but for the most part most of them been there going on twenty years. Don't you remember them?"

"I don't know. I guess not. I only remember Nicky wearing one."

"Nicky, your dad, Phil, Dean, Billy, Jake—everybody's had one of those, Katie."

Katie nodded. "I guess you're right."

"You're still pining for him."

Katie didn't answer.

"It's hard when things get cut off like that. There's never any conclusion." Sal only glanced periodically at Katie and kept at her cleaning, the gray, brillo-pad hair wisping out from its tight bun.

Katie nodded.

"Sweetheart, you know," Sal paused, shook her head. Katie knew what she was thinking: That the "thing with Nicky," as everyone called it, likely would not have lasted, if he had lived. Instead Sal said: "Well, someone's still pining for you."

Katie felt those words. "Why?"

"You don't choose who you love, Katie—you of all people should know that."

As Katie looked at Sal she could see, now, signs of the years on her face, her skin—she felt a rush of panic: it's passing, all this life she knew, into a shadow of nonexistence.

She turned to the window, looked out at the water, the old gray docks. She could again see herself standing there.

"Ain't you ever gonna get married or something, Katie?"

Sal was looking at her now. Katie smiled. "I don't know. Doesn't look it."

"Aren't there any men in that big old city?"

"I've a friend, off and on. But we can't get married or anything."

"Well, why not? He married already?"

"No—he's Chinese. He's supposed to marry someone his parents picked out for him a long time ago."

Sal snorted. "That's a bit prehistoric, don't you think?"

"Well, it keeps things simple—between us."

"Hmm. Well, if that's simple, then fish fly and bears—crochet."

"Crochet?"

"And you should know, *he's* never found anybody else."

"He who?"

"You know who."

But during the clinic, Katie saw that this was not totally true; there was a new nurse in town, and when Twigg introduced them she said to Katie: "You must know a friend of mine."

Katie lifted her brows.

"Billy. Billy Johnson."

Katie nodded. She could tell right away that the point was not whether *she* knew Billy, but that Margaret knew Billy. The nurse began to set her medical things out on the table, but she kept glancing at Katie, smiling, and Katie felt herself withdrawing, unwilling to smile back.

Soon boats began to arrive, from outlying homesteads, and children came in grudgingly, pulled by their parents. Katie sat quietly with Twigg and watched.

"You seen Billy?" Twigg asked, and even though his voice was soft Katie noticed how Margaret looked over.

"Once," Katie said. "But we didn't talk."

"You probably should do that."

"I think—what I probably should do, is leave."

"Why?"

Before she could answer Sal came in and said to Margaret: "There's a boy coming over from the village. Got a nail in his foot. They're on the way."

Margaret nodded and a short time later another boat arrived, and Katie recognized with alarm Norma's grandmother among the people in the boat, along with one of Norma's many second cousins who carried a small boy. Twigg stood, and went out to help them bring the boy in.

"Margaret, this is Alex," Twigg said when the group came in. The other families made room, and the boy was placed on a chair by Margaret. The nail was still in the boy's foot.

"Who're his parents?" Margaret asked, looking at the people who came in with the boy. Twigg replied how the boy's parents weren't there, how Norma's grandma was the boy's great grandma, and Katie felt something like a hand on the back of her head as she looked at the boy. In his face she could see Norma. In his face she saw something of herself.

Katie dug the bottle of sake out from within her clothes. She thought she would have a few sips, see if that eased the feeling she'd had of something crawling around on her insides. After Manny returned to the lodge he took Katie home, then had to "go back out" with some more clients. Katie felt he was lying. She thought she knew why.

After the boy with the nail in his foot had been brought in, at the clinic, Katie went outside to get some air. A plane landed and taxied up to the dock; before Katie knew it, a grown Dean DeVore was walking up to her, saying hello.

"How are you, Katie?" he'd said, surprising her with a soft kiss on the cheek. "We're all so sorry about your mom."

"Sorry about your dad."

"Yeah—thanks."

Katie swallowed, tried not to stare. He was better looking than she'd ever imagined he'd be—he looked fresh, with his light skin and reddish brown hair, his sky-blue eyes. When he was young he'd looked weak, snivelly, like a scrawny rooster. But no more. Katie felt, along with the foolishness of what she'd expected, a wave of guilt for the way she, Billy, Nicky, and even Norma—who liked nearly everything male—had mocked him.

"You look the same," he said.

"You don't."

"My face cleared." He'd laughed a little, and Katie noticed he had nice, clean-looking teeth and a dimpled smile. "Time does pass, doesn't it?"

"Yeah."

"For better or for worse."

"Yeah."

They'd sat, then, on the dock and chatted—of small things, mostly, of the fishing and the bears, the weather the past years and of Katie's life in Boston.

They looked up when the lodge door opened and the boy from the village was brought out with his relatives. They watched. The boy was crying a little and looked angry. His relatives were trying to soothe him as they loaded him into the skiff, which was tied to the other dock.

"Whose boy is that?" Dean had asked.

"I don't know—but that's Norma's grandmother, and one of her second cousins or something." Katie had kept her voice quiet.

"Norma's boy is older than that," Dean said, staring after the boat.

"What boy?" Katie asked. The skiff was moving now, sending waves back toward the docks, the engine a large hum.

"The boy—well, everybody knows."

"I don't."

"The boy she'd had after she'd left here. She went to Anchorage and I guess she got pregnant."

Katie, of course, remembered the pictures she'd found in her father's loft.

"That boy looks like the other," Dean said softly.

"You've seen her boy?"

Dean had looked at her then. "No—I mean, I must have seen a picture or something. I guess what I meant to say is that boy looks like Norma."

"Is Norma here?"

"Not that I know of."

But Manny had gone to the village, just yesterday. *What if*, Katie thought; *what if*.

"You're as pretty as ever," Dean had said then.

"What?"

"I think you heard me," he said, smiling at her. "You have a lot of piercings, though, in your ears—what's that about?"

Katie's hand touched one of her ears, felt the row of earrings. "I don't know. It's just something I started doing."

"Yourself?"

Katie'd nodded.

"That must hurt," he'd said, and Katie didn't answer.

Shortly after that Manny came back; he'd walked up to Katie, ignored Dean and said: "Was that a boat from the village?"

"Yeah—a boy was hurt."

"What boy?"

"We don't know," Dean had said.

Manny looked in the direction of the village, squinted his eyes. Then he went inside the lodge. Katie watched Dean watch him go.

Before Katie left, Dean had said he would like to come see her; Katie told him she would like that.

The sake was good; she heated it in a pan of water on the propane stove, poured servings of it into a small-size mason jar, her mother's past drinking glass of choice. She'd already been back to the loft and looked at the pictures again; of course it was the same boy, and yes, the two boys looked like Norma as Dean had said. So Norma had two boys. She thought it was odd how the older one had looked familiar to her, when she'd first seen the photo, when now the younger child was the one she recognized. He looked a lot like Norma, and a little like her, and a little like Manny.

So. So. Her mother was beyond this pain, Katie reminded herself. But still Katie wanted to cry, wanted to throw up, wanted to—she wasn't sure. As she kept drinking the sake she thought, for a moment, how she wished Dean would fulfill his promise to visit her and do it right then; she wanted to talk to him, she wanted to talk to anybody. If she had a phone she would even call Khoi, despite the fact that they were in one of their "off" stages, one that might be permanent, given the fact that he would soon be married.

But there was no one to talk to, anywhere, so she grabbed the near-empty bottle and took it with her down to the lake, moving dangerously down the front side of the knoll. She walked and drank, walked and drank.

Before she knew it, she was at Johnson's Point. She walked straight into the stream by the mouth of it, surprised how it didn't seem too deep or too cold, and she was easily across. The dogs were barking but Billy didn't seem to be there—she was glad, she was disappointed, she wondered if he was at his cabin or out on the lake somewhere, in Nicky's baidarka.

Go drown in your baidarka. Someone had said this to Nicky, once. One of the boys from the village.

Nicky never drowned in his baidarka.

Katie went past the point, saw the cove where Nicky's tent used to be pitched. She decided not to go there. She saw the rock in the water, where she and Nicky used to sit. She thought that would be good; she was wet already anyway, so she walked straight into the lake, holding up her bottle as the water rose up her chest.

She got there and pulled herself onto the rocks, had another drink and looked around, thought for a moment that she was happy, heard a song in her head, sang with it, danced a little then, suddenly, stopped.

There was only the wind. The wind, the water, the thick dark trees on the shore. She was wet, she was cold, the gray sky was beginning to rain.

She heard something and turned. There was a raven, flying near the shore. She remembered being out on one of the islands, looking for

Nicky. She had seen something black, on the edge of the water. Moving. She ran. Then the black thing unfolded and rose into the air. A raven, and nothing there where it had been.

"You," she said, now, to this raven. "You." There was the whisper of her voice, the faint beat of wings, then nothing again, just the soft wind, the fine drops of rain.

She sat and held her face in her hands. She wanted to sleep, but felt cold and uncomfortable. She pulled her knees to her chest and closed her eyes.

Then, suddenly it seemed, she opened them again, and the baidarka was there, on the water by the rock. It was empty. Then she saw Billy, standing near. She saw his black tennis shoes, his faded jeans. She tipped her head back and saw him looking down at her.

It was like being inside a dream. And later, when she was sober, that's how it would come back to her—like the pieces of a dream.

"Billy," she said. *Billy, Billy, Billy.* The name rolled, repeated, like water in a stream.

"You need to go home, Katie."

How funny, she thought, Nicky would always say that—*Time to take you home, skinny Katie.*

Don't tell Bill.

I'll tell him, eh? They were in the water together, swimming in the cove. It was evening and the surface reflected the gold of the sky. Mosquitoes buzzed and swarmed. Nicky's mouth was wet and cool, the taste of the lake. *Maybe you might go with me.*

Go where?

Pete's fish camp. Off Cook Inlet. Good trapping, out there.

I don't know about trapping—

There's not much I'm good at, Katie. I'm good at that.

What about Billy?

Billy'll be one pissed off son-of-a-bitch, I think—

And here Billy was now, looking down at her. She imagined saying it: *One pissed off son-of-a-bitch.* It was still raining. The rain fell on her face, fell into her eyes. "Is that you?" she said.

"It's Billy," he said. "I'll take you home."

That was who I meant, she wanted to say. *I meant you.* "Nicky's dead," she said.

"You're drunk."

"Billy," she said.

He reached down his hand. "Get up now, Katie, I'll take you home."

She hung on and he pulled. She thought maybe she was laughing. When on her feet she fell against him, and for a moment while he steadied her they were close.

"I didn't want," she said, but her words and thoughts got tangled. She wanted. That was the problem. "I don't know," she said.

Then somehow she was in the baidarka, Nicky's baidarka, Billy's legs on either side of her, her back against his chest. Her head flopped forward, then backward; he muttered something.

"Oh, don't be mean," she said.

"I'm not mean, Katie."

"Don't be unkind."

"I'm not unkind, Katie."

"You always hate me."

"No. Not always."

She put her hand across her eyes, felt the warmth there, thought maybe she was crying.

"Don't cry, Katie," he said. "Just let me get you home."

Twelve years previous

Nicky says: "Billy."

They sit on a rock in the water, wet from wading. His legs stretch out on either side of her; her back presses against his chest, and she imagines the flesh, the ribs, the thin layers of muscle—only inches between her heart and his. Her shoulder blade; she can feel his heart pounding against it.

She ignores what he said. She watches the morning, the lake and sky a wash of soft blue; the mist shrinking back toward the shore, clinging to the rounded corners of coves. There is a grebe somewhere, shrieking; there is the sound of wings on water, a pair of loons taking off, going someplace else.

She'd found him here the night before. She'd waded out to him, and when he saw her he said: *My father hates me because I killed my mother.*

Katie said, *No. He wouldn't. You were only being born.* Nicky came early in a year when breakup was late and slow, the lake covered with rotten ice. A plane couldn't land; a boat couldn't cross. The helicopter from Anchorage was too long in getting there.

Billy tries to make it up to him, Nicky said, make up for the fact that their father loves Billy the most. And then he said: *I saw her in a dream once, and she said my name.* He wasn't drunk but he wasn't right, either; Katie didn't ask. She'd held his hand and pulled him forward as they waded back to shore.

Then, at his tent, they warmed themselves by a campfire and Katie stared at Nicky's carvings. She'd said: *Do you hate me because I'm white?*

Why you say that, Katie?

I don't know. There was something about the figures, Native figures in white man's clothes, all lost and unhappy.

I'm white, too, he said. *Should I divide myself in two?*

Then he pressed his face against hers, his cheek to her cheek, their mouths near each other's ears, her eyes full of his dark curls. He whispered. She heard no words, only a sound like the wind in her ear.

Now she looks at him, feels the warmth of his face again on hers, sees how he watches the water, as if searching.

"What are you looking for?" she whispers. There is a secret.

"I'm listening."

"To what?"

"The water."

The wind pushes his hair across her eyes. She brushes it back, holds it with her finger.

He says: "If water were words, I would pull some out for you." He looks at her; there is a slight smile. "Like this." He dips his hand into the water, pulls it out, wet and dripping.

"Is that a word?" she asks.

He nods.

"What?"

"Quviannikumuit."

"What's that?"

"Inuit."

"But you're Aleut."

"If water were words it would have all the words of all the people."

"What does it mean?"

"To feel deeply happy."

"Is that something you know?"

He doesn't answer. He puts his hand back into the water, lifts it.

"Katie," he says.

"The word?"

"Yes."

"So what does that mean?"

"Quviannikumuit."

"No."

"Yes."

"Yes?"

The wind moves past. She hears a word. *Yes.*

K ATIE STOOD ON THE TRAIL TO BILLY'S, HEAD THROBBING, STOMACH UPSIDE DOWN. She wondered if she was still drunk, and that's why she was here.

She had hoped he'd be by the stream in front of his father's, splitting fish. She'd seen the net in the water, as she'd found her way across the stream, saw how it jerked in the current, jerked from the captured fish she couldn't see.

It was unlike him, to leave it. It made her angry almost, as if he had become different only to hurt her, to make her pay.

Would he even talk to her—she didn't know. Yesterday evening he'd carried her up the knoll, placed her on her bed. Or so it seemed. She remembered pieces, but not how they fit together.

She wanted to find out about Norma, and Norma's boys, wanted a second opinion as if for a diagnosis she didn't like. She woke up thinking she could be wrong.

She made her way slowly down the trail. The day was overcast and hazy; it had rained again yesterday, but she didn't remember that. Still, the trail wasn't too bad, the bushes and grasses not as wet as they could be, and it didn't matter to her anyway, as she was already drenched to the waist from crossing the stream.

Her stomach kept tensing, a feeling like the sudden downward turn on a roller coaster ride.

Everything looked so clean—the leaves, the ferns, the grass. She focused on this. Then she heard something, a thwack! and she knew instantly what it was, knew Billy was splitting wood. She could turn back; it wasn't too late; if she were here a year ago for a different reason she wouldn't be doing this, wouldn't even be thinking about it. But she found, since her mother's death, that things no longer lay quiet inside her but bubbled and seethed and demanded to be dealt with.

He didn't see her at first as he stood by the chopping block staring at a piece of wood, looking undetermined, the ax hanging limply in his hand.

Something was wrong. Katie stopped. Billy's face turned and he saw her. His chest rose with a sharp breath; he lifted the ax with one arm and sent the blade crookedly into the chopping block. Then he looked at her again. He seemed to be sweating; his cheeks were flushed despite the coolness of the day.

"Billy," she said, "are you all right?"

He tipped his head. Her heart broke.

"I need to talk to you," she said, "if it's okay. There's something. We can talk, can't we?"

He looked down at the ax, pulled at it, the chopping block tipped and he let it go.

"Oh, Katie." He sounded so tired.

"It wasn't all my fault. Was it?"

He hesitated, but shook his head. "No. Maybe I wish it was, eh?" Then: "Is this what you want to talk about?"

She shook her head.

"What, then?"

"Norma—and her boys."

"What you know about that, eh?"

"I don't know anything. I saw the one—the little one—at the clinic yesterday."

"That why you out drunk on those rocks?"

Katie looked down. "No. Maybe."

"So what do you want to know?"

"Well—who the father is. Of the little one, especially." She kept her eyes down, clenched her teeth. She heard a smirk. *Oh, Billy, don't.* Had he and Nicky been so similar?

"Take a guess."

She looked up at him. He did not look away.

Billy, where have you gone? It was a thought more than words inside her. She had an image, then, of the dream-Nicky in the water, this time with Billy there beside him. She was seeing it now, what she had so feared: That Billy had died that day, too, that his pain had been even greater than her own.

"I don't need to guess," she said. He didn't have to say any more than he did. She felt her stomach turning. "What about the other one?"

Billy shrugged. "Norma's not saying. Never did." His eyes closed, and he rubbed his hand over his eyes.

"Are you all right?" she asked again.

"I'll be right, eh?" Something Nicky would say: *You'll be right. Not to worry, eh?*

She moved closer, slowly, arm stretched toward him, palm open. She saw wrappings on one of his hands, didn't need to be close to see the swelling in the fingers.

"What did you do?"

He shook his head. "A cut."

"Is it bad?"

"Infected—pretty good now."

"Could I see?" Billy was beside his house now; she stood the width of the door from him, watching his face. He looked at her.

"Oh, Katie." The tiredness in his voice again, the weariness. He was weary of her; she felt this. Weary because even in her absence she had always been there.

He lifted his hand, held it out to her.

Cautiously she peeked beneath the wrappings, pulled back the unbuttoned cuff of his flannel shirt. She saw on his wrist a red line, coming from the hidden area beneath the gauze.

"You need to see someone."

He sighed, but nodded, and with his other hand pushed back the hair from his forehead. "I felt bad about your mom." For a moment something lifted between them.

"I wasn't ready."

"I don't think you can get ready, for things like that."

"I know." She felt color coming into her cheeks.

"You a drinker now?"

"No."

"Then why were you like you were last night?"

"I don't know." She was still looking at his hand. "Do you hate me?"

"You asked me that last night. That's what you think, eh?"

"Sometimes."

"Sometimes," he said, "sometimes you are right."

The floats hit the water and the plane jerked; he'd come in a bit too fast, reprimanded himself: *You know better*, but there was only a moment, though, when his heart beat a little faster. He had it under control. Basically.

He saw Katie and Billy on the shore at the tip of the point, waiting. Billy stood coatless in the wind; Katie sat some distance from him, holding her knees to her chest.

It was a sight natural and not at the same time, like a broken piece of pottery with the pieces glued back together—normal at a distance, but up close jagged and uneven, out of joint.

Twigg found that old feeling inside of him, hollow heaviness. They could not be fixed, Billy and Katie; like for him and Cindy, it came down wrong, and all the love in the world couldn't put it back together right.

Ruined. A word he hated, a word riddled with finality. It was ruined for them, he thought; irreversibly ruined.

He would love to be wrong.

Billy waded out and stopped the float, grabbed the wing with his good hand. Katie rose and stood on the shore.

"What's up?" Twigg said, leaning over and pushing out the door. He'd just made a flight to the lodge when Katie'd reached him there by radio and asked if he could come get Billy.

"Infection," Billy said, lifting the wrapped hand. "I should probably go in."

"Better safe than sorry, son." Twigg knew Billy knew that; he was a good woodsman, Billy was, one who knew when and when not to gamble with the realities of remote living.

Billy nodded reluctantly, looked at Katie. "You can go home, eh?"

She looked at Twigg. "I'd like to go."

"Sure, gal," Twigg said. "Fine by me."

Billy said nothing.

Twigg saw Katie measuring the distance between the shore and the plane. She was without hip boots; Twigg began to unbuckle when Billy said, after a sharp sigh, "I'll get her."

Katie said: "I'm still wet anyway," but Billy let go of his hold on the plane and trudged through the water.

Twigg could see Katie bite her knuckles. Billy walked up to her, turned around, knelt down a little, and Katie climbed on.

Twigg noticed she didn't protest much. Neither did Billy. As he watched them come through the water to the plane there was a moment like seeing back through time, and he pictured them how they once were, or how they might have been, imagined seeing smiles and hearing laughter, just for a moment. But the two people who reached the plane were like wounded soldiers trudging across an endless battlefield, too tired at the moment to care about opposing sides, wanting only to get through, one end to the other.

This was what he'd been doing, too, Twigg realized; trying to get through, trying to survive life, get from the beginning to the end of it, like a long book one doesn't want to but must read, trudging grudgingly toward those final pages—

—*God, it shouldn't be like this*—

If he could just remember, *really* remember, who he was when he'd started out.

He wished he could say now, to Billy and Katie: *Let it go. Just let it go. It doesn't make any difference anymore, what's done is done, what's gone is gone.* But this was something he couldn't even convince himself of, let alone anyone else.

He thought maybe Katie lingered a little on Billy's back, before slipping off onto the float and pulling herself into the back of the plane. Then Billy climbed in, sat back into his seat with a sigh, and stared stonily out the windshield.

It was a quiet flight, across the lake. *Between gray sky and gray water*, Twigg thought; the three of them suspended, *temporary*.

In town they all sat in Twigg's truck and drove away from the planes in the cove, which looked to Katie like a flock of different colored birds, bobbing on the waves. She tried to shrink herself, but still with the space between them she could feel the warmth of Billy's body, smell the smell of him: line-dried clothes, wood smoke, bug dope and spruce sap, skin and hair.

In Boston men smelled of pre-shave and aftershave and sheets of Bounce. Except Khoi; Khoi smelled of fish—his apron and white shirt, bleach.

Khoi didn't mind that she never said she loved him; liking was enough. They both knew they were temporary, anyway.

Katie thought about how she felt now, smelling Billy's smell. She wondered if it was because it could be Nicky's, and then she thought how she must have smelled similar to that, once: hanging on a nail in her room still was an old nightgown, left over from childhood, covered with dust and yellowed from smoke, smelling of wood smoke, of winter days feeding the fire, the smoke curling out from the open door.

The truck bumped and bounced; as they had in the plane, they sat silent. Katie wondered at this, wondered at Twigg's quietness, hoped it had nothing to do with Billy's hand, that he thought things were more serious than they seemed. They drove down Main Street, past Twigg's office, the post office, the trading post, the gas station; despite all the recent rain the town was dusty again—teenagers on three-wheelers roared past, stirring things up.

They pulled up to the little house where the nurse lived. Billy stepped out. "I'll be right, eh," he said, and closed the door. Twigg and Katie exchanged a glance, followed Billy out.

Margaret swung the door open, face full of concern, touched Billy lightly on the arm and guided him inside.

"There's coffee on the counter, Ray, if anyone would like some," she said as Twigg and Katie entered and stood awkwardly by the door. Margaret set Billy down at the table; she bustled about, pulled things out from her bag, stuck a thermometer under his tongue which Billy took out and set on the table. Margaret sighed, said: "All right. Let's look at your hand. You will let me look at your hand, won't you?"

Billy placed his arm across the table. With little sharp scissors Margaret cut the wrappings.

"Oh—I'm going to have to lance this."

"I can do that, eh?"

"No—you can't. Would you like me to numb it first?"

He shook his head. "I'm good."

"It will hurt."

"It's all right. Not to worry, eh?"

Then she said, without looking at anyone: "I need to keep him here for a little bit—at least an hour, Ray, just to watch things."

"Okay," Twigg said, "we can hang out a bit." Then, to Katie: "Wanna go get some lunch? My treat."

Katie nodded. Then Billy looked at her, and looked away. His face startled her. There was so much Nicky there. Or was it that there had been so much Billy in Nicky? She didn't know. She would never know. It was all over and done with, now. Irretrievable, unfixable, unrecoverable.

She left with Twigg; they drove through what was left of town and headed to one of the lodges along the shore. This was a log one, the oldest one, with scarred plank flooring that dipped in the corners, a bar top made of layers of clear shellac, underneath which one could see a collection of agates and Indian arrowheads.

Billy, Nicky and Katie had found many of those, trading them to the lodge for payments of candy bars and cans of soda, Twigg making deals for them, bringing back the goods on the mail run.

Nicky would not trade his arrowheads. He kept them in a leather pouch, which hung from a nail by his cot in the small dark room he shared with Billy. When he was grown he kept the pouch with him in his tent. When he died Katie went to his tent and looked for it, but it was already gone.

Twigg pulled open the heavy wooden door, and together they stepped inside. The bar was to the left, the dining room to the right; straight ahead was a hefty log staircase, leading to rooms upstairs. On the walls near the ceilings were the heads of animals, stuffed and mounted, plastic eyes dull and dusty. Bears, moose, sheep. Katie was reminded of her stuffed toys; she was reminded, too, of her mother, dead.

They went to the dining room, took a table next to a window overlooking the lake. The dining room was new, since Katie's childhood.

The day Katie and her mother arrived at Ilmenof they came here, sat at a table in the bar and watched the water. It was a gray, windy day; the waves were capped with white. Manny laughed and joked with the owner of the lodge; Katie and her mother stared out the window.

A waitress came over to the table, asked what they'd like. They both ordered French fries and coffee. As they sat there quietly with their food, Dean walked into the dining room, pulling his dark sunglasses off his face.

"Hi!" he said. "What's going on?"

"We brought Billy over to see Margaret," Twigg said. "Cut got infected. What are you up to?"

"Just business stuff. Post office and all that." He sat down, twirling the glasses between his fingers. He smiled at Katie. "How are you today, Katie?"

"Fine," she said.

"Good." He kept looking at her. Katie took a long sip from her mug and kept her eyes on his face, but she didn't smile back. He looked away.

Katie tried to remember: Did they really dislike Dean, all teasing aside? And if they did dislike him, was there any reason for it beyond his simply being from someplace else? She felt again a tinge of guilt. When he looked back at her, she was sure to smile. He smiled back. And then Katie saw something. In his smile was the boy in the photograph in her father's drawer—not the young one, but the older one. Katie quickly looked away.

Reluctantly, Margaret let him go. She stood in the doorway, watched the truck drive away. She'd done what she could: lanced the wound, drained the wound, cleaned the wound—wrapped it back up with clean, fresh gauze. A shot of penicillin, a bottle of pills for follow-up. He said he'd come back if it got worse, if the red line still crept forward. She'd asked Twigg to hold him to that. Twigg said: *I'll talk to Manny about keeping an eye on this guy.* And Margaret noticed, with that, how Katie looked downward and turned her face away.

Someone might as well have just said it, out loud, all that was between those two. Was or is. Did it matter? Something existed between them, perhaps something left over that they still carried around.

Margaret wondered how long Katie would stay.

She went back inside, sat at the table still cluttered with her equipment. She picked up the old gauze from his hand, looked at the reddish yellow stain where it had lain across the wound, felt tightness inside, like a hand squeezing her heart. Bad luck, she thought, that this Katie had to show up now. Billy was just starting to come out of himself a bit, laugh a little more—it was good for him to be with her, Margaret thought; someone he could start fresh with, a clean slate, someone with whom he could exist in the present, free of the heavy cloak of a sad history.

She'd tried to talk to him a little, while she worked on his hand.

Old girlfriend? she'd asked. It was clumsy, awkward—stupid, she realized now.

No. His response startled her; why would he lie? *She was my brother's girl. Nicky's.* He looked at her then. His face seemed to say: *Analyze that.* Thankfully, she was smart enough to bite her tongue and not say another thing.

But the look stayed with her, hurt her. During her six months at Ilmenof, she had managed to infiltrate his world a little—there had been dinners, walks, and once, over a month ago now, when weather stranded him in town he had stayed here with her, in this house, and though she'd had to work at it she finally did manage to seduce him. And it was good; it was good. And she'd played it properly cool, let him know how wonderful a time she'd had, but that she wasn't expecting anything because of it. In the morning he'd said he usually didn't do that sort of thing, and apologized. She'd assured him there was nothing to be sorry about. She'd snagged him for dinner a couple of times since, but noticed that he was careful with the weather.

When they were in bed together he was attentive and gentle, yet when he kissed her it was intense and distant at the same time, and with his eyes closed he seemed almost in pain. It was like that when he came, too, as if it was something that hurt.

She would be good for him, so good for him, if only he'd let her.

His comment about Katie being "Nicky's girl" must be a denial of sorts, she thought, originating in his own guilt over surviving his little brother, over his role in the events that led to the accident.

Still, the look on his face seemed a warning; she decided it was probably time for her to quit writing him for a while, quit sending him invitations to come to town for a visit. See if he missed her. She hoped she hadn't tipped her hand too much already. She tried to remember the details of the last letter she'd sent over there. Somewhere she'd written down the gist of what she'd said, for her own records. She would have to take a look at that, but she was sure she'd kept it low-key, just mostly an inquiry into how he was.

And, well, if he was in town, it would be nice if he'd stop by and say hello—

She tossed the soiled gauze into the trash, cleared the table and wiped it down with a disinfectant. She started to fix herself a late lunch when there was a knock on the door; she sighed. She had a feeling who it was. "Come on in, Rosie." Just yesterday Rosie had finally come to her to discuss her possible pregnancy; since then she kept coming by.

Rosie entered, stood shyly by the door, a little chubby but healthy looking, with shiny black hair and good color in her cheeks, wearing a pink anorak that stretched across her breasts.

"So how are you doing, Rosie?"

"Oh, I'm good, yeah."

"I'm just fixing some tuna. Are you hungry?"

"No, but thanks, eh?"

"You know you need to be sure to eat."

Rosie nodded.

"Rosie, are you sure you know what you're doing?" Margaret chopped celery for the tuna, moving the knife rapidly across the chopping block.

Rosie pondered the words, blinking fast. "I'm not doing anything. This just happened. I didn't mean it."

Margaret stopped, sighed a moment, then chopped again. "I just think maybe you're thinking having a baby is a way to keep Tommy."

"Keep Tommy?"

"Yes—keep him with you."

"I love Tommy."

"I know you think you do."

"I wouldn't want him to be with me unless he wanted to be. Honest." There was a quaver in her voice; Margaret turned toward her, saw how her full lips trembled at the corners, saw her dark almond eyes starting to mist.

"Oh, Rosie." Margaret hesitated, then stepped forward, put her arm around the girl's shoulder. "I'm sorry. Don't worry. It'll be all right; we'll make it all right. Okay?"

Rosie nodded, but looked at the floor.

"Are you sure you don't want some lunch?"

Rosie shook her head, said, "I'll go now," and turned and left.

"Bye!" Margaret called after her, trying to sound cheerful, but Rosie didn't look back.

Margaret shut the door, leaned back against it. She'd been terse with Rosie. Why? Most likely because Billy had been terse with her. She would have to be sure to be kinder to Rosie, next time.

She looked around. Her little house was clean, quiet—only a bit of dust on the floor where Rosie had stood, the chair where Billy had sat still crooked at the table. Her lunch was almost ready; barring any other emergencies, she had the rest of the day to herself, to do with as she pleased. But she stayed against the door for awhile, uninterested in moving, in pushing the day forward. She thought about the things going on around her, in the lives of other people—Twigg, Billy, Katie—Rosie, even. Margaret's life was so much cleaner than any of these people's. She realized the value of that but at the same time felt some kind of an absence, or seclusion, as if in a large movie theater she suddenly realized she was the only member of the audience; everyone else was on the screen, in a story of sorts, a story that was unfolding.

*When I was seventeen, my father had an affair with my friend,
Norma.*

Katie listened to the words in her head, imagined how they
would sound if she said them.

*She was Billy and Nicky's cousin, and she lived in the Native village,
which was ten miles from my house, eleven miles from Billy and Nicky's.
Uncle Pete used to bring her to visit. Pete is Billy, Nicky, and Norma's
great uncle, but I called him Uncle Pete, too—but only when I referred to
him. In person I never called him anything. If I wanted to say something
to him—which wasn't that often, I was afraid of him—I just stood nearby
and stared at him until he looked at me. He always seemed to know when I
wanted to say something.*

*Billy and Nicky's mother, Marlene, had been his niece, and she was
dead. She died when Nicky was born. There were some hard feelings about
that, between Uncle Pete and Billy and Nicky's father, Jake. It had to do
with Jake's not having wanted Pete to deliver the baby. Break-up was late
the year Nicky was born, and Jake couldn't get a plane in to take Marlene
to the doctor. Pete believes he could have saved her. Jake, I've always imagined, doesn't want to believe this might be true.*

*Because when someone is dead, that's it. Nothing can be redone, and
nothing could ever be put back the way it was.*

*But despite the problem with Jake, Pete came often from the village to
visit Billy and Nicky, almost always bringing Norma. In the summer they
came by skiff; in the winter, by dog team. Pete's team was one of the pret-
tiest, I'd always thought; some of the dogs were part wolf. The whole team
would lie silent in the snow, waiting for Pete. They would watch everything.
I often wanted to touch these dogs, run my hands through their thick, glossy
fur, but I never felt brave enough. Maybe it was because they were from the
village; the village seemed another world to me, cloaked in a sort of mystery
with all its dark-eyed residents. I often wondered what thoughts these people
thought, what someone like me seemed to them. What it was like to live
there, in the village.*

*Norma gave me a window into that world, though while I longed
to be like her—with dark slanty eyes and long black hair—after a time
I realized with some puzzlement and with a strange excitement that she
wanted to be like me. She borrowed my books and comic books and gave me*

beaded necklaces in exchange for hair elastics and pins and art supplies. She wanted my clothes, too, but she was larger than me all over and nothing fit. When my mother'd brought me a new windbreaker several sizes too big so it would last, Norma talked me into trading it to her for an old calico kuspuk. I had wanted a kuspuk for a long time. But as soon as I'd handed over the windbreaker, it (the windbreaker) seemed much nicer than I'd thought, but Norma wouldn't trade back. My mother was angry, and I found out later that Norma had swiped the kuspuk from her grandmother. I didn't want anybody's grandmother's kuspuk. After that I was more careful with my things around Norma, and she wasn't able to wear the windbreaker long, anyway; it got too small and she gave it back to me in exchange for two pairs of new knee-high socks, which were too small for her also.

I knew Norma didn't want to marry anyone from the village; it was her life's goal, to get out of the village. That was one of the reasons she read everything she could get her hands on. She said if worse came to worst, she would go somewhere and get a job. Not a cannery job, not a job on a fishing boat—nothing that had to do with fish. She hated fish, she said, though she would always eat it when it was placed on the table in front of her. Norma knew what she had to do to survive.

She liked white men, older ones. When I saw her with my father in the shed, I saw how she wanted him. I'd never believed he hit her, though she said he did and he didn't say he didn't. My mother and I never talked about it; we just left and never went back.

I regret this; I regret this omission. Like those of everyone else I have ever loved, I would see Norma's face sometimes, in the sea of faces on a Boston street during rush hour, see something familiar for an instant in a world of people I didn't know.

Katie stood in the wind on the shore, waiting as Twigg pumped the floats before taking them back across. Billy leaned against the truck, also waiting, looking cold and pale. Katie wanted to ask him if he was all right. She was afraid to. Yet she had spent most of the day with him, and nothing terrible had happened so far.

She walked toward him, shoulders stooped and head down. She stood for a moment near him, unable to decide what to say. She could feel him waiting. "Is your hand all right?" When the words came, they were barely above a whisper.

"Yes."

"Did Norma ever like Dean?"

"What?"

"Did Norma ever like Dean?"

"What do you mean, Katie?"

"I mean like him not like a friend."

She didn't look at his face, but she could feel Billy's expression of both confusion and thoughtfulness. "I don't think so," he said. "Why you ask, eh?"

"Do you know her oldest boy?"

"Yes. Nico."

"Who's his father?"

"I told you she's not saying, but you should know, Katie. Does it matter anymore?"

"He's not my dad's."

"How can you be sure?"

"He looks like someone else."

"Dean?"

"Yeah—"

He almost laughed—or smirked, Katie couldn't tell. "I don't know, Katie." He let out a sharp breath. "Manny took care of those two, Norma and Nico. Just ask."

"Took care of them?"

"Sent them money."

"Oh."

"But you should be talking to him about this."

Katie could feel anger festering inside her. She thought of all the bad apartments she and her mother lived in, all the extra shifts her mother would work.

She looked now at Billy, and he was looking at her. His face seemed softer; she wondered if Margaret had given him something for the pain. She imagined touching him, his beardless cheek, the sad place there, between his brows. She wanted, too, to ask him about the rain-coat, felt the urge trying to push its way out of her. "And Norma's back now," was what she said instead.

Billy nodded. "That's what I hear." A familiar flatness was creep-ing back into his voice; Katie felt the moment slipping.

"I was coming over to thank you for taking me home last night," she said quickly, explaining her morning appearance at Johnson's Point. "Not just to ask you about Norma's boys." And she had wanted to see him, with her own eyes again, soberly. To feel what she had a blurry memory of feeling, like something stirring around inside her.

He lifted his bandaged hand. "We're even," he said, but she saw how he didn't like the way those words sounded, and she walked quickly back to where she had been standing.

Did you know Norma was back?

Was that how she'd said it, Manny wondered; the conversation was only a short time ago, and already he wasn't sure he was remember-ing it right.

It was an accusation, wasn't it, he thought—if he knew, if he didn't know—it was all the same. Katie had long ago decided she knew what was what as far as him and Norma went.

Yeah, he'd said, hoping to let it go at that. He knew his own daughter. Knew she didn't push, only circled, like a wary bird.

She brought one of her kids with her. I guess she's got two, two boys. She'd been watching his face as she talked.

"Yep." He'd waited. He wasn't going to lie himself into a corner but he wasn't going to hand it to her, either. He watched Katie's eyes wander, from the table to the window to the floor, skipping around for a place to land, unable to find one.

When did she get like that, he wondered now, sitting alone in the dusk, smoking, while Katie was outside by herself, sitting on the edge of the knoll. She'd looked tired, pale. He thought with a smirk how she probably was a little worse for the wear; he'd been here, last night, when Billy carried her up the hill to the house, a limp rag doll in his arms. Again he wondered, when did she get like that?

He could remember a different girl. Headstrong. Bold, much bolder. Giving those boys a run for their money, taking them up on every double-dare. Getting angry—she could get angry, and wasn't afraid to let anyone know. Now he could sense her anger, but this anger was of a different breed, one that lived quietly inside her, waiting.

If she would get angry—just get good and angry. At him, at God—anything. She reminded him now of a skittish dog, lurking. He didn't like to think of her that way.

It wasn't what we'd intended. He thought of Vivian, their early years together. How she'd stood up to her family to marry him, the son of a taxi cab driver. All the jobs she held down, to get him through school. Typing his papers for him at night, though she had work of her own to do. Then there were the easy years of money, a real house, and she could finally relax but didn't—was it because of him?

Did she have that skittish look, too? Was it something that was in her—and Katie, too—or something they picked up along the way, like a dent on a car, during their years with him?

He'd often wondered if they should have stayed in Boston, but even Vivian had said, *Oh no, no—we had to go,* despite how none of it had worked out as they'd planned.

He rolled a cigarette, looked out the window and watched Katie there, on the knoll. She was no longer sitting but now paced back and forth in the wind. He was reminded of Billy, after Nicky disappeared. Three o'clock in the morning, pacing on the knoll. Katie'd heard him. He was yelling her name. Manny and Katie'd looked at him through the front window—he was like the wind, not knowing which way to blow. Manny had gone for his boots, hurried out the door and around the house, but suddenly Billy was gone. When he went back inside, Katie, too, was gone from where she'd been; he'd peeked quietly into her room, saw her huddled on her cot, knees to chest, refusing to look up.

Manny thought back beyond that time, to when Katie was little. He remembered once when they were duck hunting, and she was about nine. It was fall, freeze-up, and a thin sheet of ice had formed between the shore and most of the islands. To find any ducks they had to get to open water; the closest place was called the Shoots, a strange canyon-like space between two islands, where the currents moved river-like, wind or no wind. They'd walked on the new ice, already over two inches thick and plenty safe, he'd figured. The lake had frozen clear that year; it was as if a window had been placed over the water. He saw how Katie had hesitated, how she stared down at the distant, murky bottom.

Walk where I walk, he'd said. It was simple; there was no way she could fall through, if he didn't. He'd stayed a ways ahead of her, to check things out, turning now and again to watch her tense but deter-mined little figure come following along behind.

Then he looked and didn't see her. How long had it been, since he'd checked? There was something on the ice, but it wasn't big enough to be her. He hurried, slipping and even falling once, shaking the ice. Then he realized that what he'd been seeing was her head, her little green and black plaid cap. Her arms stretched out, hanging on. The rest of her on the other side of the ice. He stopped a short distance from her and lay down on his stomach, inched his way toward her.

Vivian's gonna kill me—

He'd grabbed her hands, started scooting back. It seemed a long time before they felt safe, clear.

I told you to walk where I walked! he'd said. Or had he yelled? He didn't remember himself as yelling.

I did!

He shook his head; he did remember that. *You couldn't have. Now how am I gonna explain this to your mother?*

Her angry little face. *I did!* she'd said. *I walked where you walked!* And then he shook his head again.

She never changed her story. Should he have believed her? *You never believe me*, she'd said once. When was that? After she'd lost the necklace, the one he thought she shouldn't have, the one he'd said she mustn't have fastened right, or that she'd snagged on the dock, both of which she'd denied.

He lit his cigarette, watched Katie pace. He knew she would ask again, about Norma and the boys. What should he tell her? He didn't know. The truth at this point seemed too little, too late.

Out on the knoll he saw her turn, look at the window, a downward tilt to her face. Did she see him through the glass? Or was he protected by shadows, he wondered. Reflections of other things.

Katie lay on the cot in her room, dozing. It was quiet. She could almost hear her father breathing, there where he sat at the table; she smelled his cigarette and imagined the smoke swirling through the room, heard the soft static of the CB radio, turned low. *What does he think*, she wondered, and her mind drifted from that to memories of her mother and father together in the house; she could remember once being sick and lying on the couch, wintertime, hearing the air suck in through the draft on the stove. Feeling that cold blast, every time the door to the outside opened. Her father, like now, at the table, talking quietly on the radio; her mother in the kitchen area, the whisper of her leather slippers as she moved across the floor.

Then, in the memory, her mother hovered over her, cool hands checking her forehead, her cheeks. Her green sweater and red lips, strangely beautiful, white snowflakes in a pattern across her chest. As Katie drifted toward sleep her mother's face became clear, almost real, and Katie heard her voice: *Would you like some soup, Katie?*

I miss you, Mom.

Oh, I know, sweetheart.

How's it supposed to be?

You'll be okay, Katie, you'll get through—

No one knows me.

Did I?

You loved me.

I know.

I don't have anybody, anymore.

Oh, Katie, don't say that.

This is where she could find her mother again, in dreams or near dreams, the voice stored inside her, words in endless combinations and tones. As if all her life she had been a recording machine, collecting sounds and images, saving. Saving.

I wish I had been there, Mom—

Oh, now, don't think like that.

I didn't know!

I know. It wasn't up to you.

Is anything?

Yes. Of course.

Katie opened her eyes. Sometimes she didn't know where her mother's voice ended and her own began. Maybe it was all her own; maybe it was all just her. She didn't like to think that. That was too much like nothing.

There were voices, now, coming over the radio; Manny turned up the volume; Katie sat and strained to hear.

Billy. His voice. And someone else, more distant, there was something about Billy's uncle—

Since when, eh? Over.

Couple of weeks, Bill. Sure hate to bother you. Over.

He's probably around. Over.

Probably… Willy Wassili, he went back there. No luck, eh. Over.

All right. I'll check it out. Tomorrow, eh? Over.

All right, Bill. You take it easy now. KBC57 over and out.

KBC83, over and out.

The voices disappeared; there was nothing but static now. Manny turned the radio down again to a whisper, cleared his throat and sighed.

Katie hardly breathed.

Katie headed out early, in the wind and rain; she knew Billy would see her, knew he would stop, would say: *Katie, whatch you doin', eh?*

What she didn't know was if she would tell him the truth: *I want to go to the village; I knew you'd be going,* or something not quite true: *I want to go to the village. I thought I'd try walking.*

He would know that she knew better. She wondered, but didn't worry about it. She didn't worry about seeing Norma, either; she only knew she was being propelled forward, by something she couldn't help—what she felt, what she didn't feel, seemed to have little to do with what she thought or didn't think, what she thought she wanted or didn't want. She was like an empty beach, at the mercy of whatever the waves pushed her way.

Katie was several miles down the uneven shore when she heard the sound of an approaching skiff. It was Billy, as she knew it would be; and also as she knew it would be, he was unable to pass her by, and instead he lowered the throttle on the outboard to a gurgle and guided the bow of the skiff toward the shore.

"Katie, whatch you doing?" he asked, sounding more like Billy—like the Billy she remembered—than otherwise. He cut the engine.

"I really have to see Norma." Wearing knee-high rubber boots, Katie waded into the water and grabbed the tip of the bow.

"You're walking there, eh?"

She looked him fully in the face. His olive skin still had a paleness to it, but his eyes were sharper than they were yesterday. "I knew you'd come by," she said, lowering her eyes. "I was hoping you would stop."

He exhaled, looked out at the water. Katie, now, could see the pain in his eyes; at once she wished she hadn't come. She had felt progress between them, yesterday, and it had made her confident, forgetful. Now her eyes stung with regret. "Billy, I'm sorry," she said. "You don't want to see me."

The water lapped against the wooden sides of the skiff. It was raining, but not hard, and a gull walked the beach nearby, pecking at the shore. So many times Katie had thought about what she would do, if she could go back. Never be with Nicky? Or never be with Billy? One had led her to the other, it seemed, but that thought was something she felt, more than something she could explain, even to herself. Her hands, now, were wet and cold where she still held the bow; her nose would be red, she knew, and dripping at the end, and her hair would be thin and flat and her ears and all their piercings would be peeking out through the strands.

"I don't know what I want," Billy said. "But—just get in now. I'll take you, eh? You've got business, so do I."

She wanted to ask him if he was sure, but instead obediently pushed the bow out as far as she could and then pulled herself up and into the skiff. With an oar Billy pushed the skiff farther from the shore, then he started the engine and they moved across the gray water.

Here I am again. The similarity of the situation slapped her in the face; she was only glad that Billy didn't know of her last trip to the village, twelve years ago, when she came with Nicky—again to see Norma. And like Nicky before him, Billy was here to see Pete.

Billy and Katie parted at the dock. Katie hurried through the village, squeaky and noisy in her raingear, feeling a sense of urgency she didn't understand, since Billy had indicated he would likely be a while. Was she afraid she would miss Norma, as she had twelve years ago? More likely she was afraid she would change her mind, chicken out, but this she wouldn't let herself admit.

She followed the wet and puddled road. Dog yards sprang to life as she passed, the huskies straining and whining at the ends of their chains. Faces looked out from behind sheets of glass, and the occasional person she saw outside stopped whatever he or she was doing and stared at her. Finally Norma's grandmother's house came into view, looking more than ever like something out of a fairy tale, the entryway sagging into the barren ground, its crooked door gaping open. Katie kept moving, was afraid, even, to pause.

Inside the entry it was dark and musty; it smelled of earth, old wood, and smoke. She felt as if she were in a coffin, struggling for breath. She pounded on the inner door.

She hadn't expected Norma to answer; later she would ask herself why she hadn't imagined this. But the door pulled open and suddenly there was Norma's moon-shaped face, older and somewhat pasty, dark eyes surprised at the sight of her, her round, full lips hanging open.

"Katie! Whatch you doin', eh?"

Katie stared as if a beam of light had found her face in the dark. As with Billy, Katie's relationship with Norma had been abruptly severed; they were friends and then they were something else. "I'm sorry," Katie said quickly, not sure why. She had felt almost indignant on the way here; over the years, imagining this moment, she had always seen herself as the avenging angel.

"Sorry?"

"I'm sorry," Katie said. "I shouldn't—be bothering you, should I?"

"Should you?" Norma pulled the door open a little wider, revealing more of herself. She left one hand on the edge of the door and put the other one on her hip. "You haven't bothered to bother me for a long time, Katie."

Katie's mouth was dry. She ran her tongue across her lips, looked downward out of the corner of her eyes.

"You come here to scratch my eyes out or somethin'?"

"I was wondering about your boys."

"My boys are none of your business, eh?"

"Please—"

"Please what?"

Katie tried to look over Norma's shoulder. She didn't want to upset the little boy.

"He's not here," Norma said.

"Is my dad his dad?"

"Shouldn't you be asking Manny about that?"

"But the other one isn't."

Norma stepped back a little. Katie felt something. "My boys aren't your business, Katie."

"I don't understand," Katie said, knowing she was talking more to herself than to Norma. She felt there were pieces of something, swimming loose like leaves and twigs in a swirling eddy, and that if the water moved and pushed them in the right way something would become clear.

"Understand? Katie, it's all long gone, okay? Me, your dad, all that. It was a bad time, eh, for everyone."

Katie looked at her then, their faces less than an arm's reach apart. "I've missed you," Katie said, unable to stop the words. Was this really happening?

Norma's eyes narrowed. She reached out and touched the side of Katie's face, grasping a clump of her hair. Katie's breath stopped. She could feel Norma tremble. Her words trembled, too, when they finally came: "I've missed *everyone*." Her hand released the hair and pressed firmly against Katie's ear, the side of her face. Then she pulled away and shut the door.

Katie fled the entryway, emerging back into the gray light of the rainy day.

How did we get here, Billy thought. *Why are we here like this?*

He stood by the river, his back to the scene behind him. The rain pelted on his dull green raincoat; the hood was down and his head was wet, but he didn't care.

She was there, on the beach, on the way here—walking along as if it were all normal, that she should be there. Of course he had to stop.

I knew you'd come by...I was hoping you would stop.

What could he say? He could have said: *No, I've got business,* but he didn't. And then she followed him here, to his uncle's, emerging from the river grasses where the trail ended just as he was walking away.

You can't leave him, out in the rain like that.

He didn't answer. She moved past him, to where his uncle lay sprawled on the ground, and began to rouse him.

He should have just left, left her here if this was what she wanted. But his old feelings of duty and obligation trapped him, again, somewhere he didn't want to be, involved in something he wanted no part of.

He listened to Katie's voice.

"Come on now, Pete, come on. Up and at 'em. Rise and shine. Looks like you've been out in the woods a few days, or something. Come on. You gotta get dry."

There was some kind of an answer this time, a groan of some sort. Then:

"Once, when I was a young man, there was a winter when all the game disappeared."

The voice startled him. He turned and looked. Katie had Pete now in a sitting position, still on the ground, but with a stump of wood behind him for support. She had taken off her raincoat and draped it over him.

"Really?" she said.

"I would walk for days, on my snowshoes, and see nothing—nothing. No squirrel track, nothing. It was as if the land had been wiped clean—wiped clean." He moved his arm as he said the word, *wiped*, knocked off the raincoat, which Katie put back on him.

"Then what happened?"

"Happened?" He shrugged, tipped his head. "Happened. The game began to come back, and the land was full again. Not all at one time. Little bit, and little bit."

"Little bit and little bit," Katie said, and Billy heard the sadness in her voice, turned from it, back to the river, but the words and tones echoed somehow, in the sound of the moving water.

Later Katie would say to him: *If you weren't going to help him, then why did you come?*

I came to see if he was dead.

That's all?

Yes.

She would shake her head, look down at the broken wood of the village dock. He would feel something, say without thinking: *What did you come here for, eh? Not to give any blessings.*

And Katie would look at him as if to say: *Is this, then, what I have done?* But instead she would say: *I saw his raincoat, there in your house.*

You shouldn't have been in my house.

But I was. And it was there.

She wouldn't say anything more, but her face would speak the questions she didn't ask.

She felt like a desert, she thought this, trying the simple words: *I feel like a desert.* Flat. Dry. Life there but hiding, away from the sun, away from the light, pulling itself deep into sand.

Sand that waits for the wind to lift it to the sky.

I want to live.

She thought this and was surprised. With the thought was the realization of having wanted to die. She remembered the night in Boston, in the bathroom, so many years ago now, the scissors in her hand. Why her hair, why her face? Later, the counselor her mother sent her to would say: *Because those are the things they loved about you, your hair and your face.*

They. Them. They who had shaped her life.

Her mother. The hero of her life. The one who said, over and over: *Someday, Katie, you'll be able to put it behind you. You will. You've just got to hang in there until then, okay?* The sound of Vivian's voice in her head brought a wave of sorrow, and she fought tears. She took deep breaths of the cold moist air, imagined her mother close, near, not gone forever. *I'm right here, Katie. Right here.* She clutched the sides of the skiff, felt the rain slanting down on her skin, closed her eyes against it, for a moment, but opened them again to watch the islands come closer, the village now miles behind.

As children they loved the islands. She, Billy, and Nicky. Norma sometimes, too. Skiffs in the summer, dog teams in winter. Over water or ice, traveling from one to the other; Katie used to pretend in her mind they were in space, going from planet to planet, exploring different worlds. Each island was never the same as the next. Some were bordered with cliffs, shooting straight down into the water; others were rimmed with beaches, sometimes soft and almost sandy, sometimes rocky and uneven.

She remembered a picnic once, on one of the nicer island beaches, in the summer with her parents. A bright blue sky, the wind from the west, clipping briskly on top of the water, cool enough to negate the warmth of the June sun.

She wondered, as she remembered the scene, why they were there. There weren't many times like that, where something was done for no apparent reason. Her mother wore a dark blue bandanna over her hair, her bangs soft and loose, blowing. Her red lipstick. She sat cross-legged on the pebbly beach while Manny leaned back on his elbows. They were talking quietly together. Katie must have been about seven, still little enough to feel the magic of a beautiful stretch of shore. They brought dried fish, cold tea and a lemon cake.

Her mother would have remembered the picnic, what it was about. Katie doubted her father would.

She went over the fragments of memory, trying to determine if her parents were happy then. She thought so, then doubted herself. She had always thought things were fine, with the exception of a fight or two. Quiet. She could remember a lot of quiet. She thought of kerosene lamps. Quietly burning, the wick, the flame, perched atop a pool of calm clear liquid, inches away from explosion and disaster, chaos.

Pow!

The sight of Norma had filled her with pain. She wasn't sure why; she had expected pain, but of a different sort, a pain laced with anger, not feelings of sadness and grief.

Outside Norma's house, as she was leaving, the wind had come and echoed through the old washtubs leaning against a silvery gray wall. Katie had looked at the clothes hanging on the line, waving. An old calico kuspuk (how long can that woman live, she wondered). A black bra and a low-cut T-shirt, wide corduroy jeans. A little flannel shirt, tiny boy's underwear. How could Katie be angry at that? She had seen Norma's longings—and poverty—on the streets of Boston, even in

Marsha Ray's attempts to look a certain way that her money wouldn't allow. An image of Norma as a teenager came into her mind—Norma washing, washing washing washing her few clothes. Water was free, and Ilmenof had plenty of it.

Now in the skiff she and Billy moved slowly over the green-gray water, waves growing in the rising wind. Katie didn't look behind her, though she longed for the sight of Billy's face. There was something. He'd seemed angry, as they stood together on the dock, but there was also something else, some other kind of tension. She held the look on his face, the infliction in his voice, inside her like something precious, delicate—a treasure, a stirring beneath dry sand.

Katie was in her room lying on her cot listening to the wind when her father came home. She'd been tired after the village, and had tried—but failed—to sleep. She'd started thinking about her mother, and how the end of her life was the end of her story. How once her mother had been a little girl, full of hopes and dreams, holding her own mother's hand as she skipped down a street. Katie then thought of her own oblivious happiness in that child-world, the strong, safe feel of her mother's hand holding hers.

And she thought about all the time, all the wasted time, in which she would not let herself be happy with her mother because of what happened to Nicky. It hadn't occurred to her that she could lose someone else, too.

She'd kept thinking there would be some kind of a point that she would get to where she would be a different person in a different world, and she would make up that time with her mother. They would get out of that city and live somewhere nice—an old house in the country or maybe even Alaska again—and Katie would help her mother as she began to face old age, pay her back for all the care she had given Katie, for all the worrying Katie had caused her. But now she couldn't make anything up; she still couldn't bring Nicky back and make that right, and now it was too late to grant her mother the simplest of wishes: the wish her mother had had to see Katie happy again.

Katie—it's Friday—why don't we go out to a movie or something?

Sure, Mom—

Katie, how about going shopping this Saturday—just bop around and look at things?

Sure, Mom—

Katie, can I get you anything?

Sure, Mom—

It would have been so easy. Katie knew this, even then, but her devotion to her own pain took precedence—it was her addiction, it was something that she felt defined who she was.

Her mother's pain—which surfaced sometimes in cries in the night—seemed, to Katie, just more proof of all that had been taken away from her—*her*, her mostly, for didn't she lose more than her mother? Her father *and* her best friends.

The image of Norma's aged, almost beaten face twisted around in Katie's heart, and she knew the struggle revealed in the old clothes on the line. Norma's dreams of rising above poverty had never come true.

Her mother as a little girl. Where had those dreams gone?

The morning newspaper, the afternoon news—all those sad stories; a young man Katie once saw on the subway, looking so tired and so sad; the fat man who came into the restaurant every Thursday at 5 p.m. and sat by himself at a table with a wealth of food in front of him, so alone. The old woman who lived down the hall from them in a lonely apartment. How could Katie have thought her pain was so special? Khoi—Khoi tried to tell her, in his own sweet way. *There is sadness in life, Katie—not many escape that. It is why you should be kind, when you can. You never know what someone may have suffered.*

Now Katie listened to her father walking in the door. He began taking off his wet raingear; Katie heard snaps unsnapping, heard the squeaks of the rubberized material.

"Katie? You home?" he asked.

"Yeah—" She sat up.

"I was home earlier—you weren't here."

Katie walked over to the doorway and pulled back the curtain. "I went for a walk." She had imagined telling him where she went, but now she felt afraid to; it was one thing knowing what was inside a box—another thing opening the box to the light of day.

Manny turned and looked at her. His eyes were narrowed. "You took a long damned walk."

"What do you mean?"

"Katie, come on. I'm not going to cat and mouse with you. You think no one around here talks to anybody else? You got something you want to ask me—ask me. Don't lie to me."

"You've lied." Katie's heart was beating fast.

"Well, you've got me there," he said. He pulled a chair out and sat at the table. "But just remember, Katie, we've all been a little guilty of that."

The words hit like arrows. Katie felt off-balance. She retreated back into her room, let the curtain fall. The words, *please, please please*, chanted inside her. Please what? *Please, please, please.* She heard her father rise from the table, the scrape of his chair on the floor. He walked over and stood beside her doorway on the other side of the curtain.

"Katie, I'm sorry. I shouldn't have said that. I apologize. You were just a kid; I was an adult with no excuses. You should not have had to pay so hard for that mistake."

"He wasn't a mistake!" The words blurted out with a spill of tears.

"All right; all right. That's not what I meant. Everybody loved Nicky. You know that. We all know that. That's not what I meant. I didn't mean anything—Jesus Christ." He sighed long and hard. "Katie, I'm no good at this. Maybe if I was I could have explained things better to your mother." He paused, as if waiting for her to say something. "So—you want to know about Norma's boys." Another sharp sigh. Katie continued her silence. "Well, Alex is mine—he's the one you saw at the lodge—another mistake between me and Norma, but one that happened only long after I gave up on getting you and your mother back…. The other boy—Nico—well, some people think he's mine but he's not. That's all you need to know about that."

"You could have told me," Katie said.

"Well, I'm telling you now."

"Someone should have told me I had a brother."

"Katie, you already weren't talking to me. You and your mother just cut yourselves off from me." His voice seemed to tremble. "I wrote you letters. I dumped years' worth of change into the pay phone across the lake. I didn't get a lot back, Katie. You two treated me as if I was dead."

Had they, Katie wondered? Those years after they'd first left were so long ago. She could remember the phone calls, and how they just upset her mother and led to the eerie cries she would hear coming from her mother's room in the middle of the night. And there was all that business about Manny hitting Norma, and how the troopers questioned him about Nicky's disappearance. She'd thought, for years, that maybe Nicky did go to the village, that his skiff was there, and that he caught Manny hitting Norma and then he and Manny fought again, and that's what happened to Nicky. But Manny didn't have a scratch on him—just bruised knuckles from where he'd hit Nicky earlier that day, from where he'd supposedly hit Norma after she admittedly attacked him. It was all so strange, and as Katie thought about it now she realized how very strange it was. It was as if the violent wind of that day lifted them all off the ground into a whirlwind of confusion from which they would never wholly return. From which they would scatter and run.

"I'd thought you might have killed Nicky," Katie said. She could see the curtain that covered her doorway move just slightly.

"Sweetheart, I didn't kill Nicky. I was mad as hell at him, but not that mad. Christ—didn't you know me at all?"

"Well, you hit Norma."

Several moments passed. In between the gusts of wind Katie could hear Manny breathing. "That's—that's another story, Katie, okay? That was just another unfortunate thing that happened that just needs to be forgotten about."

"Billy has Nicky's raincoat."

There was a pause, then: "He does? What makes you think that?"

"I saw it. In Billy's house."

"How do you know it was Nicky's?"

"He'd cut it with Mom's pinking shears."

"Well, maybe Nicky'd worn something else. I think Billy would have said. Christ, he spends his summers looking for him, did you know that? Not going fishing because they can't find someone to watch the place is just an excuse. Jake doesn't know what to do. Billy's just letting his whole life go. Now—do you want to come out here and have some tea or something? Supper?"

"I'm tired," Katie said.

"You gotta eat."

"I did. I'm fine." She watched the curtain. Manny continued to stand there. "I don't think we know what happened."

"To Nicky? No—we don't, Katie, but we know what's likely. This stuff happens. It just does. And it's not the lake. The lake just *is*. All of nature just is, and we don't always fit."

"I keep thinking there's a piece missing."

"Well, you need to let that go. It's over and done, whatever happened."

Katie nodded, though she knew her father couldn't see her. Did it really matter anymore? Shadows, shadows, shadows. Katie thought of the sunny place she used to think she—and her mother—would one day find. Where things were clean and clear and somehow put away, tidied up and resolved. Now she saw it as a place with no one in it; an empty land, dry as bone. She realized she wanted her shadows; in those shadows Nicky still lived, still haunted, still reached for her in her dreams.

Dean's plane came in fast and low; from where she sat at the table Katie could see it splash onto and across the surface of the water near the mouth of the cove. Manny, who had not yet left for the day, saw the plane come in; a look of confusion and what seemed to be anger clouded across his face.

"What the hell is he doing here?"

"He—we're—going to go on a picnic."

Manny looked as if he had just smelled something sour. Katie waited. "He's not what he seems." Manny's voice was steady but grim sounding.

Are any of us? Katie thought, but said nothing. She slipped on her jacket as she stood, grabbed her sunglasses even though the day held no promise of sun. Manny watched her walk to the door. She lifted her hand in goodbye and hurried outside.

Dean was tying the plane to the dock when Katie appeared.

"Hi," he said. "You set?"

Katie nodded.

"Good." He put on his dark glasses and she put on hers, even though the day was as gray as gray could be.

They flew over the islands; Katie could remember every one. She kept her face forward but let her eyes slide around, let herself look at Dean. He chatted and smiled often; Katie wondered why her father disliked him so much. She remembered again how they made fun of Dean, remembered how they thought he would be nothing but a loser. Clean and neat, bright and chipper, Dean seemed to have outdone them all.

So what if something had happened between Dean and Norma. Katie was realizing it had nothing to do with anything, except maybe that the joke had been on her father. Of course. That's what happened; Dean had come between Manny and Norma, made Manny feel the aging fool he was. Katie was at once relived and disappointed; it was so mundane.

Maybe Manny and Norma had simply fought; maybe Nicky had grabbed the wrong raincoat, and the wind had simply blown. There was no one there to see his red mitten and pull him back to the air. It could all be as simple as that.

It was, she thought again, time to go home. Back to Boston, her apartment, her job at the restaurant and the small bit of time she had left with Khoi before he got married. It wasn't much—especially now without her mother. But she had gotten used to her life of no expectations.

Dean brought the plane down in a sheltered waterway between two islands and taxied up to a quiet-looking beach. He hopped out and rode the float as the plane approached the shore; before the floats could hit bottom he stepped down into the water and held the plane steady. Katie climbed onto the opposite float; having remembered to wear rubber boots, she made her way to the shore with the rope Dean tossed to her.

After securing the plane they walked down the beach a ways, then headed into the woods. Katie knew where they were going. This was an island that dipped towards the water on the one side, rose sharply on the other, where it faced the lake with a glittering cliff face. It was full of pyrite; Katie couldn't believe it the first time she saw it—the first time Billy and Nicky took her there—the way it sparkled in the sun.

She also remembered the time they took Dean up there.

Hey—look. Look at those sparkles!

Where?

There—look! It looks like gold!

Wow, yeah, sure does, eh—

We need to get some—let's get some—show our dads—Holy cow!

It was winter. A Saturday. Phil and Dean had flown in just as Billy, Nicky and Norma were arriving with the dog team to pick Katie up for an afternoon of adventuring. So they had to bring Dean along. There were looks exchanged, a few careful whispers. A swift ride across the wind-packed snow on the lake, a quick climb with young legs.

We could be rich—you know that? We need to show my dad.

Katie could remember holding her breath as Dean stood dangerously near the edge. Billy stood nearby, struggling to keep a straight face, and Nicky slunk sullenly a short ways away. Norma almost gave it all away with her giggles. The next thing Katie knew Dean was on his stomach, trying to reach over the snowy lip, and Billy lay beside him, pretending he would do it, too, but staying safely back from the edge.

Dean was head and shoulders over the edge. Katie'd said: *Stop! Dean, come back! It's not gold! You're gonna fall!*

Then Dean was stuck; he couldn't move backwards. *Help! Pull me up! Help! I'm falling!*

Katie lunged forward and grabbed him by the boot. Billy held Dean's coat and together they pulled him back up. Nicky and Norma were giggling; Billy could no longer suppress his grin. Dean's face was pale, then red, and he was shaking and his nose began to bleed.

You could have killed me!

Ha! We got you, eh? Billy.

Fool's gold, get it? Norma.

Sucker. Nicky.

Katie didn't say anything, and her cheeks burned. She found some toilet paper in the pocket of her parka and handed it to Dean for his nose, and worried that he would cry.

Now Dean said: "Haven't been up here in awhile." They had reached the top of the island, and stood not far from the place where Dean had been tormented all those years ago. Katie searched his face for some reaction, but saw none. Then he turned toward her and smiled, and Katie could see there was something there; there was something there.

"Why didn't you ever come back, Katie?"

"I don't know."

"You never answered my letters."

"I know. I didn't—answer anybody's letters."

"You remember that day up here—when you guys tricked me about the gold?"

"Yes."

"Thank you."

"For what?"

"For not laughing. I always remembered that."

He had taken off his glasses and was looking out at the water beyond the island. The wind was strong; Katie could see the beginnings of whitecaps on the tops of the waves. "Is your life all right?" she asked.

"All right? Yeah, I guess you could say that. I miss my dad, but I'm getting used to it."

"You married?"

"No—"

"How come?"

"Waiting for the right girl, I guess. Waiting for you to come back." He winked quickly, said how he was joking. But Katie noticed how, as he leaned back on his elbows, outstretched, his foot tapped nervously in the empty air, sometimes increasing, sometimes decreasing, in speed.

"So did you know Norma's back?" Katie asked.

"She is?" The foot tapped fast.

"I saw her."

"You did?"

Katie nodded.

"You know, this wind is really kicking up. We'd probably better go soon."

"All right."

"But I have something for you."

Katie felt her face frown. What was this, now?

Dean reached into the breast pocket of his chamois shirt. Suddenly a necklace dangled from between his fingers, and Katie's lips parted in surprise. It appeared to be the necklace she'd lost, the one she thought she saw at Billy's.

"Did you find it?"

"No—no. But I saw this one in a shop—before you left, actually, and I was going to give it to you for a going-away present, for when you were going to go to college. It's like it, isn't it?"

"Yes—as far as I can remember." She held out her hand, and Dean dropped the necklace into her open palm. She stared at it. How could he have found one so similar?

"You're welcome."

"What?"

"I said, you're welcome."

"I'm sorry—I'm just surprised. Thank you. It's very nice."

"You're very nice, Katie. You were always nice to me."

Katie wasn't, though; she laughed along with the rest of them, most of the time. She felt the blood gathering in her cheeks. Why had they gotten so much fun out of making fun of someone else? But the joke had been on them, hadn't it, all of them.

"Katie."

"Yes?"

"You should smile more. You used to smile." Dean stood and began packing away the remains of their lunch. "This wind's not going to stop," he said. "We'd better get moving."

Katie nodded and rose to help him. The wind now was a constant pressing force.

"I used to wish," Dean said, "that the wind would blow this island and all its fool's gold away."

He looked at Katie, and smiled.

———————————————

When Twigg had met Cindy, he suddenly felt so not alone. It was something he couldn't explain—even to himself—as in those first years of their acquaintance they hardly talked, hardly saw each other. She was the married sister of his friend, Andy, who he played softball with. She would come to the games, sit in the bleachers in the sun. Tall and willowy, her bones so slender she almost seemed a stick figure with a tumble of thick brown hair. But it wasn't how she looked that got to him. It was the way she'd jump up and holler at a good play or a good hit or a good slide into home, the impish look on her face when her husband, who sometimes came with her, would try unsuccessfully to get her to sit back down.

Once she went out with the team, after a game, and Twigg had never known a woman could laugh so much.

As the years went on she laughed less, but she came to the games more and more, pregnant, then with one baby and then another, her husband often absent, busy with his work.

Twigg began to notice the difference in her, when her husband was with her and when he wasn't; they seemed to get on all right, but there was something about his presence that was like a cloud over her sun; even Cindy could never quite understand it, this effect he had on her.

She'd always told Twigg it wasn't all because of him. That sooner or later she and her husband would have divorced anyway, that something about the marriage left her hungry, starving, though her friends often told her how lucky she was to have what she had.

Twigg had realized his feelings for her one day during a tournament when the opposing team was up at bat, and he happened to catch sight of her face, tipping toward the sky, watching what was a beautiful hit, but then she turned suddenly, her eyes drawn to something else, a flock of small birds, flying fast. He didn't know what it was about that moment, but it was as if the whole world came alive, right then, with the turn of her head.

When he was with her—even before he realized she had feelings for him, too—he felt like someone knew him. That between them the curtains were for some reason pulled wide open, and they had a clear view of each other. It was the most wonderful thing. Not to feel alone.

Now he looked at the message delivered to his office only moments ago, though it seemed hours ago already. A telegram, from his mother. Who knew he had a phone in his office, but who still believed in telegrams, when it came to bad news.

son-andy-travis-has-passed-heart-failure-very-sudden-services-soon-call-home-your-loving-mother

Stop.

He thought of Andy on the field, saw a ball flying into his glove.

He felt tired, tired of being alone. He wondered if he could let himself not be.

He sighed and looked out the window at the street. The trees—scrub spruce, short and scraggly, ancient looking—bent steadily. *Christ,* Twigg thought. Maybe today he'd better step outside and look at the lake. He felt uneasy, on edge. But of course he would. The telegram.

And with it the thought that he should call home. Not to his mother. Call Cindy.

As he stood the phone rang. It startled him; he hesitated before picking it up. Margaret's voice, restless.

"Ray—it's Rosie. She's swallowed a bunch of pills. I think I've a got handle on things, but could you stand by in case I need to fly her out of here? I just called the airport and the plane from Anchorage has left already."

"Christ, Margaret, it's blowin' like a son-of-a-bitch out there." He realized one thing that was bothering him about the wind was the thought of the bodies buried in the water, that the lake would start spitting up skeletons.

"Oh, I can see that. I think we're okay. Damn it! Go find that Tommy Wassilli and shoot him, would you? I could have told her—did tell her—that she was going about things all wrong!"

"Margaret—"

"Well, that's water under the bridge. Next time she'll know better. So you'll stay by the phone?"

"You need some help?"

"No—she's got a cousin here, has some EMT training. I think we'll be okay."

"All right. I'll be here."

"Great. Thanks, Ray."

The click, the flat tone of the empty line. He stood looking at the phone. Then he set it back down.

The wind kept on, relentless. He felt that it was knocking on his brain. No wonder the Natives made myths of the wind, he thought; it did seem, at times, to be more than just moving air.

Despite what he told Margaret about staying by the phone, he realized he'd better go check on his plane. He'd hurry.

He put on his vest, buttoned it up, left his baseball hat on his desk.

He drove to the cove, parked by the water, and watched. As he suspected, even if Margaret called there wouldn't be a damned thing he could do. Not even a fool would fly in this.

He closed his eyes, felt a squeezing on his heart. Andy. How could so much life have gone by? What had he thought—that when he left Georgia the world he knew solidified and stilled, would be forever as he knew it to be?

He should go back. No. He shouldn't. There was no reason; every other year he bought his mother a Hawaiian vacation, met her over there. He didn't need to go to Georgia.

The wind rattled his truck, shook it, even. He should open his eyes and look at the plane. But he didn't. He felt very tired; his mind started to drift.

He dreamt of a feeling, a feeling like a leaf in the wind, blowing. His memory reached for him, like ghostly hands. He saw the staircase of his old home, his childhood home, then the sunny patch of yard where he'd played with his toy trucks in the dirt, his mother there, playing too. Then suddenly there was a softball game, and he was watching it; he couldn't tell if he was big or little, then his plane started to move on the water, broke loose, it was sinking, he was in it, but he looked and there was the Windego, pulling him up and into the air—

He jolted awake. Looked around quickly. He was still in his truck. The wind was still blowing. And there in the cove was his plane, still safe, moving with the water, breathing with the air that rushed and swirled beneath its wings. For a moment he thought he could see it. The wind. For a moment he thought he could.

———————————————

"How are you feeling, Rosie? Rosie?"

The girl opened her eyes, smiled a little.

"I think we should get up and walk around again."

Rosie only smiled.

"Come on, you'll get through this. And then you'll know. Nothing you'll ever feel for anyone is worth hurting yourself over." Margaret put her arms around Rosie, tried unsuccessfully to pull her forward into a sitting position. She sighed, looked over her shoulder, said: "Sophie?" The room was small and dark, closed in. The curtain across the doorway moved. Sophie, Rosie's cousin, slipped in quietly.

"We need to get her moving again. You up for it?"

Sophie nodded. In the dim light Margaret could see the young woman's long beaded earrings swaying between her thin neck and her fine, black hair. Margaret thought how Sophie was quietly mysterious, unlike Rosie, who walked around with her insides on the outside, always. There was something about Sophie that made Margaret feel clumsy, large, and intrusive. Still, she was grateful that Sophie was here.

Margaret had been sitting at her table, drinking a fresh cup of herbal tea, before the phone rang. She had been thinking about Billy. She wondered what it was that made him still love Katie, after everything that had happened. Maybe she'd read it all wrong—the look on his face—but she didn't think so—even though it just didn't make sense.

After Sophie's phone call she'd grabbed her bag and run out the door, into the wind. She'd never been to Rosie's house but remembered Rosie pointing it out to her, a dreary-looking shack with rusty three-wheelers and broken-down cars sinking into the tundra in what should have been the backyard.

She couldn't believe it. What had she missed? She didn't have Rosie pegged as a possible suicide, though she'd been warned about the high rate of those deaths among the young Natives.

"What did she take?" Margaret had asked, when Sophie opened the door for her.

"Maybe some pain killers. Walter had some around, for his back."

Walter, Margaret remembered, was Rosie's uncle and guardian. She didn't think he was Sophie's parent, either; from what she understood Walter had no children of his own.

"*Had some around?*" Margaret said. "Doesn't he know where he kept them? Doesn't he know he should keep prescription drugs somewhere where she couldn't find them?"

"Rosie's not a child."

"Where is he now? Where is Rosie?"

Sophie's dark, narrow eyes met Margaret's. "We're not so stupid, eh? We know some things. I'm an EMT, and Walter's had some training. He's walking her around."

"Oh—good. I—I didn't mean—"

But she did mean, she realized; she did.

Now Margaret and Sophie were working together, pulling Rosie off her low-lying cot, steadying her into a standing position, moving through the curtain into the main room and toward the door. Outside the three women walked, linked together, around the rim of the dog yard; the huskies watched quietly, silently, peering out from their tunnel-like houses made from rusty 55-gallon barrels split in half. Now and then the smell of shit came to Margaret's nose, when the wind calmed a little, making her feel nauseated and headachy.

"Tommy," Rosie said, and started to cry.

"Tommy's not here, Rosie," Margaret said.

Then Sophie's voice, soft and gentle: "He'll come soon, eh? The wind's up bad; the lake's no good right now. But Walter said he'd make sure he'd get him word."

Margaret looked past Rosie's head, said to Sophie: "What makes you think he's going to show up?"

"He loves Rosie."

"What—because she's pregnant?"

"She's not pregnant."

Margaret paused, considered, asked: "Then what's this all about?"

"Rosie gets very sad sometimes."

"Sad?"

"Yeah, sad."

"What kind of sad?"

"Sad like you don't know why the wind blows. That you think there is no point to it, just blowing around like that."

"Isn't this all because of Tommy?"

"No—why would it be because of Tommy? Tommy makes her feel better."

"Why?" Or how, she thought; she had not seen any proof of this.

"Because she loves him."

"Why?" Margaret asked again, though she already had this one figured: Low self-esteem.

"Because he loves her."

Margaret sighed, turned her face away, tilted it down against the wind.

The wind had been building all day, and by evening the lake was a frothing gray moving mass. Manny came home early and parked himself at the table, radio on, listening. Katie cornered herself in her room, trying to draw. Draw the wind, the Windego, moving around the house, trying to engulf it. When she was little the big winds that blew through Ilmenof would excite her. Now she knew to fear them.

When she was little she would run out to the edge of the knoll when the wind blew like this. She would whirl around in the wind, let it blow through her clothes.

When she was little.

She adjusted her book on her lap and felt again the sharp stab of the infected piercing in her belly button. As she lifted the bottom of her sweater and shirt she felt how it stuck to her T-shirt; gently she separated the cloth from the skin.

"Shit," she whispered as she looked at the angry red skin surrounding the stud; she pressed the inflamed skin and pus oozed from the hole. "Shit." She might have to give up on this one eventually.

As she cleaned the piercing with alcohol and swabs, she noticed Manny had turned up the CB. There was a voice, one she didn't recognize, and, as on several nights previous, Billy's answering tones.

Someone had found part of a skiff. An old skiff, water logged and rotten, something that had been in the water for a long time—

Katie was in her doorway looking at Manny. "What do you think?" she said.

Manny squinted his eyes as he thought. "Could be. There are traces of red paint—"

Katie's heart began to beat so fast it was as if it had suddenly come alive and was in danger of escaping out her throat. Without even thinking she moved toward the door and began to put on her old rubber boots.

"What are you doing?"

"See Billy—"

"You stay off the god-damned water!"

"I will!"

"You keep him off it, too—"

"That's why I'm going."

Katie ran. She was afraid she would see him, in the skiff on the water, heading out into it, in search of something—someone—who wasn't there.

She thought about what Manny had said, about always walking through a graveyard. Graveyard below, sky above. She pictured Billy moving across the lake, and down through the water she imagined the bottom, covered with crosses and tombstones.

Would it make any difference if Nicky were in the water or out of the water, his white bones finally washed ashore?

She used to think yes, it would. There would be an ending. But she realized it wasn't so. Nothing ends. Things change, shift, mutate, but all we have known is all we have known, forever.

All that had happened, had happened. That was the beauty and the crux of the past. It was *certain*.

As she neared the point she saw him there; it was as she expected but it seemed a sort of dream—a projection of what she had imagined, made real.

He paced the shoreline, down where the mouth of the stream spilled into the lake. The skiff was nearby. She could almost feel how he wanted just to go, just go; he had waited so long for something, any-thing—

But where had he found the raincoat?

Katie knew he would see her, soon, but she kept moving, went up the stream a ways and started to cross, then on the other side she walked without stopping over to where he was, stood facing him, the skiff between.

She shook her head. "There's no hurry. Just wait."

He looked down, then back at the water.

"Where did you find the raincoat, Billy?"

He looked at her, looked at the water, back to her, then walked away. Katie sat down, pressed her forehead against the bow of the skiff, closed her eyes and listened to the sound of him leaving. She stayed there a long time. It got later and she got cold. Once he would not have let her do this; once he would have said: *Come on, Katie, you're cold, eh, come on, let's get you warm.* She remembered him wrapping blankets around her, remembered laying her head on his shoulder, remembered Nicky, too, remembered the way Nicky's hands were always in her hair—

But Billy would be so still, as if she was a bird that at any moment might fly. Maybe he was afraid; she hadn't thought that before, that maybe he was afraid of her, or afraid of what he felt for her, too much.

She got up and walked the trail to his house. It was quiet, dark behind the window glass. She slid the latch on the door and stepped inside. He was in bed, his wet clothes piled on the floor by his cot. He turned and looked.

"Billy—"

"Oh, Katie—"

She slipped off her coat and went to her knees, rested her head on the blankets beside his chest.

"I'm tired," she said. "I'm just so tired."

He didn't say anything. But after awhile his fingers began to move lightly through her hair. She closed her eyes, tried to check her breathing. There was a low fire in the stove; she felt its warmth. Then he shifted slightly and his face was close to hers. His breath on her skin. He whispered. "Did I lose you, Katie, because you thought I didn't want you like Nicky did?"

Their eyes, close in the dark, searched each other. "No," she said, her eyes not leaving his. "It was more than that."

He blinked against the pain. "I'm glad," he said. "I'm glad it was more than that." He brought his hand to the back of her head, let his fingers wander in her hair. Then his lips pressed against her forehead, ran down the bridge of her nose. He put his arms around her and lifted her onto the bed, onto him, and they began to kiss each other, slowly, then less so, and piece by piece her clothes came off and joined his where they lay, disheveled and temporarily forgotten, in a scattered pile on the floor.

The wind blew through the night. Even where Billy's cabin was, tucked back in the woods, the trees bent and shook and Katie lay sleepless, listening while beside her Billy slept and she dared not move. Where Manny was, though, on the knoll, the wind was hitting the house with all its force; *Too much, Manfred, too much*, was what Vivian would say to him, when things reached extremes, and now these were the words he himself thought, as he lay awake thinking of her death: *Too much, Vivian; too much.* How could the world now be without her?

Twigg, too, was sleepless through much of this night, his mind filled with images of what the wind might wash up on the lake's many shores. When it subsided he would have to go, he knew; already he'd heard of the piece of the skiff, already he knew of all the wondering there must be. Toward morning he fell into a fitful sleep, but was awakened not much later by a fast knocking on his door.

As in a dream, he opened it. As in a dream, Margaret was there.

What does it mean to have a good life? This was what she was asking, as he sat her down and patted her hand and untangled his thoughts so he could follow hers. "I don't know anymore," she went on, "and I don't know why I don't know. I keep thinking I know what I'm doing! I know I'm a smart person and I'm not impulsive at all. I'm always telling myself, 'Aren't you glad you're not this person, or aren't you glad you're not that person?' I thought that about you. I thought that about Rosie. But now I wonder, do people think that about me? I think that about me!

"I'm sorry—I'm sorry—I've been up all night with Rosie and now this damned wind—I'm so tired and I just can't sleep, I can't stop thinking…"

"It's all right, Margaret."

"All the terrible things that have happened to these people around here—to you—yet I would be Katie, Ray, just to have that, for one moment, someone to look at me the way he looks at her. And oh how terrible your story is, Ray. Oh, what a nightmare, what a nightmare—but it wasn't your fault, it just happened, and I know it cost you everything but you know—you *know*, you know what it's like to have someone know you. Isn't that part of it—why we need it—to know that someone knows us?"

"It's all right, Margaret, you're just exhausted. Here, lie down here. Just lie down and I'll—I'll look over you. You need some sleep."

"I'm not drunk or anything—"

"I know. You're tired. We've all been there."

"The wind is driving me crazy."

"Just don't think about it. Here—I'll play you some songs. One of my uncles"—*Jesus, that was such a long time ago*—"he would sing me to sleep, when I was little, just listen to the words, to the story in the words." After some fumbling he found his guitar, and after some more fumbling he got it in tune. He strummed quietly, and sang with a voice that hadn't sung in awhile, but which used to know how—

Slow up doggies, quit roaming around,
Spread away out on this big open ground.
My horse is dead weary and I'm kinda tired,
But if you get away I'm sure to get fired.
Hold up, doggies, hold up—
Hi-you, hi-you, hi-you

And in that way Margaret finally closed her eyes and drifted off to sleep.

Twelve years previous

The wind is howling; she dreams of wolves hiding in the shadowed spots beneath trees. She thinks: Not wolves, wind. She is aware that she is dreaming, aware that she is thinking; she is in and out, weaving.

It's only the wind—

Why is that familiar? A flitting image of a candy house, a little boy in suspendered pants—

Hansel and Gretel.

It's only the wind.

There is another sound, a voice; her father, the static of the radio. She rolls over, pulls the covers tight over her ears, she doesn't want to hear his voice, she has heard his voice, she thinks, enough for the rest of her life.

Take your hands off my daughter!

You piece of shit! Piece of Indian shit!

His words of the day before.

She turns again, longs for deep sleep, but feels herself rising up out of it, her father's voice tugging her, the words lining up in order.

There is something about Nicky. She opens her eyes and sits up.

"And he's not with Pete, then?"

A pause. Static-laced words she can't hear.

"And not in town. It doesn't make sense…. Maybe he's camping somewhere. Let's not jump to conclusions, here, it's a bit soon for—"

Katie stands in her doorway. When he sees her Manny says: "It seems the boy's gone missing."

"Wouldn't you?" she says, imagining Nicky on one of the islands, safe and away from her father.

"Well," Manny says. "I'm sure he's around somewhere. Billy's a bit nervous about it, so I think we'll take a bit of a spin once the wind dies down."

Katie moves to the door and slips on her boots.

"Now what do you think you're doing?"

She doesn't say anything, just wants to be out of there, figure out where Nicky's gone, find him and talk to him.

"You just stay put, missy."

"No," she says. Her voice is small.

"What?"

She shakes her head, looks at the floor.

"Look, he and Billy'd got into it a bit after they got home. I'm sure he just went out somewhere to cool off."

Silence.

"Look, missy, you've made enough of a mess out of things. If it turns out we have to go looking for Nicky, I don't want to have to be wondering where you are!"

What her father doesn't know is that she left the house last night—she went to Nicky's tent, but he wasn't there. She saw how the skiff was gone; she saw how there was a gash in the baidarka, the precious baidarka, only recently completed. She remembers now the bad feeling she'd had, when she saw that—what had happened? Where were Billy and Nicky? Yet she hadn't been brave enough to run down the trail to Billy's.

"All right," Manny says, in response to her silence. "Go on. But don't take the skiff; don't go out on the water. If Nicky's in trouble, you'll only hurt things if you do."

Katie grabs her raincoat, pulls open the door and begins to run.

She runs to Johnson's Point. She sees Billy. He paces the shoreline. She doesn't stop.

Then it is as if she leaps forward, through time and space, and is near him, and he turns his angry face to her, and she sees his lip swollen and split, the scabs like red paint on a gray photograph, and she knows, she knows—

Things have been broken.

I N THE MORNING KATIE SAT IN THE QUIET EMPTINESS OF BILLY'S HOUSE, WATCHING THE BIRDS FLUTTERING AT THE FEEDERS OUTSIDE THE WINDOWS. There were so many; some she identified, some she didn't, and though she had seen these birds all her life she realized she didn't know all the names.

Was it important, she wondered, the names— would it make a difference to how she saw them? They would still be only what they were.

There was a moment, as Billy had reached for his door, when his hand stilled on the latch, and his head began to turn. There was a moment, when he was like that. Between the past and the future, hesitating. She could have said something, and he would have looked. But she let him go.

So she stood now, deciding she had stayed long enough, had taken into her memory the view from his cot, the smell of him like a lingering shadow on her skin, hanging on. She smoothed his blankets, pressed her nose against them, breathed deep.

Then she remembered something, stepped over to his shelf, touched the necklace that hung from a nail. It wasn't hers. It was similar, but it was not hers. The petals were smaller, rounder. In her pocket she still had the one Dean had given her. She pulled it out, looked at the two together. Beside the one she knew wasn't hers, the other looked remarkably like the one she'd lost. Had Dean taken it that day?

What happened, Katie?

I'll help you look—

She didn't think he would have had opportunity. She put the necklace back in her pocket, pulled it out again, looked at it some more. She could almost feel it around her neck. But how could it possibly be the one she'd lost? She put it back in the pocket. She didn't want to be taken away from these moments here, now. She was filled with the feeling that she would not ever be here again.

She walked slowly to the door, and when she got there she saw that Nicky's raincoat was no longer hanging beside it. She wondered what Billy had done with it. She pulled the latch and lingered in the open doorway. The wind that had blown so hard a few short hours ago was now a whisper of what it had been. Maybe today, she thought; maybe today. She knew where Billy had gone; Manny, maybe, was there, too, and she imagined Twigg had heard and would come see. She would hurry home, turn on the radio and listen.

She pulled the door closed and pressed her forehead against the rough wood as she slid the latch. She would draw this scene, eventually, and in the picture there would be birds and there would also be Nicky, standing nearby in the trees and the brush, watching her leave.

Was he here now, she wondered? What would he think? Was he with them last night, in Billy's bed? It had seemed, for that brief time, that he wasn't, that the moment was encapsulated in itself, separate.

But with the return of the day, the return of consciousness, Nicky returned to the scene; he was there in Billy's wordless slip out the door, there in Katie's inability to speak.

Her forehead began to hurt, and she was acutely aware again of the unhealed piercing in her navel. With her forehead still pressed to the door she felt for and pulled apart the stud that stabbed through the infected hole. She could do without this, she thought; she could do without this. She let the pieces fall on Billy's doorstep, knowing he would never see them, knowing they would always be there. Then she turned away. Birds scattered and flew.

There was still pretty good wind. The skiff lurched in the waves; Billy watched the water carefully.

Spray hit his face. He felt he was a part of the skiff. He felt the skiff was part of the water.

He tried not to think beyond the *now*, beyond the direction of the wind, the roll of the waves. The grip of the outboard's tiller in his hand.

The island was ahead of him. He was almost there. The distance was short but time seemed slow; then finally the bottom of the skiff grated across the gravelly bottom, bow touching shore. Quickly he leapt out, grabbed the rope and secured it to a tree.

He paused a moment. But when he did the feel of Katie's skin against his returned to him, and he bounced between desire and despair, despair and desire.

How could he have let that happen?

Now he felt it all over again, as if he was full of holes and bleeding.

But that was not how he had felt last night, as her body slid against his, her breasts against his chest, soft and warm. All the warm places of her. She seemed to go beneath him, into him, as if their bodies had no substance and their cells mingled and meshed.

He felt none of the old anger and pain, then.

Then.

He started to walk the beach.

This was the last island, the one on the outside edge of the bay. The last stop before the open water, like a bridge between worlds, between what was home and what was town. The dangerous place you have to cross, to get to the other side.

He wondered, looking out at the miles and miles of gray water, what he had already wondered over and over: How far did Nicky get? Was he way out there, in the desolate middle of it, or had these islands, these shores, been in his sight, been for him hope as the waves crashed over his head?

Billy used to ask Nicky if he remembered falling through the hole in the ice, falling down into the dark and the cold. He would always only say: *I remember coming up. I remember coming through the light, and I remember your face, and I remember the snow was huge and bright, falling everywhere.*

Sometimes Billy wanted to go down there, below the ice, to see where Nicky had been. Just last winter he had fallen through, what was solid beneath his feet vanishing suddenly, but as he plunged down his arms shot out and stopped him, grabbing the icy edge, pulling him out. It was over before he could even think about it.

Why hadn't Nicky done that, he wondered, spread his arms like wings, saved himself? The hole in the ice was not so big, a fluke, the edges solid. He almost would have had to lift his arms above his head to pass through, even as small as he was. Billy's imagined image of Nicky's fall is something so with him it is alive in his memory, as if he had really seen it; he even wondered sometimes if he did, though he knew he didn't, he didn't; he was back behind the curtain of falling snow, looking for what was not there.

Nicky, little Nicky, stands in a swirl of white, as if suspended in nothing. Then he lifts his arms above his head, hands together in extended prayer, and begins to vanish, from the bottom up, into another world.

The red mittens that used to be Billy's, that his mother had knitted before she died, the one still on his hand, like a beacon there, reaching. Billy's earliest memory was of those mittens, his mother's voice:

You like, eh?

And the mittens on his hands, soft and warm and red. Without those mittens he would never have seen Nicky. Without those mittens he, Billy, would have known a different life.

He stopped himself before he wished the world had been otherwise. He knew that was not what to want.

He saw something now, up ahead of him on the beach, and began to run, the shore wet and slippery and uneven. Gradually it became clear, focused: The stern of the skiff, the skiff Nicky had used, he knew because of a once-silvery metal patch, screwed into the wood and still there, hanging on, discolored and eaten by rust.

He knelt beside it, his breathing rushed and ragged, touched the rotten wood, placed his hand across the patch.

Later he would search every inch of shore, throwing rocks in frustration, calling Nicky's name, wanting him back, even just part of him, something. It had been so long, he had looked for so long. All for a piece of metal, a piece of old wood, a raincoat in a place it should not have been. A question he did not want to ask. An answer he did not want to know—

And he would see something, in his mind:

Nicky, bare hands above his head, falling down down down through water.

He would never find him. Once was all he was to be given.
He would look at the water and know: *He will always be there.*
He would think of Katie and know: *He will always be there.*
But he, Billy, wouldn't have to be.

There was no way of knowing.
Twigg had told himself this, over and over, for the past nineteen years. It still seemed possible. It still seemed that things should not be the way they are, that this really wasn't the way his life was supposed to be. There was a mistake somewhere, a siding off the main track that he had taken and kept going on and on and on and on, running alongside the life he should have had.

His father had died before Twigg was born. Out of the blue, out of left field, renegade blood cells in his veins. And his mother always saying: *It was never supposed to be this way.* But the way it was seemed how it should be to him; it was the world he was born into, and he had never known it to be any different.

He had bailed on Cindy. Had he? *It was never supposed to be this way.* Leaving was the only thing he could think of to do, and he had done it for her. He always told himself that. How could they ever go back to any kind of life together? By leaving, he had given her another chance.

There was that party, years ago, crowded and noisy. They were pressed together into the same space. She had turned toward him, laughing at something, and on impulse and from too much beer he grabbed her face and kissed her. In front of God and everybody. It was at that moment she became his responsibility; wherever she wanted to take it from there he would stand by her, stand by any decision she made.

There was just no way of knowing.

He felt the wind against his plane. Not too much; it was as if it had blown itself out, clearing since morning, clouds spreading, thinning, moving on. There were moments when he could see down past the reflection of the sky into the water. He flew low.

Everything gets shaken loose, gets washed up sometime. He circled the islands, scanned the shorelines. Late afternoon now; he'd been flying on and off all day, breaking for lunch and to refill the fuel tanks.

It somehow seemed necessary to do this. He thought maybe, if he could find Nicky, it would change things. For Billy and Katie, maybe Pete. It would change things. Just as Nicky's disappearance into the water changed the world forever, finding his remains would change it again.

There was a difference, between the missing and the dead, though everyone in this case knew they were one and the same. There was a difference.

But there were too many miles of shore, too many coves and bays and cliff fronts that dropped straight down—

He thought of something, a place. Where the lake was tunneled like a river between walls of cliffs. A place where the wind funneled through. The last place to freeze, the first place to thaw. A tricky place for a boat; a bad place for a plane. The Shoots. He was nearby; he tipped his wing and turned.

They had searched there, of course, for Nicky. And for Colleen Smith, too. But it wasn't just that the wind seemed to be pulled in there; there was some kind of current thing going on, below the surface; even on a calm day the water moved, river-like. He decided against trying to fly between the cliffs, chose to find a place to land instead.

What he noticed, after landing and hopping down onto his float, was a lonely sound. The wind moving around all those cliff faces, he figured. Maybe it had been too long since he'd been out in the middle of it.

He took a deep breath and eased himself down into the water. It came to the top of his hip boots, sloshed over the edge of one, soaking his thigh. But he didn't dare bring the plane in any closer. He couldn't afford to buy new floats.

He moved carefully toward the shore, a long rope in his hand to tie the plane to a tree, watching the wind on the water, hoping it wouldn't push the plane into the rocky shallows.

He stepped up into the edge of the woods. He noticed how thick and dense the trees were; the forest floor covered with soft moss, in varying shades of green. He hated to step on it. It was perfect, untouched.

He secured the rope to the base of a spruce that leaned toward the water, bending in a way that seemed unnatural. Twigg thought about its growing that way, deforming itself to meet the sun, thrusting out of the darkness in which it was born. He looked for a moment into the shadowed woods, at the long strands of hair-like moss hanging off the older trees, at the small shards of sunlight slanting down through the branches.

He stepped back onto the sliver of shore below the bank, began to walk. He had to keep going into the water, had to keep stepping up into the woods. Now and then he yelled into the trees, in case of bears. His voice was strange in the quiet. It did not reassure him.

He came up on one of the cliffs, the mouth of the Shoots, tried to estimate the depth of the water around the front of it. He could climb over the top, and come out on the other side, but he wouldn't be able to really see down into the water along the face. He found a long piece of driftwood on the shore, a pole to help keep his balance, and began to work his way around, sticking his feet down between the large, green-covered rocks sitting silent and ancient below the surface.

He wasn't even half way around when his hip boots reached their limit; he let them fill. The water climbed toward his chest. When he got home tonight, he told himself, he'd put on some long johns and a pair of clean wool socks. Read a book. Maybe find that bottle of rum he had lying around somewhere, fix himself a hot drink.

He felt the water moving around his legs, a pulling and a pushing. He tucked his walking stick under his armpit and placed both hands on the face of the cliff. The rocks there were warm from the sun. They were smooth, and they sparkled. Sparkled golden. Pyrite. Fool's gold in the shale. He felt for a moment that he was in a dream. The warm sparkling rocks. The water wrapping and tugging his legs. The lonely sound. The dead.

He pulled himself around the front of the cliff and heard a crashing in the thick forest.

He tried to take in everything at once, hands still on the warm face of the cliff. The dark forest, where just recently something crashed through, now closed up and silent again, like nothing had ever been in there; the lonely sound. And then the cluster of large rocks, dark gray, half in, half out of the water. A good place to look. With his eyes on the woods he moved toward the rocks. He slipped and nearly fell forward, stirring up the muck. A glimpse of something white. He grabbed the walking stick, which floated beside him on the water. He pushed it down, toward the white. There it was.

Oh geez, oh, my, oh, God—

"Colleen," he said.

Perfect teeth, except for the chip in front. He always remembered. Like Cindy's.

"Colleen, your daddy wants you home."

Katie and Manny had easily found the piece of skiff still on the shore of one of the islands, but Billy was nowhere to be seen. His tracks wandered the shoreline, and at times it appeared he had been walking in circles. Katie and Manny lifted the waterlogged and rotten remains of the boat into their own skiff. They didn't know what else to do.

Again, not knowing what else to do, they took the piece of skiff to the lodge, where Dean and Sal stood around with them, looking at it. The news that Twigg had found human remains was spreading through the area, though so was his assertion that they were those of Colleen Smith. They had seen the local trooper's plane flying toward the Shoots; some time later a trooper helicopter headed the same way. Always, there are people missing in Alaska; always, there are families who want to know.

As Katie stood with the small group that kept vigil over the rotten wood that was once a piece of skiff, she thought about how, as she had left Billy's and walked the trail, she'd felt something in the woods there with her. She'd stopped, listened, looked over her shoulder and saw a wolf, a gray wolf, big yellow eyes looking at her. In that moment she felt oddly unafraid. The wolf turned quickly and disappeared, into the green-leafed berry bushes. Into the slender white birch trees. Into the umbrella-like devil's club and the lacy green ferns. Katie realized, in that moment, as she imagined the wolf's swift walk through the dense forest, that she could not live in Boston anymore. That there was too much in Alaska that was in her, and that here she could always find them, both of them—Nicky. And Billy, too.

And that had been the reason she'd stayed gone so long.

Now, at the lodge, clouds were moving in though the wind was keeping its peace. A boat from the village was coming, with relatives of Nicky's from the village; as the boat neared the docks Katie could see that Norma was among them, but not Pete. Norma sat in the bow, black hair flying. She swung herself out of the boat even before it came to a complete stop. She approached the wood as if it were Nicky's actual remains.

"Oh, Nicky, oh, Nicholas!" she moaned and sank to her knees. Dean took a step backward; Katie found herself doing the same, and also found herself having to fight the urge to cry. Norma's pain was enormous, like a huge wave crashing onto the shore.

Then Norma looked up and her face changed from grief to rage. Katie saw with surprise that she was looking at Dean—

"You get away from here! You get away from this! He would have killed you and you know it! You know it!" She began to rise as she spoke. Manny took a swift step toward her.

"Norma! Norma Jean!" he said, and grabbed her lunging form.

Katie looked at Dean. His face was down and turned away. Katie looked at Sal. Sal looked at her and shrugged, eyes wide.

By then the others who had been in the boat had made their way over; they ignored Norma as if that was all normal, nodded their heads in greeting, and Katie shook a few hands that were held out to her. She could remember some of the faces, some of the names: they were second cousins, third cousins, all men except Norma who seemed, after being taken aside, to be calming down. Now she glared at Katie, but not at her face; Katie realized it was her throat she was looking at, as if trying to see something that wasn't there.

A light rain began to fall. Katie felt someone touch her arm and now Sal stood beside her, saying quietly: "Let's get us some raincoats,

Katie." Katie nodded and followed Sal in through the front door. They both looked out the window to the scene they'd just left.

"Why did Norma say that about Nicky and Dean?" Sal asked as they stared.

Katie shook her head. "I don't know—I was going to ask you."

"I guess they never really cared for each other that much—"

"Maybe Norma was just being dramatic," Katie said, but she kept wondering. Dean was still standing there, though Katie couldn't imagine why. It was as if he felt he had to—head down, still as a statue.

"Though you know, he'd looked for Nicky as much as anyone. And he still looks, too."

Katie glanced at Sal, then, but briefly; her attention was fixed on the scene out the window.

"What are you looking at?" Sal asked. They were both speaking barely above a whisper.

"Dean."

"Boy, he looks a little shell-shocked, doesn't he?"

"Where was Dean," Katie asked, "the night Nicky disappeared?"

"Here, I guess."

"You don't know?"

"I was stuck in town—remember? I went to see that doctor about my foot, couldn't make it back 'cause of the wind."

"How'd you get there?"

"Where?"

"To town."

"Dean flew me—remember? And then he saw Billy over there, and flew him back here."

"That's right." Katie remembered. How could she forget?

"He'd also got that delivery from the doctor, for the village. Antibiotics, for some infection or something."

Katie looked at Sal, who handed her a raincoat off the wall.

"So Dean went to the village?"

"Yeah—before the wind came up, after he dropped Billy off here."

Katie slipped the raincoat on. There were those gray hours, those lost hours, between when Nicky left Johnson's Point and whenever it was his boat went down. Before the wind got extreme.

Katie thought then about how Norma had seemed to be looking at her throat. Katie put her hand there, near her collarbone, remembered suddenly how Norma had so coveted Katie's necklace, before she'd lost it—

Something felt strange, a tickling under her chin. Katie pulled her hand away, looked at the sleeve of the raincoat and felt the jolt of her heart like a pull on a bell—

Nicky's raincoat.

Twelve years previous

I killed him.
No, I didn't.
Yes, I did.
No.
Yes.
If water were words, what would they say now?

But she can't hear the water. She is away from it, up the mountain, in the forget-me-nots, sky above, earth below.

The silence. The search over. The planes that were everywhere—twisting buzzing, swooping—gone. They were like birds. Terns. *Twisting, buzzing, swooping.* Boats on the water. The sound of them, always.

Looking for Nicky.

Nicky, who is in the water.

The lake, calm since it took him. Calm because it doesn't want to give him up.

Snagged somewhere, someone said. Who? Manny maybe. Maybe Twigg.

She remembers Nicky, drifting in the skiff on the water. What was he doing? Listening to loons. She'd watched him from the knoll.

Now she thinks: *He is drifting, he is in the skiff and he is drifting, there beneath, there where we can't see—*

Loons dipping their heads look at him.

The fish circle around him, are his friends. The salmon know. They are on the way, too.

And the light filters down, shattered and broken but soft and diffused; when ravens fly over him their shadows fall down down down, touching him.

And in the winter—she is not sure she wants to think of winter, of the ice sealing him off from the sky—

She feels someone, there on the mountain with her. She pulls herself out of her bed of flowers. She looks and knows: Black eyes.

Black hair in the wind—
    Nicky—
    No.
    Billy.
    She turns for an instant. When she looks back he is gone.

    Billy runs down the mountain, thinks of jumping, sees himself with the birds above the trees. Cawing with the ravens—yes, they would know—wing tip to wing tip with the magpies, then down by the water with the seagulls and terns, and to each one he would ask:
    Have you seen him?

    It is getting late, and she has been gone all day.
    Manny sits at the table and smokes. He listens to Vivian pacing in the kitchen area. He wishes she was sitting here, at the table, and they were worrying together, without all those miles in between. They had gotten through so much together—weathered the storms, as they used to say—they were good at that, getting through things.
    When did the distance start?
    They had gotten too comfortable, he thinks; they had quit moving. And they'd never intended on staying in one spot: they wanted Alaska, all of it, not just Ilmenof.
    But the first years were so hard, and they'd almost lost everything. Then things evened out. They began to like it that way.
    Was that, then, what the Norma thing was about? A pebble—no, rock—tossed into water that had become too still, stagnant.
    Vivian had said: *I think Katie and I will go home for awhile.*
    He knew Vivian. She was going to fix this, but not necessarily *them.*
    They had waited all day for Katie to come home. The search was over and she had not wanted to hear that.
    Out of the corner of his eye he catches something out the window, there on the water: a skiff. *His* skiff. Empty, it seems—he runs outside, Vivian saying *What? What?* Runs to the edge of the knoll, sees:

Katie in the skiff, flat on the bottom of it, drifting.

What the hell is this, now—

He goes straight down. The face of the knoll is so steep it is like falling. He rushes out into the water.

Aw shit, Katie—

"Katie!"

In water to his chest, and he grabs the side of the skiff. He pulls. The bottom is slippery and his legs shoot out; he worries for a moment he will tip it.

"Christ, Katie, what is all this now? Come on, come on, now, we all feel bad, we all do. Don't go doing crazy things now, Katie—we'll get through, your mother and me, we'll get you through this…"

He finds the bow line, leans forward and pulls, turning the skiff back toward shore.

"It's okay. It's okay—everything's gonna be okay."

Katie hears the water against the skiff. The gentle touching of it. The soft breathing movement of it. It is a sound she imagines comes with death, with the quiet falling of death.

 **W**HY DO YOU WANT TO DIE, ROSIE?

I don't want! I don't want!
Honey, don't want what? To live?
I don't want to be here anymore! There is too much!
Too much?
There is too much.

Margaret was home, mixing chocolate frosting for a chocolate cake. An odd thing for her to be doing. Expensive, too—she didn't have any of the ingredients she'd needed, so she picked them up at the trading post where everything cost twice as much as it should.

There is just too much. And Rosie didn't seem to mean too much bad, too much pain—just too much, period. Margaret thought about this. The world to her had always seemed even, balanced.

Rosie, becoming coherent again, had clung to her like a lost child. Then Tommy Wasilli showed up, so quietly it was as if he appeared out of nowhere; Margaret was holding Rosie, there was a soft tap on her shoulder, she looked and there he was, finger to his lips, saying: *Shh.*

Margaret slipped out of her spot, let him slide in. Not much more than a boy. Round, whiskerless cheeks, untidy hair. Rosie's hands gripped his jacket; she pressed her face against his chest, and he began to talk to her, quietly, and so gently it filled Margaret with a feeling of absence and longing for something she couldn't even identify.

Shhh, Rosie, shhh. You be right, eh?
There is too much, Tommy! There's too much!
I know, Rosie, I know, there is too much, there is so much. But don't go, eh? We'll be right, we'll get through it, there will always be too much but that's the way and it's okay, it's okay… Don't go, eh?

Margaret stood in the shadowed doorway.

Now Margaret took the two layers of cake and began to smooth the frosting over the tender surfaces. It had been so long since she'd baked a cake—at least anything besides carrot. The cake was for Rosie. Margaret thought it might cheer her up. Chocolate had a way of doing that, for some people; it was chemical, Margaret knew—chocolate was full of endorphins, the same chemical that feelings of love release into the brain. But maybe, and more important, Rosie might feel better knowing Margaret did this for her, baked her a cake.

As she worked Margaret thought about her life, the facts of it, the relationships she'd had, though carefully not thinking of her appearance at Twigg's. There didn't seem to be anything that shouldn't be; it was all idyllic, even—her parents stayed together, were still together, had been and were supportive and indulgent with her; she was mildly popular in high school, successful in college, where she had predicted and then realized her first love-adventure with a nice young man with whom she is still friends, still in touch, though he has been long married with several children, half grown by now. There was never too little, and there was never too much; like the baby bear-sized bed in Goldilocks, everything seemed to fit, everything seemed just right.

Even coming to Alaska. It had been time for her to reach out a little, expand herself. Round out the experience of her life, have a little adventure. Then go back, find a job again in some doctor's office—not in a hospital, no; a family practitioner, maybe, or even a pediatrician—maybe she was ready to have children in her life. And there would be male doctors, and male nurses, physician's assistants, dinner dates, staff parties, Sunday barbecues, everybody always wanting to hear what it was like for her in Alaska.

What would she say? She suddenly wondered if there was anything she could say, really.

There was a girl who wanted to die because there was too much—

How could she explain what she didn't understand?

The wind would come up off the water, bend the little spruce trees, then when it came through the leaves in the tops of the birch—

Were there words for that, that sound?

I think I was in love. The thought came uninvited. Had she—did she—love Billy?

The whole town was buzzing now, about what the last night's winds had washed up. She tried to imagine what Billy went through, every time anything like this happened, and she worried about him now. Did he ever think of her, when he was unhappy?

An image came to her, of a day when she had seen Billy at Dean's lodge, and they'd stood in the entryway talking. It was after their night together. She could see Billy struggling to say something to her that would be right. One hand was shoved in his pocket; the other hung loose and his fingers unconsciously fumbled with the sleeves of the many raincoats that hung from the pegs. He looked her in the eye and asked her how she was. She chatted casually, tilting her head coyly. His cheeks reddened a little. "Margaret," he'd begun, but then his face changed and his eyes went down to the sleeve of the raincoat he was fingering. He seemed to go white. She'd said: "Billy, about the other night—it's all right. We don't have to make a big thing of it." Then he looked up at her as if he hadn't heard a word she'd said.

It was senseless. She had been able to see, though she didn't understand, where his heart was. She stopped for a moment and closed her eyes, felt the ache and let it be. It was okay. The pain filled her and hot tears pushed their way past her eyelids. But it was okay. She stuck her finger in the frosting and brought it back to her lips. It was good— it was so good. She had forgotten. She had some more, and then some more while her tears spilled down her cheeks and over her upper lip and into her mouth, their salty warmth mixing with the cool sweetness of the frosting. It was okay.

A little while later Margaret stood outside the door of Rosie's house. She'd put the cake in a basket and walked the two miles, surprised at how heavy the cake turned out to be. Before knocking she lifted the cake from the basket, so that when Sophie answered the door she looked at the cake first, then at Margaret. Sophie's forehead frowned and she seemed a bit taken aback, and Margaret was about to start explaining herself when she heard Rosie's voice coming from the darkness inside the house.

"Sophie, who's there, eh?" A form began to emerge from the shadows, approaching the light in the doorway. Margaret's heart beat, and she smiled.

"You're wearing the necklace."

"Yes." Katie raised her hand to it, aware of the jagged edge of the raincoat's sleeve, wondering if Dean would notice it.

"It looks nice."

Katie smiled, studied his face. How did it all fit? A necklace, a raincoat, things from different eras of her past. Were they messengers? Was she crazy? Was her dream of Nicky simply a dream?

She tried to get something out of Manny—anything—after he returned from taking the piece of skiff to Johnson's Point, from which Billy was absent. She was on the edge of the knoll when he returned and told her he couldn't find Billy, though the skiff was still there; Katie then asked him about Norma and Dean, why Norma seemed so angry.

"Katie, you don't want to know, and that's *all* you need to know," he said. "It's got nothin' to do with anything." With that he went back into the house.

About the raincoat, he'd seemed to think that Katie could not be sure.

Dean had appeared suddenly and unexpectedly. She watched him fly in, knew he saw her on the knoll. He bypassed the house and came directly to where she was. Katie could see Manny behind the glass of the front window, chugging white wine and peering at them through smoke and glass.

"I was feeling restless," Dean said, "and thought I'd fly around a bit, see if there's—anything. Want to come?"

"Sure," Katie said.

"Katie—"

"Yes?"

His hand touched the sleeve of the raincoat, and Katie quit breathing. With a finger he lifted the jagged edge a bit, pushing it up her arm. "Why the tattoos?" He looked her full in the face. He didn't seem to have noticed the raincoat at all.

"I was—I don't know. Trying to remember Nicky."

"Nicky?"

"They're *N*'s. The shapes are all *N*'s."

"Oh, I—I didn't see that. It looked kind of Aztec or something— the pattern." He looked away then, and Katie thought his face was troubled.

Manny poked his head out the doorway as they passed the house. His head was moving in something between a nod and a no. Again, the wineglass looked out of place with his grizzled appearance.

"I'll have her back in an hour," Dean said. "We're just going to look around." They kept walking, and Manny didn't seem able to come up with a reply. Katie waved as if everything was normal.

In the plane, in the air, they circled islands and followed shorelines. Katie thought about what Sal had said, about how Dean always looked for Nicky. Katie felt touched and confused at once. The day had been full of confusions—the raincoat, Norma. Why would Billy leave the raincoat at the lodge? It had to have been deliberate. But why put it somewhere it would disappear?

She could imagine, though, a story behind Norma's being angry with Dean. She reasoned it went something like this: Sometime or another Norma and Dean got together, Norma got pregnant, and Dean didn't come through for her. Maybe the fresh rush of grief heightened her anger. Norma could be volatile; that was the one part Katie could believe about her father's having hit her—Norma could fly off the handle at times.

Dean was pointing at something up ahead on the water. Katie looked and knew at once what it was: Billy in the baidarka.

Dean looked at her.

"Let's leave him alone," Katie said, straining to be heard above the sound of the engine. Dean continued to fly as if Billy wasn't there.

"What do you think he's doing?" Dean asked.

"I don't know," Katie said. He was still in the islands, but heading steadily away from Johnson's Point. Katie looked over her shoulder and watched him for as long as she could.

Shortly after that, they flew back to Katie's, and after taxiing into the cove Dean killed the engine and let the plane drift on the water. The sudden silence rang in Katie's ears. She looked at Dean. His head was tilted slightly downward, and beyond the frames of his dark glasses Katie could see his brow was furrowed.

"How did we get here?" he asked.

"What do you mean?"

"I mean—how do things happen to people? I remember—all those times, my dad and I flying in to say hello during the winters, and

I remember all I wanted was to grow up so I could live here all the time and hang out with you guys."

Katie stayed quiet.

"It's just not how I thought it would be," he said. "Everybody's gone—except Billy, and he might as well be.... I don't even have my dad anymore, and I never thought that would happen." He looked quickly at her, still wearing his aviator glasses. "I'm sorry. I know you know how that feels."

Katie nodded.

"I've been thinking about going somewhere."

"Where?"

"I don't know. But what have I got here? An airplane, and a lodge that seems to decay a little more every time I touch it." He took off his glasses, rubbed his eyes and said without looking at her: "Katie, would you come with me?"

She looked away from him, out the side window, and tried to process what he'd said. "Why?" she asked. The tight space of the plane felt thick and heavy; Katie longed for air.

"Well, I've always liked you—wasn't that obvious? I don't know—I just feel like I want a new start. I thought maybe you might, too. It's just a thought. When you think about it, you can change your life, you know, even change who you are. You just have to let go."

"I can't let go." She'd said the words faster than she'd thought them.

"Of Nicky?"

Katie was silent. After a moment or two Dean said: "Billy."

"Both."

"Both." They looked at each other. His eyes were moist. "I guess I haven't been able to let go of them, either, Katie. They're with me all the time. Both of them. And you."

"And what happened. I can't let go of what happened."

"That wasn't your fault, Katie."

"Nicky's raincoat was at the lodge."

"What?"

"Nicky's raincoat. I found it today, hanging there with the others. This is it. I'm wearing it."

He looked at the coat. "Katie, that's impossible. Why would Nicky's coat be there?"

"I don't know. Billy had it. He left it there and I don't know why."

"Billy had it?"

"I saw it, at Billy's. Then today it was at the lodge."

"Is his name in it? How could you know it's his—we've got half a dozen that look just like that."

"Here." Katie lifted the sleeve. "He did this. With my mom's scissors."

Nicky, what are you doing?
Cutting my coat.
Why?
Because I want to. Look, see—cool, eh?

"But he was wearing the coat, wasn't he?"

"Yes."

"But where did Billy find it?"

"I don't know. He wouldn't tell me."

"Katie, that's—that's something, isn't it? That's weird. But you know if he'd been wearing that coat, it would be trashed by now, being outside…" He didn't finish. He looked at the coat, then looked at Katie, and to her surprise he reached out and touched the side of her face, brushed her lips with his fingers, then touched the necklace where it lay across her collarbone. Katie didn't know what to do, felt her blood pumping fast.

The plane had drifted nearly to the dock. She could see this without moving her head. She swallowed. Her eyes stayed on Dean's face. "I guess I should go," she said. Her voice was weak and whispery.

There was a moment of stillness, then Dean nodded. "It's been quite the day." He slowly lifted his hand. He smiled at her, but he did not look happy.

"I'll see you around," Katie said. She unbuckled and fumbled for the door latch. He reached around her and helped her. The door opened. She slipped out onto the float and was able to hop from there to the dock. She stepped back as Dean started the prop, and waved goodbye through the wind and the noise and the whirring blade.

When she walked in the door Manny said: "All right, all right, I'll tell you." He was in the kitchen area facing her, his hands on the counter, his weight leaning forward. He was still drinking and smoking. "I didn't hit Norma. Your little pal Dean there's the one who did."

———————————

"You know I still can't believe you and your mother thought I did that—Jesus Christ, didn't you know me at all? All right, I'm a lot of things. I wasn't the best father and I was a cad of a husband. But I don't beat young girls. Anyway, Dean beat her—he beat her, he raped her—yeah, that's where little Nico comes from—hell, I don't believe in that Windego bullshit but there was some bad wind blowing through here that night—" He paused to drink, his eyes narrow and staying on Katie.

"Now don't go thinking this has anything to do with anything—I know what you're thinking." Again a pause, but this time just to look at her. "Well, maybe I do. Norma keeps thinkin' she saw Nicky that night, but I tell ya, those kids were drunk as hell—it was a miracle Dean managed to fly the god-damned plane back to the lodge. Puke-faced drunk. If she wasn't bruised all over, I tell ya, I don't know if I'd a known what to think—she couldn't even really remember what happened.

"But it was somethin' like this: She was all in a stink 'cause I'd come to my senses and realized I just couldn't bring myself to take up with someone young enough to be my daughter and that I wanted my family. Hah! Lot of good *that* did me—anyway, Dean shows up there at the village and starts crying to Norma about how he loves you but Billy was back—blah, blah, blah. They find Phil's stash in the plane and have themselves a party—remember granny's gone with the rest of the world to see Dr. Trueheart or whatever the hell his name was over there at the clinic—and all Norma knows is they were having fun until she told him about you and Nicky—she'd figured that one out—and then Dean just loses it and suddenly they're not having any fun anymore.

"Why'd I lie and say I did it? She asked me to. I went to see her first, when we were looking for Nicky. She was all torn up and all ashamed and didn't want anybody to know what happened. I owed it to her. And I knew I'd fucked up and didn't want her turning on me. Your mother already knew something but she didn't know the whole of it. So it was a tradeoff, and we concocted a story: I rejected her, she flipped, I hit, end of story. Nobody saw most of them bruises. The little bastard went to town on her. So you just stay away from him. He's one fucked-up little Boy Scout."

"The part about Nicky—what did she say about Nicky?"

He chugged down the rest of the wine in his glass. "That's nothing. We checked it out."

"We?"

"Me and Phil. She was saying someone came in sometime or another and pulled up what was left of her clothes and put her on her bed. Spoke to her. She said she remembered thinking it was her father's ghost—not that she ever knew who the hell he was. But then she said it must have been Nicky—him or his ghost. Personally, I think she was just fucked up—then when Nicky disappeared suddenly everything was about him."

"But there was that boy—"

"That saw Nicky's skiff? He wasn't that sure, either, Katie, and you know—what difference did it make? If he was there he left, 'cause he obviously got in trouble out on the water. Bottom line."

"But what if he went to the lodge—after Dean—"

"Of course I thought about that. I asked. I investigated. I chose to believe Phil on that one. Dean came home drunk and upset, puked his guts out and passed out. That was their night. We searched that area, you know, being where it was. We searched everywhere. There was no answer but the lake."

"And Dean just—he got away with doing that?"

"Oh no, oh no. We dealt with it. He went to counseling. Helped out at the old folk's home. Worked shit jobs and had to send the money to Norma."

"Billy said you sent money to Norma."

"I sent Norma *Dean's* money."

"Oh."

"So it never occurred to you that I'm not the one who hit her?"

"I—"

"Hell, Christ. That was the worst of it. I told your mother, you know, several times, that I didn't hit Norma."

"What did she say?"

"She told me to shove it but I think she might have believed me a bit—she did, didn't she?" His expression hung suspended.

"She said—she said there might have been things we didn't know about."

"There you go," Manny said, nodding. "There you go." He poured himself more wine, lifted the glass toward Katie. Her heart beat fast. If only she knew, if only she knew, if only she knew. If this, then that. If this, then that. If Nicky went on the water, because of Norma, because of Dean—then Katie alone wouldn't have caused it. Then it wouldn't have been all her fault.

———

Twigg sat in the silence of his office, staring at the phone. It was evening of the day he'd found the bones of Colleen Smith; some of the bones, anyway; he wasn't sure of what all had been recovered, it was in the troopers' hands now, and they were probably still out there, looking.

It was a sign of sorts, he thought; how else could he have just found her like that?

He was supposed to call home.

But he was being ridiculous. He was thinking it was a sign for him to call because that's what he really wanted to do. You can read anything any way you want, he'd learned; make yourself believe the wind is blowing the direction it does just for you.

But did he really want to call? The thought twisted his stomach. He didn't know anything about Cindy's life now, only that she'd gone to law school, like he was going to, and that she'd moved to a familiar town in a nearby county. He'd told his ma he just didn't want to know. She'd honored his request.

But now, suddenly, he was tired of the unknown, tired of always shoveling to keep his past from rising out of the hole he'd buried it in—he was tired. And what had happened, happened; nothing he could ever do would change it or make up for it—that was just the way it was.

But he could call her, and he could say: *I'm sorry.* About Andy. He could do that.

He'd said that, the day he left her: *I'm sorry.* So lame. And he'd said it so much, by then. Silently she watched him leave; there was nothing she could do.

He reminded himself of the deal he'd made, while still out in the Shoots waiting for the troopers to come: He would call Colleen Smith's father only after he'd called Cindy. So he wouldn't be able to keep putting it off.

He picked up the phone, dialed long distance information—Georgia, the name of the town. He blurted out the name and a machine gave him the number.

Just like that.

He dialed it fast.

Somewhere across the miles a phone was ringing. In some house he'd never seen, through a phone touched by her hand. He could hardly breathe.

A clicking noise, then Cindy's voice:

Hello, you've reached the home of Cindy, Bill and Danny. Sorry to have missed you, please leave us a message and—

Then a voice, young, male, breaking in—

"Hello?"

Twigg hesitated, hand shaking. The machine finished its message. "Hello?"

"Hi—Cindy, please. Can I talk to Cindy? Is she—"

"Yeah—hold on."

A fumbling sound. Then: "Mom! Hey, Mom! Phone!"

A distant voice: "Okay, honey, I'll be right there—"

Twigg closed his eyes. Ages passed. A fumbling sound again, then suddenly her voice, right in his ear, alive, vibrant, and it is twenty years ago, he is twenty-three years old—

"Hello?…Hello? Honey, there doesn't seen to be anyone here. Hello?"

He hung up the phone.

He sat. The scene fleshed itself out in his mind: The house, older—she liked those old houses with creaky porches, uneven floors—the phone, the boy—twelve? fourteen?—Cindy unchanged, still the same, the stick figure with the tumble of chestnut hair—

He slapped his hands over his eyes, shuddered as he breathed. Leaned forward in the chair and rocked himself back and forth, back and forth—

Just let her be happy, let her be happy…

Time passed. Gradually he remembered the other call, searched the top drawer of his desk and pulled out a small folded piece of paper. He opened it and read the numbers, old and faded, written down by a sad hand so long ago. He tried to figure what time it would be in Idaho, then remembered:

Anytime, day or night, call us please, if there's anything—

He dialed. The phone was picked up on the fourth ring. Mr. Smith. A voice he'd never forget.

"Sir, this is Ray Twigg calling, from Alaska, you know…Well, yes, yes sir, I've got news, we've had some pretty good wind up here and…Yes; yes. Looks like…Oh, those teeth, you know, that chip in the front there—"

The two men talked for a long time.

———————————————

Billy was gone. He had been seen several more times from the air in the baidarka, moving across the water, camping along different shores. Going someplace. Most recently he had been seen crossing the portage, a slab of land separating Ilmenof from the salty waters of Cook Inlet.

The fish camp, Katie thought; *he must be going to Pete's old fish camp.*

She hoped. It seemed the safest thing.

It had been two days since she'd seen Dean, since her father's story, since the finding of the piece of skiff and the raincoat. Katie had expected to see Dean again and waited to hear from him, though not without some dread. But there was no word. When Manny returned from a trip to the lodge he said Sal told him that Dean took off, shortly after he'd brought Katie home.

Now Katie was in another plane, this time with Twigg and Margaret, flying to the village. Katie had asked Twigg if she could ride over there with him when he did the mail run. She didn't know Margaret would be along.

Katie sat in the rear of the plane with the sacks of mail, her thoughts lost in the hum of the engine. "Forget what I told you," Manny had said, in the morning when he'd sobered and remembered what he'd told Katie. But of course Katie couldn't forget. For twelve years all she had wanted was to know those hours, those gray and unknown last hours of Nicky's life.

She would try, if possible, to not let Norma know all that Manny told her. She kept trying over and over to decide what to say and how to say it.

There was a strange feeling of peace in the plane, Katie noticed; the nurse had greeted her with a friendly smile, and Twigg seemed quietly happy and a little pale. He had cut his hair; Katie felt off-balance by it at first—he had always only looked a certain way. It was a straight, simple cut that fell just below his ears, and free of the weight of length it curled in loose, golden ringlets. Katie kept looking at him. She noticed Margaret did, too.

Margaret was going to the village to discuss with some of the elders the idea of a permanent clinic somewhere at Ilmenof; Margaret explained to Katie how she thought it was badly needed, and how she decided to take it upon herself to submit grant applications and explore federal funding possibilities. She said she wanted to make more of a permanent difference during her stay at Ilmenof.

Katie almost envied her. The idea of a mission, a quest that could better other people's lives, was something she had often dreamed about when she was young. She'd wanted to be a nun, or maybe a Peace Corps worker; she'd also wanted to be a nurse. She could remember that feeling, the feeling that all she had to do was choose. It was only now beginning to occur to her that she still could. She thought about what Dean said, about letting go. She knew she wouldn't be able to do that, no matter what she might find out about Nicky, but maybe she could move a little, get up again from where she fell on the field, and put one foot in front of the other.

She imagined Billy inching his way across the portage, carrying the baidarka and everything else he was taking with him.

As the plane neared the village, Katie stretched her neck to see. Several toy-like three-wheelers buzzed down the length of the wide brown ribbon of the main street, and beyond the village stood a row of tundra-covered hills. On these Katie could see the graveyard, the simple white crosses against the reddish tundra. She had been there before, with Norma. From the graveyard you could see a mass of mountains, white and distant and frozen. Somewhere to the right of those was the sea.

A cluster of children playing by the water spotted the plane as Twigg came in low for the landing. Some scattered, running up into the village, while the others waited by the docks, wide-eyed with their hands to their mouths. As the plane taxied closer, many of the houses that Katie could see emptied as the villagers came out to greet the mail plane.

It was like Christmas. The children jumped and waved and everybody smiled. Twigg stood on the float and waved like a celebrity, calling out to many of the children by name: "Well, Tommy, how's it going? Junior, you catch that record pike yet? Hey, Sharon, hey—you lost your tooth! Well, Berta! Look at you in that dress!" Katie and Margaret watched and smiled.

Then at the edge of the crowd Katie saw Norma. She stood apart a little, a soft smile on her face as she watched her own little boy joining the other joyful children. Katie had to stay in her seat until the mail and Margaret were both unloaded; Norma, by this time, had quietly slipped away.

"I won't be long," Katie said to Twigg.

"It's all right—Margaret's going to talk to some folks, so take what you need."

Katie noticed Norma's grandmother among the elders that had gathered around Margaret. She resisted the urge to run but walked at a steady pace, Nicky's raincoat flapping loose around her in the wind.

Again, she entered the dark entryway. Again, she knocked on the door.

Norma answered, looked with surprise at Katie's face, looked with increased surprise at Katie's neck, reached out and ripped the necklace from Katie's throat.

Katie stepped backwards, stumbling, her hands going to where the necklace had been. She looked with disbelief at Norma, who groaned and slapped herself on the forehead.

"I can't believe I just did that!" Norma said. She seemed to almost laugh. "Katie, I am sorry, eh? Christ. I don't know about myself sometimes!" Her face now had softened, and she actually smiled, then her eyes went to Katie's neck. "Oh—I hurt you, eh? Look, there's some blood!"

Katie touched the side of her neck where the chain from the necklace had scraped across her skin as it broke. "It's nothing," Katie said. Her hands were shaking from surprise.

"I can't explain myself," Norma said.

But Katie was beginning to think she could. Something was coming clear. She was beginning to think that the necklace, the raincoat, Norma and Dean all had a part in the story she was trying to learn.

"You took the necklace."

"Here—I'm sorry. Take it back."

"No—I mean you took it, before. When I'd lost it."

The smile fell from Norma's face. "So he tell you that, eh? That little bastard tell you that?"

Katie shook her head. "No—I just realized it. I should have before. I'd looked so hard—I knew it couldn't have just disappeared."

"Why not? Bigger things than necklaces disappear, Katie."

At that Katie and Norma looked at each other, and time slowed.

"I loved Nicky. It wasn't a game." Katie's voice was whispery and low.

"I loved him too, eh? Nothing—nothing broke my heart like that."

"How did Dean get my necklace?"

"Ripped it from my throat—like what I just did."

"Why?"

"Why do you think? You were one popular flat-chested girl, Katie. He saw me wearing that necklace, and—" She paused, and her eyes wandered as she thought. "And you don't need to know the rest. It's so crazy. I'd kept that necklace hidden for years, feeling all bad about it. Then the one time I wear it—it was like a curse."

"I need to know—"

"What?"

"I need to know if Nicky was here, that night. The night he left. I just need to know."

Norma's eyes narrowed. "If I knew that, don't you think I'd've said?"

"I had this dream of him, that he didn't drown. That there's blood coming out of the back of his head."

"If he had been here, what would that tell you?"

"I think it would tell me where he went, from here."

"What do you mean?"

"Dean was the one who hit you."

"Fucking Manny!"

"No—Norma, please. Please. Don't get mad. Just listen. If Dean hit you, and Nicky knew, he'd go there, don't you think?"

"Of course I think! What do you think, eh? Nicky loved me!"

"Please tell me! Please! I can't do anything, Norma—and Billy can't, either—we're both spinning in it still—"

"And you think I'm not? I lost more than just my cousin that night, Katie. I paid for your necklace, more than anyone should have. I paid for hurting you and hurting your mother. I paid for all that wanting to be someone I wasn't—I paid. And now, what you want me to say—that because of me, Nicky's gone? That because I stole your necklace, a long time ago when I was a little girl who was so sick of you and all your stuff, that because of that, my Nicky is gone? And why—to free you? I should suffer and you shouldn't? Is your pain more special than mine?"

Katie felt the words like raining stones tumbling over her. She looked down at the damp dirt floor of the entry. "You're right. I'm sorry. I was looking—I was hoping—that there was some other reason than because of what he and I had done."

"Hear what you say."

"What?"

"He and I."

"What about it?"

"What if you had been the one that drowned? Then he would now be you, blaming himself. Would you want that? Like you said, there were two of you doing what you did. Not just one. Not just you. And Billy—well, he should have seen that one coming. I saw it. I knew my Nicholas. I watched him, eh? I knew what he wanted." Norma breathed a sigh, leaned against the door frame. "He might have come here. I don't know. I was very drunk. I remember someone helping me. I remember someone telling me it was all right, it would be all right." Her eyes welled with tears, and her lips trembled. "I wish I knew. Manny always told me it wouldn't matter, if he was here or not. Manny said it didn't look to him like Nicky went to the lodge. But I always thought, why would Nicky go to town? It seemed like, if he was upset, he would come here, to me or to Pete. I always thought that." Norma then looked beyond Katie, to the rectangle of daylight in the outer doorway. "Oh, Alex! You back, eh? Come in, it's all right. This is my old friend Katie."

The boy slipped past Katie and stood by Norma, leaning back against her. Katie smiled and felt an urge to touch him but held herself back.

"There's a letter from Nico, Mama," he said, handing a small bundle to Norma while his dark eyes stared at Katie. "There's mail for Gran, too, and then you got another letter, too."

Norma took the mail without looking at it. "Thank you, Alex. Go play now, okay?"

"I was going to ask that anyway!" the boy said, giving Norma a toothless grin. His big eyes fell on Katie again as he hurried back out the door.

"My boys—I look at them, and then I think, I don't have it so bad," Norma said, her eyes on the lighted area Alex had just passed through. "I can't believe the stupid stuff I used to want." She looked again at Katie, handed back the broken necklace, then quietly closed the door.

Back at the dock Katie looked out at the water as she waited for Twigg and Margaret to appear. Down the beach a ways Alex played with other boys—it was some kind of a catch game, and they squealed and laughed as they chased each other over the rocky shore. Katie felt wrung out from talking to Norma, and she wanted to see her father. Manny was spending the day helping Sal do some maintenance work at the lodge; she would have Twigg drop her off there and would wait to go home in the skiff with him.

So Norma wasn't sure. Would anything, ever, be sure? All Katie had heard was what she already knew.

Soon Twigg and Margaret returned, along with an entourage of villagers, all laughing and talking. As Katie joined them beside the plane, Margaret looked at her and said: "Oh my goodness—what happened to you?"

Katie's hand went to the side of her neck, which was sticky with blood. "Oh, nothing," Katie said. She rubbed her torn skin. Margaret handed her a tissue. "What's with these jagged–edged raincoats—is that some kind of an identification thing?" she asked.

"What?"

"Oh, Billy found one like that, over at the lodge one day. I guess that's one way to tell them apart, but permanent marker would do just as well."

Katie looked at the sleeve of the raincoat, at the silly cuttings on the edge. Margaret was still saying something, but Katie wasn't listening. She was aware of a hot stinging in her eyes. *Oh, Nicky, Nicky.* And in her mind she saw him, charging across the water in the skiff, heading for the lodge, heading for eternity, heading toward the last hours of his life—

Heading toward whatever it was that happened to him there.

———————————

Norma watched Katie leave from a small dark window. She thought about her behavior and cringed, then told herself to let it go, let it go. There was more than that moment to be fixed between them.

She had thought about returning to the dock to talk to the nurse real quick before she left, but she didn't want to confront Katie again. Norma wanted to make sure she wasn't going to kill Pete as she tried to cure him.

Actually, it was Pete who was doing it to himself, Pete who decided to quit drinking again. He said he wanted to come back. So he was shaking and sweating, teeth chattering. When Norma left him last night he was a little better, but not much. It was worse than a bad birth, and it was like the alcohol was truly a demon inside him that had to be exorcised from his body.

One of the cousins stayed with him last night. Norma would go back there in a little while with some soup she was making and see how things were.

She remembered Alex saying there was a letter from Nico in the mail, and she smiled. Soon she would have to go back to Dillingham, when the basketball camp ended. It would be hard to leave. Each time she managed to come, it got harder to leave. She'd heard rumors about the lodge, about Dean not doing so good with it. If he sold it and cut his ties to Ilmenof, then she could start to think about coming back.

How funny, she thought, to want to come back to someplace you had once so badly—more than anything in the world—wanted to leave behind. Her life had been nothing more than a loop in a path she thought was going someplace else.

But she does have Nico and Alex. And though her world wasn't what she'd wanted, what would she change? Even that awful thing, to get rid of that, and then she would not have Nico, a thought more awful than anything. She ran her finger across the dust that had gathered on the windowsill, wrote out her name. *Norma.* Norma Nicholi. *This is who I am in this life.* Raised by her grandmother in the village of Okhonek, on the western shore of the great lake Ilmenof. Unknown father, worthless mother gone long ago. This was who she was; this was where she was from.

She had thought she would be someone else, some other person. That her life would be normal: she had always been so hungry for that, *normal.* No village life for her, but a life in a real town. A husband with a job, one that didn't involve catching fish, or canning fish, or selling fish. A washing machine, so there would always be clean clothes. She couldn't imagine anything more wonderful than owning a washing machine. It didn't seem so big a dream to have.

Well, there was a laundromat in Dillingham, of course, but here she and Alex did their laundry in tubs of water and hand plungers and old fashioned wringers, just like she used to. And Alex liked it; he liked to see the clothes go through the rollers on the wringer, liked to watch the water come squeezing out. They did laundry just yesterday. The sun was out a little.

What if I came through that wringer, Alex asked. *Would I come out all flat like that?*

You wouldn't fit, Norma had said.

But what if I did?

Then you would hurt, yeah, as you got all flattened.

Would I be dead?

Oh, I think so. You can't live without your blood. You can't live all smushed up like that.

Well, I guess I won't do it, then. He'd put his hands on his little hips, said this very seriously.

Norma had laughed. *Good idea.* Then she'd realized something; she saw their laundry days becoming part of him, part of the story of his life—

When I was little, and we went to visit my great-grandmother in the village, my mother and I did our laundry in an old metal tub and there was this wringer that you put the wet clothes into, and turned them through these rollers, and all the water would squish out and the clothes would come out flat, like bad pancakes.

And she'd felt good then, about her life, how it had been and how it was, and she'd seen that it was good, and could be good. There were things to look forward to, simple things. Good things.

And maybe Pete could get back on track now. There were others he should think about. There had always been others, besides Nicky.

Later, at Pete's, Norma would sit with him by the river, and though he still trembled, he would be better. She would hear, mixed with the sound of the water, wind coming; she would look upriver and imagine it blowing down from the mountains, where the river began, following the water like a trail; she would imagine all that it passed and touched, on its way toward the lake: The barren foothills; the high-country forests where the spruce grew big and where the grizzly bears made their dens; the dips and valleys filled with white birch and red birch and devil's club and skunk cabbage; misty swamps where maybe moose were feeding, where salmon berries grew close to the soggy earth.

The wind would come and blow through the leafy tops of the birch, bending the river near where she sat with Pete. His breathing would begin to sound more regular. Norma would kiss him, pull the blanket up tighter around his shoulders, then go inside to put on a kettle for tea.

Now Norma moved toward the stove in her grandmother's house and stirred the pot of soup she would take to Pete's. It smelled good, and she felt good about this. Then she remembered again her mail, the letter from Nico. As she shuffled through the small stack Alex had brought she saw the other letter addressed to her. Her heart felt like it stopped. The letter was from Dean.

"If Billy'd already found the coat, then why'd he bring it back here?"

"I don't know—"

"Are you sure, Katie, that that's really his—all these coats look alike to me."

"Yes, I'm sure. I watched him do this. He had my mom's pinking shears—"

They were in the entryway, Katie and Manny and Sal. When Twigg had dropped Katie at the lodge, she'd found Manny and Sal sitting at one of the tables in the dining room, drinking coffee and taking a break. As Katie entered quietly and joined them, they didn't react to her unexpected appearance but had seemed distant and distracted.

"What's going on?" Katie had asked, her voice like an intrusion in the room.

Sal said, "It seems Dean's getting rid of this place."

Katie looked at Sal, then at Manny. "To who?"

"We don't know yet," Manny had said. "But the bastard probably stole those investors right out from under me!"

Then Katie said: "I think Nicky came here."

"When?"

"That night."

"Well," Sal had said, "If he did, that would be the best kept secret this lake's ever seen."

Now they stood around in the entryway, as if it could tell them something. But there was nothing, of course—nothing, just a coat that seems to have been there, then taken, then put back for some unexplainable reason. Manny and Sal returned to the table, and the talk returned to the mystery of Dean's getting rid of the lodge. Sal had received a brief note from him, when Twigg had stopped at the lodge earlier with the mail, warning her that a change of hands would soon be occurring. Manny's mail Katie had put under a bucket near the dock when Twigg came by; she wondered now what it might contain.

Katie looked at the two people at the table with her and felt a squeezing on her heart. What would they do? For Sal especially the lodge had been home. Katie could remember visiting Sal once, in her rooms in what would be considered the attic of the building. There was a big, soft chair with corduroy patches scattered here and there over the worn fabric, and walls stacked with books. Sal had served her tea in a cup with red roses on it.

"What will you do, Sal?" Katie asked.

"I don't know—I've been here so long I don't think the rest of the world would have me at this point." She laughed. "It's not a surprise, Katie, really. Dean just doesn't have it in him to give this place what it needs. He was always uncomfortable here, as if the walls were breathing down his neck."

Katie then looked at Manny. His eyes were narrow and he was looking out one of windows. She followed his gaze to the tree line beyond the crescent curve of the shore. The trees looked dark in the grayness of the drizzling sky—dark, spruce-green silhouettes, jagged and uneven. Katie could see them—the trees—as they would be in winter, darker still against a steel cold sky, bending against the harsh winter wind.

If Manny left Ilmenof, then her family's story here would be over. Eventually, it would be as if they had never been here; they would disappear as surely as Nicky had, fading into a hazy memory. At the table they grew quiet; after awhile Sal went into the kitchen and fixed dinner. "Food, well, you need food," she said as she placed a pot of stew and a loaf of bread on the table. "No matter what happens, a body needs its food. One of the few things in this world that doesn't change."

Later, at home, Manny flipped through the bucket of mail. There was, as expected, a letter from Dean, mailed from Ilmenof the last day he was here. Manny opened the envelope and pulled out, along with a letter for him, another envelope. This was addressed to Katie. Manny handed it to her with some puzzlement but was distracted by his own letter. Katie took the letter out to the end of the knoll. She opened it with shaking hands. She knew before reading that this was it; this was what she was looking for.

Dear Katie,

This letter will come as a surprise to you, but it's one that I have written in my mind many, many times before. I hope one day you will forgive me for not writing this sooner; I did try, you know, to initiate communication between us when you were in Boston, but as you know you didn't respond to my letters.

But that's no excuse for me. There are no excuses for me. And don't think it was the raincoat that now has me suddenly confessing; it was your pain, Katie, your pain and seeing it face to face, seeing those tattoos and all those piercings, and knowing that I could do something to help make it better. I have not done much good in my life. I keep telling myself that—beyond the events of that night—I have not done any harm, either—but that night caused a lifetime's worth of harm, for which I have not yet properly paid. I am tired of it. I have been tired of it.

I didn't kill Nicky, if that's what you're thinking, but I know some things that are factors in his disappearance. That his raincoat was there the whole time astounds me. It must have gotten mixed up with the ones that fell off the pegs, got put back with them, and stayed there until, apparently, Billy found it.

Nicky came to the lodge that night because of something that happened between Norma and me. It is something that I tried for many years to deny, then forget, then to understand— all with no success. I don't remember much, as we'd been drinking heavily and neither of us had done much of that before. But I remember I noticed your necklace on her neck—yes, the one I just "gave" you, and when I said something she started laughing about how she'd had it, right under your nose, all this time. I must have started to become upset; I remember her then laughing at me for liking you—laughing at me not because of you and Billy, but because of you and Nicky, something of which I'd had no idea. I can't remember after that. Maybe I choose not to remember. If there is a monster inside of me he showed himself that night—how many times I have looked at my face in the mirror, looking for the person that did what I was supposed to have done; how long I have lived my life alone now, for fear that I might do something like that again.

I was sick when I came back to the lodge, and my father threw me a blanket and made me stay outside in one of the Adirondack chairs. I remember a little of that. Then all at once—and I don't know how much later—I was yanked from the chair and thrown up against the wall. It was Nicky. He threw me around like I was nothing. Then one hand came up around my throat. That's when my father appeared.

He thought Nicky was killing me. He grabbed a rock off the ground and hit Nicky on the back of the head. He'd knocked him out, and there was some blood. We carefully brought him into the entryway, out of the weather. I remember

*the raincoats falling down everywhere. My dad yelled at me
to turn on the radio and try to raise someone and to get the
first aid book and the first aid kit. As I was stumbling around
inside he started asking me what was going on—he'd heard
Nicky yelling at me. I told him I didn't remember, but some
horrible images were appearing in my mind. He kept at me
and I started saying things. He began yelling at me and for
a short time we forgot about Nicky, there on the floor of the
entryway. When we went back there the door was open and
Nicky was gone. We couldn't have left him for more than five
minutes—at least it didn't seem that long. But he and his skiff
were gone. My dad went after him in our skiff but couldn't find
him, and couldn't get far because of the wind.*

*Katie, you don't know how it's haunted me, wondering
what happened to Nicky. Was it because my father hit him—
trying to stop him from giving me what I deserved—or was it
just because of the wind and the water? Maybe you think I've
looked for Nicky so I could find him first. That's not true. I just
want to know. My father wanted to know. For the most part,
we chose to believe it was the water that got him. That's the
only way we managed to live with it.*

*But I suddenly have realized that I could do something for
you. You see now how it wasn't your fault at all. Whether the
hit on the head had anything to do with it or not, Nicky was
where he was because of me, not you. Please let my telling you
this be the one decent thing I've done in my life. Please let it
help you let go.*

*I'm going to go away for awhile, and I don't know what I'll
do. I had, you know, considered flying my plane into the side of
a mountain, but I found I hadn't the nerve. I don't know what
should become of me. I will leave a copy of this letter with my
lawyer, should it be necessary he see it.*

*I hope you will be well, and I hope someday you will be
happy. I will always think of you no matter where I am, and
remember you as a sweet light in my life.*

Dean

Katie thought: If Dean hadn't attacked Norma, if Norma hadn't worn the necklace, if Norma hadn't stolen the necklace, if Katie hadn't lost the necklace, if her parents hadn't given her the necklace, if the people who made the necklace had made the clasp stronger—would Nicky be alive today?

But there was another way to look at it, too. Katie backed up the list: If she and Nicky hadn't been caught together, then Nicky would not have fought with Billy and would not have gone to the village. Norma would have been the story of the next day, not Nicky.

She closed her eyes and was eleven years old again, on the dock, the necklace bright around her neck as she and Norma played pirate, the dock their ship on the wide ocean. The sun was bright as Katie pranced about, a stick for a sword, and she felt the necklace move, caught a glimpse of it as she twirled around with her arms spread wide, her face to the sky.

That was the last time she could remember seeing the necklace, of being aware it was still on her person.

Was that the moment that changed her life? Or had there been another moment, a different movement, that sent the necklace flying into the world of cause and effect, of this, then that, of shaping a future beyond anything Katie would ever imagine?

We are so careful, Katie thought; we try to be so careful and yet so little can matter so much.

She thought about Nicky, those lost hours taking shape now in the gray of the unknown. The village, the gentle placing of Norma on the cot, Nicky back in the skiff, in the wind, going to the lodge, to Dean and to a man who would protect his son, then back to the water again.

Was he cold in the wind, without his raincoat? Did he stand and fall, tumbling from the skiff and into the waiting water, or did he collapse on the bottom of the skiff, blood spilling from the back of his head?

Or did he simply stand and leave, all right and intact, and judge it wrong, underestimate the churning of the waves—

She was aware, then, of Manny's approach on the knoll. "Hey, it's raining out here," he said, then he looked at her face. "Well, what the hell are you crying about now? I'm the one out of a place to work!" She handed him the letter, and he began to read.

And Katie closed her eyes and twirled again with the girl on the dock, whose necklace shone in the sun.

It was the longest day of the year, Katie realized; a night that was barely dusk, a dawn that was merely a brightening of what already was. She'd spent most of it on the knoll after the rain subsided, unable to sleep. She'd thought of Billy, she'd thought of Nicky, she'd thought of Norma, she'd thought of Dean. But Nicky, mostly. Nicky the ghost of her dreams, Nicky in that haze of memory where he continued on unchanged.

Katie had thought she was stuck, thought Billy was stuck, but she realized that wasn't so. They were each far from who they had been. They had each altered themselves to the world a necklace and a windstorm had created twelve years ago.

When she slept that night, that briefest night that paired the longest day, she dreamed of Nicky. She was looking for her necklace off the end of the dock, her face down in the water, and found Nicky instead. He swam by amidst a school of sticklebacks. He disappeared. She fell into the water. The muck was thick and green.

Then she couldn't breathe and she twisted her way toward the surface, but the muck was too thick and she no longer knew which way she needed to go. Then suddenly the water cleared and she could see. She broke through the surface and there was Nicky, swimming in the cove as they did the night before he died. There was soft evening sun, golden. The trees were so green. She lifted her hand to wave, but was pulled back under the water. There Nicky was again, now in green shadows.

You didn't drown.

Didn't I?

And the red swirls in the water by his head were strands of yarn, from a red mitten that was unraveling.

When Katie woke up, she returned to her solstice vigil on the knoll and watched dusk fold into dusk, mists form and disappear, and listened to a loon somewhere on the water cry out.

Now it was morning—real morning, and the lightest night was slowly slipping away. She thought about her dream, smiling to herself. Dean's effort hadn't freed Katie; it had only filled in the hours. She would never let go.

She would go down with it—the ship, the boat, Nicky's skiff.

But not to stay down, not still; she would also, she realized, get up and start walking. Toward what, she didn't know.

Still on the knoll, she watched the long morning continue on. Manny was up inside now, peering at her through the window, and no doubt the weasel was scurrying about. Katie wondered where Billy was, and she wished him the beauty of the day.

She placed a warm mug of coffee that she'd brought out from the house against her navel and let the heat soothe the itching of the healing hole. If she needed to pierce something again, she would have to choose something else, though any of the options left were unacceptable to her for one reason or another. Maybe she could pick up the tattoos again, but she didn't like the idea of having tattoos when she was older, which she realized she someday might be. She may have been stuck, but the years continued on, and not without her. Thirty would soon turn to forty, forty to fifty, if her luck held at all.

As she sat she began to hear something—a motor, though she couldn't tell what kind at first. Then it distinctly became the sound of a skiff, coming from the direction of the village. Katie rose. She had an old green army blanket wrapped around her and it slipped off her shoulders onto the ground as she stared. It was Norma, in the stern with hair flying, hand on the throttle of the outboard, steering the skiff into the cove.

Katie hurried to the house.

"Norma's coming."

"What?" Manny's fork stopped between his plate and his mouth. "Here?"

"She's pulling into the cove."

Manny set his fork down. "Well, I wonder what the hell she wants!" He stood and adjusted his jeans, tightening the tuck of his shirt. Katie pretended not to see as he darted past a mirror and ran his hand over the top of his head.

Norma didn't waste any time, and was soon knocking on the door. Manny answered, with Katie standing behind him, and a moment passed where Norma just looked at them.

"I got some news, eh?" she said.

Katie and Manny exchanged a glance.

"We already know," Manny said.

"About Dean?"

Manny nodded. "Yeah, yeah. I never thought old Phil would lie to me, but you know, you just never can tell about people—"

"And Dean told you about the lodge, eh?"

Manny nodded again. "I kinda thought he'd be sellin' it."

"He's not selling it," Norma said. She handed Manny a folded letter. He looked at her suspiciously, opened the paper and began to read. His brows arched and his head pulled in toward his neck. He looked at Norma and looked back at the paper.

"You were right, eh, Katie," Norma said while Manny read. "That Nicky went there." Their eyes met.

Katie said: "But it was still because of me—him and me—that he was at the village." They looked at each other, then at once looked away.

"Well, Norma, well," Manny said, after a few moments passed. He handed her back the letter. "You deserve it. Got some work cut out for you, though—he didn't take good care of the place."

"I know—I was wondering if we could talk, eh?"

Manny nodded, and gestured toward the knoll. Katie looked at her father.

"Dean didn't sell the lodge," he said. "He gave it to Norma."

With that they left Katie and walked like two old friends out to the edge of the knoll. Katie went back inside and stood back from the window a bit, watching. Norma's hair whipped behind her in the wind, and she stood with one hand in the back pocket of her dark jeans. Katie could see how weight had settled on her, but she could also see that there was a substance to Norma, a look of solidness uncharacteristic of the hungry and often silly girl Katie once knew. Katie wondered what words passed between them. It wasn't long before Norma left, and Katie walked out to the knoll to talk to Manny.

"Well, I could let her be my boss," he said when Katie stood beside him. He smirked, pulled his tobacco pouch from his shirt pocket. "Aw, hell, I don't know. I was getting kind of set on leaving." He turned his back to the wind and began the process of rolling a cigarette. "She said if I wanted to sell that the Native corporation would want it. It's a bit of a sore spot in their kingdom, you might say. But they'd want us to tear down the house."

"Why?"

"Let the land go back to itself. That's why they'd want to buy it."

"What about the Japanese people?"

"You know if I sold to them they'd just put Norma out of business. I can't do that to her any more than I could have done that to Phil." He struggled with a match in the wind. "But maybe if I'd a known he'd lied to me all these years, I'd of felt a bit different."

Katie looked at the water. "I'm sure they thought maybe Nicky'd just drowned."

"Maybe he just did." Manny sucked in some smoke, blew it out into the wind. "What do you think, Katie? We could get enough to start over somewhere, and then some."

"What do *you* think?"

His eyes narrowed and he scanned the water. "All these years being without your mother, and I don't really know what it's like to be without her."

Katie looked at him.

"I mean, everything I ever did we did together. We did this place together, created this existence for us. I've got no fucking idea of what I can do on my own."

"Then sell. Find out."

"Well, we can talk about it." Manny was looking toward where the view disappeared, and Katie wondered what he thought. They stood together in silence, then Katie walked back to the house, went inside and leaned against the wall near the table and the window.

She thought about the house, this land, without them. She thought about the house no longer existing, as something that lived only in memory, a few photographs here and there. It would be another ghost living inside her. Would there be anything of her, living inside the boards and in the glass, in the insulation between the rafters in the ceiling, the studs in the walls?

Owens Corning, Corning Owens, glass-Fiber-Fiberglass-lation-Insul-Owens Corning Fiberglass Insulation—

Red letters on shiny silver, stared at in the light of summer nights, trying to find sleep, trying to turn thoughts from the wanting to be outside, in the wind and the green, in the wonderful softness of midnight—

The light of now, summer. In six months it will be all opposite; she tried to picture it, six months into the future, the only certainty the dark and the cold; *that* will be here, whether the house was or not.

Three weeks from that moment Katie would stand again in that same spot, looking for the last time at the table in its old place by the window that was once much of her days. After a time she would go outside, gather wood for the stove in the tent Manny set up at the bottom of the knoll by the cove. She would see her father's weasel come through the now doorless doorway, watch it disappear into the woods.

The sun would shine sharply on the windows, then recede slightly as the sun moved toward the west.

Not even August, and already there would be signs of summer's ending.

She would realize she was hungry and tired. With an arm full of wood she would begin walking down toward the tent.

It is the same tent the three of them—Katie, her mother and her father—lived in while they built the house, rushing to beat the swift onset of winter, and she would see it from the top of the trail, faint among the trees below. Then suddenly it would light up—glow—but would fall dark again. Katie would know what it was—Manny trying to start the old Coleman lantern, the one her mother used to read by.

She would then think briefly of a movie she saw once, with Khoi, which showed the Chinese Festival of the Dead—bright lanterns floating down a dark river.

Then the light would come again, and hold.

But now she stood, watching her father through the glass. He was cross-armed in the wind, looking at the view that had been his for over twenty years. She touched the table, ran her fingers over the nicks and scratches embedded in the varnish and the wood, wondering what would happen to it if they moved. She could see herself at this table, as a girl, watching the seasons unfold, the different faces of the water: the bright blue of a July day with the west wind blowing the surface into crisp, choppy waves; the glassy stillness of the first freeze; the white sheet of winter, and the chunky, restless churning of the lake during break-up. She could see this. And she could see the others there, too—Nicky, her mother—Billy as he used to be; Manny as a man with a family.

Like her mother's ashes, could she take this table with them, she wondered, wherever it was they were going to go?

Twelve years ago Nicky sat at this table, in a chair across from her, as midnight approached and brought what was to be the last day of his life. They were quiet, together; they could be that way. They'd been swimming in the cove; Katie's mother was in town and Manny was on an overnight guiding trip. Nicky's wet hair rained tear-shaped drops onto the surface of the table.

She wanted to go inside him, to be him, but she didn't know how to do this. The boyish youthfulness of his slender shoulders hurt her in a way she couldn't explain, made her want to fold him into her arms, tell him it was all right, the world was all right, she would be the bandage across his wounds.

He stared out the window, arms folded; she couldn't quite see where he looked but soon realized he wasn't looking anywhere in the place they were. He felt her watching him; his eyes flickered then brushed across hers; she looked down. Now he looked at her; she could feel the way he tipped his head, lifted his brows.

Once, I tried to be a white man.

She looked up. His face was turned already, back to the window.

My uncle said, Can't you see me? But I'd had enough by then, of the Old Way; I'd had enough of my own people, the ones my age, laughing and making fun.

Pete said, They are out on the water. They can't see us old people on the shore, calling them.

I said, The old people are dying, Uncle.

I went to the city.

I would have a flush toilet, I said. Wear a tie. Go to a college.

Picture that, eh? Me in a college.

But people looked at me, and they didn't see me in a college.

They saw me downtown, Fourth Avenue, with the drunks and the whores.

Here he touched the window with his finger, where his reflection was on the glass. Then with a soft voice:

I worked in this hotel once, and I used to watch them—the drunks and the whores—from the windows. I was way up, eight stories, and I could see pretty far.

Fourth Avenue, it was one block away.

One block away, and eight stories up, that's where I was.

Twelve years previous

Nicky moves through the dark entryway, cautiously peers through the partially open doorway. "Norma?" Then his eyes take in the scene—a chair overturned, broken glass—Norma. He rushes to her, feels her throat, gently pushes the hair back from her face. Blood comes from her mouth, from torn skin on her neck. Her bra is pulled to her collarbone; her shirt is ripped and hangs in shreds from her shoulders. Her jeans are tangled around her ankles. Everywhere is the smell of alcohol.

"Who the fuck did this, Norma, who the fuck did this," Nicky chants softly, busily covering her nakedness with anything he can find within reach. She stirs. "Daddy," she croaks.

"No, Norma, no—who hurt you, who did this to you, eh?"

"Katie," she says.

"What you sayin', eh?"

"Everybody loves Katie. Everybody." Her eyes open, roll around and close again.

"Who hurt you, Norma."

"Nobody loves me."

"I love you, Norma. Billy loves you. Pete. Grandma Nicholi. Lots of people."

"Dean can have the necklace."

"Dean? Was Dean here, Norma?"

But she passes out again, and Nicky tries but fails to wake her. Then his eyes see something, crushed there on the floor beside Norma. Glasses, dark glasses, Dean's sunglasses, he knows them, would know them—

Quickly he examines Norma, checks her breathing, feels the beating of her heart, determines she will be okay for awhile, until he comes back. He lifts her and carries her to her bed, lays her down, props her up in case she vomits. Quietly and quickly he leaves the village, careful not to be seen. He doesn't want anyone to try to stop him.

He curses the wind. It makes the going slower, but once out of sight of the village he stands and works with the mounting waves, and when he points the bow toward the lodge there is a time when the wind is with him and he gains speed.

When he gets there, he will make Dean wish he had never been born.

He finds Dean passed out in a lawn chair between the docks and the lodge. Without a pause he grabs him by the shirt around the throat, lifts him from the chair, carries him a few short steps and slams him against the wall of the lodge. Dean's eyes open. His mouth opens. Nicky slams him again, then holds him by the throat and watches his face as he struggles for air.

Then he thinks of Katie, and thinks how he cannot kill Dean. He will help Norma get better, then he will leave and hope that Katie will come with him. Hope that Bill will forgive him.

He loosens his grip on Dean's throat, and suddenly there is pain and bright light and nothing.

When he wakes he thinks at first he is back in Anchorage, he'd been drinking and shooting up and now he didn't know where he was. But then he remembers as he hears angry voices in the room nearby: he is at the lodge, he isn't drunk, he isn't high—he is okay, he hasn't done anything, he is okay.

He carefully touches the back of his head, feels how it is wet and sticky and warm.

Behind him the door is open. He crawls through the doorway, over dirt and pebbles and old woodchips, down to the dock. He tumbles into his skiff, pushes it away, pulls the outboard to a start and twists the throttle. He needs to get Billy, needs to get Billy and get back to Norma. Billy would know what they should do about all this.

The wind is laced with rain. His raincoat is gone somewhere; he doesn't know where. The waves keep coming. He needs to stand. His legs push him upward and he is in the wind and in the rain and the last thing he knows is dizziness and a bright warm light as he opens his arms and falls.

BILLY CAME AROUND A BEND, SAW THE BAY, LIKE A THUMB STICKING OUT FROM THE REST OF THE INLET. The water calmer, the old fish camp there, somewhere on the far side. He was tired of carrying the baidarka, lowered it off his shoulder and set it onto the beach. He lay down in the sand and closed his eyes, the surf a roar in his ears. His arms ached. All his muscles, aching. He had come a long way.

He was hungry, he realized; he sat up and reached into the baidarka, up into the bow. Took out a smoked salmon, two halves joined at the tail, ate the whole thing. He thought about the fish camp, remembered times spent there, years ago, set-netting with Pete. He and Nicky running down the beach. Then that low tide, one time at night, when they found a small octopus. Its long tentacles wrapped around a rock, the water far away. They wedged a stick under it and tried to move it. There was a sucking sound.

He drank from a canteen, studied the strip of beach he was on, the pale sand faded and washed in the evening light. He wondered if there was good walking all the way to the other side of the bay. Probably not. And it was a long way. It would take a long time to walk, another day or two. He thought about shoving the baidarka into the water, just going for it.

He looked in the other direction, where the waters of the inlet seemed endless, but he knew that somewhere out there, past the horizon, were the Aleutian Islands, where his mother's people were once from.

Nicky had wanted to go there, in the baidarka, a crazy idea. But as Billy looked he thought: *That is a way to go, too.* The world would become the water, the wind, himself, the baidarka and his paddle. What was left of his supplies. What might be swimming there, down below the surface, in places he couldn't see.

But for now, he was tired. After awhile he would gather up some driftwood and start a fire. There was no hurry. He lay back down.

Just over two years later, there would be a letter from Katie. Billy would still be living at the fish camp; Pete would be there with him. Twigg would fly over, bringing the letter. Billy would walk the windy beach as he read.

Dear Billy—

The handwriting so familiar.

> *I think of you, as much as I think of Nicky. Maybe more, as my thoughts of you hold hope of one day seeing you again.*
> *I thought I wouldn't write. I thought my family's leaving Ilmenof would be what you needed, but I heard you have not gone back. It seems I was once more an instrument of unhappy change in your life. Is there anything I can do to make it okay for you?*
> *I have accepted, now, finally, how that catastrophic event in our lives had forever altered what my life would be. But I have found that joy can come in time, and in the quietest of things. It will never be right. But it will be okay.*
> *I know you've heard that Manny found land in the Interior. We found it together, actually, on a lake like a puddle compared to Ilmenof. It's within walking distance of a small town, if you have a whole day, and of course a shorter trip by snowmachine in the winter. We started to build the fall after we left, but winter came on soon and strong. I went back to Boston of all places, and Manny went with me. After Christmas I started at Boston University, in an art program. Manny stayed miserable like a bear without a den until the weather warmed enough for him to return. I followed and helped him build, but returned to Boston in the fall.*
> *As I am doing again, writing this letter in the Anchorage airport waiting for my flight. I have the strongest desire to find a plane going to Ilmenof, like a salmon being called back to the*

stream where it was born. But there is nothing for me there, though I would dearly love to see Twigg. And I heard Norma is doing wonderfully well.

—It snows in Boston, in the winter, and with the damp it gets surprisingly cold, though not like Ilmenof. There isn't the wind, for one thing, but down by the water it does blow, and you can feel it, and of course it reminds me—

All right. Enough of that. I hope you are well.

Love,

Katie

Billy would fold the letter, hands shaking, put it in his back pocket and look over his shoulder to where Twigg and his uncle stood talking. Then he would look out again at the rolling ocean, feel the wind that came off of it, and he would be struck by an image of Katie as he'd never seen her—walking down a city street, snow falling in her hair—her face in profile, a woman's face, and she would turn to speak to someone there, walking beside her—

He saw her smiling, he saw in her face the Katie of his childhood, the curve of her long, slender neck where once he placed his kisses—

Where Nicky did, too.

And he would think suddenly how they are together, he and Nicky, in her—in the memory of her mind, the memory of her skin. The way the land remembers where water once flowed, they are there.

He would imagine the scene again, of Katie on the street, and he would know at once who it was walking beside her in that city far away—

Him. It would be him.

Waves would break on the shore, pull away, and come again. Billy would watch the sand near his feet, catching sight of some pebbles, caught in the water, rolling and tumbling, pushed up, pulled back, there because they were.

Billy was a long way from that moment, as he lay on the beach by the baidarka, Ilmenof behind him. But it would come. For now he rose, brushed the sand off, and slowly walked the empty beach in search of driftwood, dry and discarded, left on the shore.

McRoy & Blackburn, Publishers

• literature • mysteries • thrillers • tales of the Bush • tales of the sea • adventure • tall tales • satire • humor • children's books •

fiction from the North: books for young and old

To order our catalog, please contact us at:
P.O. Box 276 • Ester, AK 99725
www.alaskafiction.com
907.479.2774 • (fax) 907.479.2707
also available through Alaska Small Press or Amazon.com

Other books from M&B

MYSTERIES, ADVENTURES, AND THRILLERS:

Alaskans Die Young

by Susan Hudson Johnson

Heather Adams set out to write her mystery novel, but slowly, she began to fear that her fiction was becoming far too real for comfort—or for safety. If an actual murderer did lurk out there, the would-be author was right on track for becoming the next victim.

"The publisher describes *Alaskans Die Young* as one of a series of "cold cozy" novels, neither noir nor gory. The book delivers on that promise, managing to convey both a sense of dread and a touching respect for the dead without lurid scenes. It is perfect for a relaxing read in an easy chair with a mug of steaming coffee on the side."

— SHANA LOSHBAUGH, *FAIRBANKS DAILY NEWS-MINER*

Cut Bait

by C.M. Winterhouse

Death, gossip, and shifty luck plague the quiet weekend Leona Skavitch expected to share with her husband on their little boat in Alaska's Prince William Sound. Leona butts her way into what even she has to admit are other people's affairs, and soon has gotten herself tangled in

"C.M. Winterhouse, the newest writer on the Alaska mystery scene, has created a meandering and irresistible sometime sleuth in her debut novel, *Cut Bait*. ...Unlike some Alaska mysteries in which the only local color is the landscape, *Cut Bait* is filled with characters and situations that seem convincingly Alaskan."

— SANDRA BOATWRIGHT, *FAIRBANKS DAILY NEWS-MINER*

Happy Hour
by Don G. Porter

A tale of merry mayhem and murder with cocktails, this novel set in 1970s Anchorage features embattled barkeepers fighting off "insurance" salesmen with the help of bush pilot and amateur investigator Alex Price.

Happy Hour is a good-time entertainment set in urban Alaska. [It is] a new twist on an old-fashioned shoot-'em-up action tale, set in the recent Wild West of Anchorage and Fairbanks in the 1970s.... His descriptions of flying a small plane across the landscape show deep affection for the great land...By Alaska standards, *Happy Hour* is great, guilty fun. Like a night on the town in the "big" city, you might not want to explain *Happy Hour* to your mother, but reading it will provide hours of enjoyable escapism.

—SHANA LOSHBAUGH, *FAIRBANKS DAILY NEWS-MINER*

Raven's Prey
by Slim Randles

The police are satisfied that the murderer of four men at a remote camp in the Talkeetna Mountains will not long survive Alaska's wilderness. But Jeep George, hunting guide and best friend to one of the victims, is not so sure, and decides to track the killer.

"*Raven's Prey* is a compelling read, a novel that satisfies many tastes without pandering to any of them."

— DAVID STEINBERG, *ALBUQUERQUE JOURNAL*

"Readers will enjoy the mystery, a wonderful cast of characters, and the Alaskan trivia they will absorb along the way [in *Raven's Prey*]. Randles' descriptive skills do credit to his deep knowledge of Alaska, the people, and the way of life, as he takes you along on the hunt of a lifetime in the far north."

— GAIL SKINNER, *ON THE SCENE* MAGAZINE

The Wake-Up Call of the Wild
by Nita Nettleton

"Amnesia is a cliched plot device. Wolverines are not. Mix in a remote Alaska cabin and odd neighbors and you have the quirky fundamentals of Nita Nettleton's debut novel...It is a bit mystery, a bit self-discovery, and a lot of gutsy, womanly wit...It has great momentum, with its fluid prose and unexpected developments...*The Wake-Up Call of the Wild* is a lark, a gentle and witty tale...it is well written and a charming entertainment."

— SHANA LOSHBAUGH, *FAIRBANKS DAILY NEWS-MINER*

HUMOR, SATIRE, AND TALL TALES:

Battling Against Success
by Neil Davis

Alaska at midcentury offered great opportunities to the restless and ambitious people who had survived the Great Depression and World War II. Some of those who came North succeeded; some came and left; some came and managed to beat down every opportunity that raised its ugly head.

In this often humorous, but mostly matter-of-fact autobiographical novel [*Battlling Against Success*], Neil Davis tells the compelling story of growing up on a homestead near Fairbanks in the 1940s. It's hard to tell who's real and who's imaginary in this tale, for Davis does an outstanding job of bringing all the characters to life."

— MELISSA DEVAUGHN, *ALASKA MAGAZINE*

"[H]is sense of humor and detail are engaging.... By the end of *Battling Against Success*, I was won over by this mature young narrator."

— ELLEN MOORE, *FAIRBANKS DAILY NEWS-MINER*

Caught in the Sluice: Tales from Alaska's Gold Camps
by Neil Davis, illustrated by Alice Cook

"*Caught in the Sluice* [is] a collection of entertaining stories about Alaska characters... usually their hearts are in the right place—except when blackened by greed and treachery... The author's style reflects his sense of how these tales would be told by literate miners. He does not overdo the folksy touch, nor strain for vintage slang, yet still manages to convey a sense of a particular time, place and occupation."

— BILL HUNT, *ALASKA MAGAZINE*

The Great Alaska Zingwater Caper
by Neil Davis

Meeting by accident in Mexico, a lawyer, an accountant, and a government researcher hatch a plot to scam money from the Alaska public trough.

"[*The Great Alaska Zingwater Caper*] is a very clever and very Alaskan story... Davis' book is a triumph because of how perfectly the characters fit their roles... It's an intriguing novel from a man who's been inside and seen the soft underbelly of the Alaska government, and wants you to know about it. And most important of all, as is so essential for life in Alaska, it is a great ride!"

— RICH SEIFERT, *THE ESTER REPUBLIC*

"*The Great Alaska Zingwater Caper* is likely to tweak the state's movers and shakers. But for the humble folk who look askance at how the power brokers conduct their business, this pointed satire is a hoot.... [It is] a penetrating critique of state business in the form of comic fiction.... The book's strongest suit is Davis's shrewd analysis of Alaska's boondoggles and shortcomings."

— KENAI PENINSULA CLARION

The Long Dark: An Alaska Winter's Tale
by Slim Randles

The little towns of the north are the last great secret of the Last Frontier; true Alaska living is found in small villages full of scruffy cabins and original characters. In this classic of Alaska fiction, the array of mushers and pilots, cheechakos and sourdoughs are exuberantly true to life, as are their adventures, from the hilarious to the horrible. In the season of the long dark, it is the small town that lets Alaskans fend off the isolation and chill of winter near the top of the world.

"*The Long Dark* sits squarely in the classic Alaska tradition of sourdough literature, and reading it is a pleasant way to pass a winter night."

— SANDRA BOATWRIGHT, FAIRBANKS DAILY NEWS-MINER

"Slim Randles can set one heck of a scene... He just sinks you in there, and hopes you'll be willing to swim. The receptive reader is very willing to follow his lead... A quiet undercurrent of humor keeps the reader contentedly turning pages, looking forward to the next clever plot development. He has a good hand with a yarn."

— ANN CHANDONNET, JUNEAU EMPIRE

"...every person bitten with the 'Alaska' bug can send *The Long Dark* to family members in the lower 48 who cannot understand why people stay here... Suitable for all ages, it is a small book by an excellent story teller, well worth your time and money."

— JEANETTE GAUL, THE ALEUTIAN EAGLE

CHILDREN'S BOOKS:

The Birthday Party
by Ann Chandonnet, illustrated by K. Fiedler

After the birthday party on Mrs. Atkins' lawn, a little girl in a purple kuspuk recounts her adventures there to her mother, who sinks slowly down into her chair as the delights unfold in rhyme. This illustrated romp through the perils of peppermint pie, leaky garden hoses, compost heaps, and large numbers of young birthday guests stimulates the imagination and tweaks the funnybone.

"[In *The Birthday Party*], Chandonnet's use of rhyme and meter keeps the story moving along toward the punch line..."

— Nancy Brown, Peninsula Clarion

Bucket
by Eric Forrer, illustrated by Eloise Forrer

Bucket the cat was a reincarnated pirate. He lived with Ellie Kulikan, who owned a boarding house at the end of a dock in a fishing village where old men with floppy hats told tales of such inventiveness that they became the truth and were passed down to the local children as the history of the town. But one day the cool, dreamlike sea turns dangerous, and an adventure falls into the life of Bucket and Ellie and their woodchopper friend Olaf.

"Although *Bucket* seems to be a picture book, it is really a sophisticated romance. The heavy satiny pages are pleasing, but it is the illustrations made with colored carbon paper and a household iron which keeps one studying each page.... This book has a strong Alaska flavor...it could take place almost anywhere along the Alaskan coast, wherever halibut is fished. This is a very special book that should be seen and read."

— Sandra Strandtmann, Newspoke Alaska Library Network News

"[*Bucket*] is a tale parents won't mind reading again and again...Eric Forrer's writing is as rich as an old-time fairy tale... Eloise Forrer's unique, whimsical illustrations were done with colored carbon paper and an iron. The effect is something like woodblock printing, textured and lovely. Refreshingly, the book has no moral or lesson, except that sometimes you should let a story just take you away."

— Donna Freedman, Alaska magazine

Keep the Round Side Down
by Tim Jones, illustrated by Susan Ogle

A grizzled old fisherman raises a boy of mysterious origins on the shores of the spectacular, resource-rich but unforgiving Prince William Sound.

"Tim Jones grounds this sea-based adventure [*Keep the Round Side Down*] with a touch of realism... His novel for young adults borders on the magical..."

— Debbie Carter, Fairbanks DailyNews-Miner

"...[*Keep the Round Side Down*] is great reading..."

— Nancy Brown, Peninsula Clarion